ATTACK!

The sabertooth sprang from cover just as Vickers bent to pick up the partridge he had shot. Holgar Nilsen shouted as he leveled his Mauser. He would have had an easy shot—except that Vickers' own body blocked the Mauser's line of fire.

The thud of the cat's paws crossing to leap again warned Vickers an instant in advance of Nilsen's cry. He was holding his shotgun at the balance, not ready to fire—and not that bird-shot would have affected the 500-pound killer.

The cat swung down its lower jaw, locking out of the way everything extraneous to stabbing with its six-inch upper canines, as it made its third and final leap. Its bared palate was white as bone.

Vickers flung himself backwards, trying desperately to raise the shotgun. As the sabertooth sprang, its forelegs splayed and the ten black claws shot out of the pads. Every tense muscle of the cat's body quivered in the air. Its weight slammed Vickers' torso against the stony ground . . . .

From CALIBRATION RUN

STARHUNTERS: VOL. 1
DAVID DRAKE

MEN HUNTING THINGS

BAEN BOOKS

MEN HUNTING THINGS

This is a work of fiction. All the characters and events portrayed in this book are fictional, and any resemblance to real people or incidents is purely coincidental.

A Baen Books Original

Baen Publishing Enterprises
260 Fifth Avenue
New York, N.Y. 10001

First printing, April 1988

ISBN: 0-671-65399-7

Cover art by Pat Ortega

Printed in the United States of America

Distributed by
SIMON & SCHUSTER
1230 Avenue of the Americas
New York, N.Y. 10020

Dedication

To Charles G. Waugh and Martin Harry Greenberg.
Teachers by example; and exemplary teachers.

Contents

                Introductions by David Drake

Acknowledgments

People have been awfully nice as I got into what for me was a new endeavor. Among those whose help is specifically reflected in the contents are: Karl Edward Wagner; Richard Dalby; Richard Minter; Leslie Flood; Janet Morris; Jim Baen; Charles Waugh; and Marty Greenberg.

Introduction

IT'S A LOT
LIKE WAR

David Drake

A hunter and a soldier on a modern battlefield contrast in more ways than they're similar.

That wasn't always the case. Captain C.H. Stigand's 1913 book of reminiscences, HUNTING THE ELEPHANT IN AFRICA, contains a chapter entitled "Stalking the African" (between "Camp Hints" and "Hunting the Bongo"). It's a straightforward series of anecdotes involving the business for which Stigand was paid by his government—punitive expeditions against native races in the British African colonies.

Readers of modern sensibilities may be pleased to learn that Stigand died six years later with a Dinka spear through his ribs; but he was a man of his times, not an aberration. Richard Meinertzhagen wrote with great satisfaction of the unique "right and left" he made during a punitive expedition against the Irryeni in 1904: he shot a native with the right barrel of his elephant gun—and then dropped the lion which his first shot had startled into view.

It would be easy enough to say that the whites who served in Africa in the 19th century considered native races to be sub-human and therefore game to be hunted under a specialized set of rules. There's some justification for viewing the colonial overlords that way. The stringency of the attendant "hunting laws" varied from British and German possessions, whose administrators took their "civilizing mission" seriously, to the Congo Free State where Leopold, King of the Belgians, gave the dregs of all the world license to do as they pleased—so long as it made him a profit.

(For what it's worth, Leopold's butchers *didn't* bring him much profit. The Congo became a Belgian—rather than a personal—possession when Leopold defaulted on the loans his country had advanced him against the colony's security.)

But the unity of hunting and war went beyond racial attitudes. Meinertzhagen was seventy years old in 1948 when his cruise ship docked in Haifa during the Israeli War of Independence. He borrowed a rifle and 200 rounds—which he fired off during what he described as "a glorious day!", increasing his personal bag by perhaps twenty Arab gunmen.

Similarly, Frederick Courteney Selous—perhaps the most famous big-game hunter of them all—enlisted at the outbreak of World War One even though he *wasn't* a professional soldier. He was sixty-five years old when a German sniper blew his brains out in what is now Tanzania.

Hunters and soldiers were nearly identical for most of the millennia since human societies became organized enough to wage war. Why isn't that still true today?

In large measure, I think, the change is due to the advance of technology. In modern warfare, a soldier who is seen by the enemy is probably doomed. Indeed, most casualties are men who *weren't* seen by the enemy. They were simply caught by bombs, shells, or automatic gunfire sweeping an area.

A glance at casualties grouped by cause of wound from World War One onward suggests that indirect artillery fire is the only significant factor in battle. All other weapons—tanks included—serve only to provide targets for the howitzers to grind up; and the gunners lobbing their shells in high arcs almost never see a living enemy.

The reality isn't quite *that* simple; but I defy anybody who's spent time in a modern war zone to tell me that they felt personally in control of their environment.

Hunters can be killed or injured by their intended prey. Still, most of them die in bed. (The most likely human victim of a hungry leopard or a peckish rhinoceros has always been an unarmed native who was in the wrong place at the wrong time.) Very few soldiers become battle casualties either—but soldiers don't have the option that hunters have, to go home any time they please.

A modern war zone is a terrifying place, if you let yourself think about it; and even at its smallest scale, guerrilla warfare, it's utterly impersonal.

A guerrilla can never be sure that the infra-red trace of his stove hasn't been spotted by an aircraft in the silent darkness, or that his footsteps aren't being picked up by sensors disguised as pebbles along the trail down which he pads. Either way, a salvo of artillery shells may be the last thing he hears—unless they've blown him out of existence before the shriek of their supersonic passage reaches his ears.

But technology doesn't free his opponent from fear—or give him personal control of the battlefield, either. When the counter-insurgent moves, he's likely to put his foot or his vehicle on top of a mine. The blast will be the only warning he has that he's being maimed. Even men protected by the four-inch steel of a tank know the guerrillas may have buried a 500-pound bomb under *this* stretch of road. If that happens, his family will be sent a hundred and fifty pounds of sand—with instructions not to open the coffin.

At rest, the counter-insurgent wears his boots because he may be attacked at any instant. Then he'll shoot out into the night—but he'll have no target except the muzzle flashes of the guns trying to kill him, and there'll be no result to point to in the morning except perhaps a smear of blood or a weapon dropped somewhere along the tree line.

If a rocket screams across the darkness, the counter-insurgent can hunch down in his slit trench and pray that the glowing green ball with a sound like a steam locomotive will land on somebody else instead. Prayer probably won't help, any more than it'll stop the rain or make the mosquitos stop biting. But nothing else will help either.

So nowadays, a soldier doesn't have much in common with a hunter. That's not to say that warfare is no longer similar to hunting, however.

On the contrary: modern soldiers and hunted beasts have a great deal in common.

"Death of a Hunter" originally appeared in Fantastic Universe, *a magazine that paid only half or a quarter of what a story would bring in the better SF digests.*

For a variety of reasons, stories appear in salvage markets whose terms or rate of pay is such that a writer sells there only after he's exhausted all other alternatives. Sometimes the writer is new—often unpublished. Editors who have a choice buy comparable stories from writers with more of a track record.

Sometimes the story is simply a bad one—every writer has an off day. If the writer is well enough known, he or she can still sell the piece to an editor who can't afford really publishable work by a writer of that stature.

And occasionally a story is excellent and makes a powerful statement—but none of the established markets will touch it because that statement is unpleasant to the orthodoxy of its day. This third category is unusual, because very few stories are good enough to have that degree of impact.

"Death of a Hunter" *is that good.*

1

DEATH OF A HUNTER

Michael Shaara

Nielson sat within a bush, out of sight, his head bent low and his eyes closed. A few feet behind his back the forest opened onto a wide stream, and on the other side of the stream was a steep, bare rise which flattened out at the top into a small plateau. There were several men on the plateau. If Nielson had looked he would have seen them, sitting among the rocks at the top. He did not look but he knew they were there. On the other side of the forest there were more men coming toward him. They were firing into the bush as they came and occasionally he could hear the quick snaps and hisses of their guns. It was late afternoon. Nielson raised half-closed eyes to stare at the sky. No sign of rain. All day long he had hoped for rain. Still, it was already late afternoon and if the men coming toward him were cautious enough they might not get to him before the sun went down. He rested his head again on his chest, breathing slowly and heavily.

For three days he had not eaten, because he had not had time to stop and get something. He was also very

3

thirsty. He thought of the stream a few feet away, the dust in his throat, the streaked stiff dirt on his face. Briefly he thought of what it would be like to go swimming. But the thought did not last. He was very tired. He wondered if he went to sleep in the bush here they might just possibly pass him by. And then he would awake in the middle of the night, the dark lovely night and stars shining through the trees, and all alone he would be, and then he would go swimming in the stream . . .

The psychologist sat on a rock at the top of the plateau, staring down into the forest. He was a young man, dressed in street clothes, bushy haired and nervous, unarmed. If the hunters captured the man down there alive, or if he lived for a while after they caught him, it would be the psychologist's job to find out why the hunted man was what he was. But the odds against them getting him alive were very small, and besides, the spectacle of many men hunting another is never uplifting, and the psychologist was gloomy now as well as nervous.

Near him on the ground was the leader of the hunt, a much older man in rough clothes, heavily armed. This man's name was Walter George. His hat was off and his silvery hair shone in the sun. He had a small portable radio by his side, into which he spoke from time to time, but mostly he spent his time looking from the sun to his watch to the forest. He also was nervous.

"How much light is there?" the psychologist asked.

"About an hour and a half."

"How does it look?"

"It'll be close."

"And if you don't get him before night?"

"Then we light up the woods as well as we can and sit it out until morning. He'll try to break out during the night. We'll have to keep very quiet."

The psychologist fidgeted.

"No chance at all of him giving up, I suppose?"

The older man shrugged.

"You're sure everyone knows that he's to be taken alive if at all possible?"

"Take it easy," George said. "Everybody knows, but don't expect anything. If you get him you get him, if you don't you don't. I been hunting him myself already for three years."

"And now, at last, it's become politically important," the psychologist said wryly. "Three years to get one man."

"It's a big continent," the older man said, apparently calm, "and he's an odd man."

"You said it," the psychologist muttered.

"The longer you look at it the odder it gets. The whole thing. You know how many men we have out there?" He waved an arm crookedly at the woods. "More than ten thousand. Ten thousand men spread out along a fifteen-mile front. Almost a thousand to the mile. Sometimes in the last three years we had even more. And helicopters and dogs and professional hunters. And altogether he killed twenty-seven of us and I don't recall as anybody ever saw him. Man, after a while you get superstitious."

"He's only a man."

"True. But a man can be a remarkable thing."

The psychologist looked up for a moment, frowning. Then he looked down into cool shadow of the stream.

"The unfortunate thing is that why he did it will die with him. How can we stamp that sort of thing out if we don't know the reason?"

"I wonder if he knew himself," the older man said.

"Listen," the psychologist said. "They told me back at the base that you might be able to tell me something."

George looked at him without expression.

"At least you spoke to him once or twice. That's more than anybody else around here."

"Yes," George said. He breathed once deeply and squinted into the sun. "I guess I could tell you something."

The psychologist took out a small black notebook.

"What was your impression of him? Were there any particular habits . . . ?"

The older man spoke as if he hadn't heard.

"I guess I really might just possibly be able to tell you something. Sure, now, I might just as well. Anyway, if we sit here all afternoon we can't help thinking of him down there in the dust, can we? So I might just as well tell you a little about it. It ought to help pass the time of day."

He leaned back comfortably and folded his arms across his rifle, ignoring the psychologist, who was staring at him with surprise. He was not sure yet just how much of it he would tell, but, as he said, it may have been after all that now was the time.

"Well, now," George said, "if the facts are of help, I have a great many. But what kind of man Nielson was? He did not know himself. Son of a government clerk, he was of a thin gloomy Swede father who collected stamps and buried his family for twenty years in a dim dark home on one of the lower levels of New York and of whom it is said that he never once saw a leaf in its natural state or peered upwards once into the sky, or wished to, from his tenth year on, but passed his life reading books on philosophy and the care of ancient paper. And so he unwittingly imparted to his young Swede son a serious emptiness which the chance sight of a real jungle later on was certainly not enough to fill, but more than enough to magnetize, so that the young man possibly went into the woods as a flower turns to the sun because of that, because of too much closeness and dimness and pressure as a boy, but perhaps not for that reason at all. Perhaps for some reason lost with the now-lost books of his father, which he read and made a serious attempt to understand while too young, and from which he no doubt derived too much misunderstood philosophy too young. At any rate, a woodsman, a professional hunter. And yet more, for it is a long, long complicated path he led to the woods in which he sits now below, and there is about it a strange brutal darkness.

"So who was he?

"A hunter. A man who chose for his lifelong profession the killing of animals. A man who chose mostly to live alone.

"How came he to Morgan? Why?

"Well, these are the facts.

"He came to Morgan in the first year, when it was still young, just after it was discovered and before the colonists landed. When he came there were only a few thousand men on the planet: a motley bearded construction crew building the first city, some properly enthusiastic scientific teams, one bewildered professional hunter, and also the Morgans, which were not men but very close to men, who killed a good many of us and who had us seriously worried that they might be intelligent, which luckily, as the report turned out, they were not. He came at this moment, then, Nielson, a good, raw moment, because Morgan was new and wild and badly needed for its substance and its living room.

"Why did he come? Well, Director Maas said he came to hunt for us free, without pay, had volunteered his services merely to look at Morgans, which on the face of it was ridiculous, since hunters do not do Game Control work for nothing, so there must have been another reason, and another, but nobody knows it, not I, not even Nielson, who thought he came to help a friend. What brought him to Morgan to meet what can only be described as fate? But I see I confuse you. Let it go.

"And what did he look like?

"A matter of record. A Swede, thick all the way down like the bole of a tree. Round stomach as a wind reserve and heavy thighs built up by walking many hundred miles. Strange shape for a woodsman, not slinky at all, more like a big heavy bomb. Blond hair, bullet head, close shaven, and in the Swede blood somewhere something dark, for the eyes evolved coal black. Muscular out of proportion, the kind of man that other men stood near with a sort of tense unconscious caution, a man who when he moved made you inadvertently start to jump back. Yet, for all the steely mean look of him a cheerful man and after all really only a boy, not yet thirty, rosy faced and clean. Only the dark eyes strange in the lighted face, a man to remember and ponder over, if you are the type to ponder, which no doubt you are. But still only a boy, this Nielson, Joe, complete with a great happiness at being alive and a lurking rage at conformity and an as yet untapped determination to go his own way. And eventually a killer. How many is it altogether? Let's see. Something like forty.

"And the events?

"He came to Morgan to hunt and Maas called me and had me fly him out to where the other hunter, Wolke, was, somewhere out across half a continent, and I did. On the plane on the way out he fell asleep instantly like an animal and so I never said a word to him at the beginning, and when he got out at the camp he armed himself and went immediately into the woods, not knowing where Wolke was, not knowing anything about the Morgans except that their danger lay in their ability to sneak up on you and kill you with a rock at fifty feet. But he had no fear of anything sneaking up on him, not on *him*, not of anything in the woods, for he was a professional and hunting is now almost a science, and so off he went. And there it began, although I did not know it then, watching him go off into the trees of Morgan on the way to be hunted simply because he came to help a friend, and moving so quietly even the birds in the trees around him continued to sing."

"Well," the psychologist said stiffly. He was dazed.

"Digest it slowly," George said. "It takes time, but in the end it's worth it. You'll get more than you bargained for."

"Well," the psychologist said again, groping. "You say he didn't come just to hunt?"

"Of course not. We already had the hunter Game Control had sent down, Wolke, and Maas knew that ethically it was not right to let Nielson in, good kind Director Maas, and though he was usually very strict about visitors before a planet was ready, still he let Nielson through, which was unlike him. But then, Nielson was unique. Maybe Maas was just in a hurry to get the job done."

"Wait a minute," the psychologist said. "Simplify it. What do you mean?"

"Well, look at it on the surface. Young hunter comes to Morgan for own reasons. Why? To help a friend. Director gives him permission. But that is unlike Director. Why? Ah! Now we begin to get the point. Now ask me about the Morgans."

The psychologist blinked.

"Well, what about the Morgans?"

George settled back, smiling oddly.

"I'm glad you asked me. Having discovered the planet, you see, one could not help but discover the Morgans, much as we would rather have not. Vicious things they were—long, lean, apelike creatures of great cleverness. They took a dislike to us and killed us whenever they could—which was only natural, as we were doing the same to them. The law concerning dangerous game is that specimens are to be taken and the rest destroyed, so that the whole planet is safe for parks and such. Then the specimens are taken and put on a huge reservation, which is kept exactly as it was when the planet was discovered. That was the way it was to be with the Morgans, but they proved difficult. They managed very quickly to avoid our traps and our poisons, and to kill us with rocks whenever we were incautious. They were indiscriminate. They killed women and children impartially.

"Game Control sent one man down to clear them up. He did very well, captured several and seriously depleted the rest by the hundred, and then one day several apparently ganged up on him and we found him in pieces. His successor was Wolke, but Wolke did not do well at all. He was an amiable, cheerful man, not really a very good hunter, but simply a man who loved the open life and who was very well liked because of his cheerful nature. He had a wife and two children. He took the job with Game Control because he needed the money—he was paid by the head. But the Morgans had already learned a great deal before he came, and what few were left mostly evaded him.

"And there, you see, was the reason Nielson came.

Wolke was failing, and if he failed he would not get paid and his reputation would suffer and he would get no more guide jobs and would have to leave the woods. So he wrote for help to the only really good hunter he knew who would understand what it meant to remain a hunter, and who would come.

"Nielson came. His visit was unofficial. Maas let him come, you see, because on the surface he was anxious to have all the Morgans cleaned out and the job completed. But the truth is that he was more than anxious, he was sincerely worried. He used Nielson's visit to get rid of the Morgans as quickly as possible. And now, you see, we are getting to the point. He thought the Morgans were intelligent."

The psychologist's eyes widened.

"Yes," the older man said, smiling oddly, "that is the real point of it, the question no one ever answered. Not really. Not scientifically. The thing was, you see, that the Morgans *couldn't* be intelligent. Morgan was such a beautiful planet, and we needed it so badly, and besides, they showed no sign of intelligence, no culture. They did not band together, they had no tools, no gods. And they did not respond to tests. When we caged them they would not even move, just sat and looked at us and ignored the tests. But they couldn't be intelligent. All that land, you see, all that living room, all those wild, green, ore-rich plains, we would lose all that if they were intelligent. The law says we cannot dispossess an intelligent people, no matter what their cultural status. So Maas was very relieved, we were all relieved, when the psychologist's report came in and said that the Morgans were only animals after all."

The psychologist stared with mounting confusion.

"But what do you mean?"

"I don't know," George said, still smiling, "nobody knows. Or will know. But was there a little fixing, do you think? Did someone in authority realize the simple, practical truth quite early, and send down Word that the Morgans could not be intelligent? And after all, was there really any blame? Here was room and resources, land and prosperity, sunlight for children, here was a home for ten billion people and another stepping-stone to the far stars. Alongside this what are the claims of a few thousand naked beasts?"

"But who was the psychologist? You'll have to verify your charges!"

"I make no charges," George said softly. "I verify nothing. You wanted the story. I tell it as it was. No one can really say if the Morgans were intelligent. But if anyone knew, Maas did, and Wolke did, and later on, certainly, Nielson did. That's what makes it interesting. Picture now the way it might have been down in the forest with Wolke and Nielson.

"If the Morgans were intelligent and Wolke knew it, what happened then must have been interesting. There was Wolke, a nice, decent, genial man, greeting Nielson with open arms, Nielson, the man who had come across light-years to help him. What would Wolke say?

"'Oh, Joe, dammit,' he would say, 'thanks for—I appreciate—' and he would break off, because there would be no need to say that. Then, perhaps, as they sat together in some sheltered place from which they could not be seen but from which they could see everything clearly, he would tell Nielson about the Morgans. He would say that they had been too smart for him, surely, and other things. He would say that hunting them really should be easy because they had been cleared out of every area except one long dense wood below the great northern mountains. For some reason they never left that area, perhaps because they did not really know any other, and therefore you knew in general where they were. But you could not get close to them, no matter how hard you tried or how softly you moved, and you had to keep a close watch behind you, especially at night. They were not hard to kill, but if you got in a shot you better make it good, because you would not get a second one. This Wolke would say, or something like it, but what then? Talk about the family, the wife, the weather? Talk about the theory he had that all the dinosaurs had disappeared off Earth because

once, long ago, someone had hunted them out? Talk
about Nielson's latest clients, whose wives he had slept
with? Yet clearly, if anyone knew other than Maas,
Wolke did. But could he mention it? Which was more
important—the wife, the job, or the friend? And after
all, in the end, did Nielson really care? Oh, it's all very
interesting, and very complicated. And I really don't
know what happened. But surely, before long Nielson
knew some of it. He learned it in the woods that very
same night . . ."

And the old man stopped his musing and went on
with the story, telling it now with his eyes closed as he
began to lose himself in it, telling it in great detail and
realizing now that he would have to tell it all, and not
caring.

"That night they decided that they should move out
as soon as possible before too many of the Morgans
knew that there was another hunter in the woods. But
little Wolke was overjoyed to have Nielson with him
here and wanted to celebrate a little, so he went out at
dusk and silently killed four partridgelike birds, and
they sat on a high knoll munching bones until late in
the evening. They had maybe two or three hours to talk
and then they moved out.

"Now understand, they were very well equipped, for
hunting is a science. They had soft tight clothing which
would not scratch on twigs as they moved and a cream
which coated their bodies and removed their scent so
they could not be smelled. They had lenses for night
vision and pills for endurance and chemicals which
made their own nostrils sensitive. Each carried two
guns—an electron handgun and a rifle. Like most
hunters, Nielson preferred a missile-firing rifle to an
electron one; he told me that the blaster causes too
many fires and too much smoke, and though it cuts a
hole right through whatever it hits, even rock, still, it
does not have the shock effect, the vital stopping power,
of a solid ball. Therefore Nielson had a .300 H. & H.
Magnum along with his handgun. But most of all, of

course, what Nielson had was that magnificent inborn skill which comes to very few men—certainly not to Wolke—that ability to move quickly and be unseen, to be silent but very, very swift, which Nielson had to an almost unbelievable extent. And so armed they were.

"Wolke had located a group of Morgans in a valley to the north. He briefed Nielson carefully on the terrain and then the two of them moved out together. The way Wolke had chosen to go down into the valley was through a narrow ravine—not through it, really, but along the sides. When they reached the mouth of the ravine they split up, each taking one side, timing themselves to arrive at the end together. It was a fairly cold night in autumn, and very dark, for Morgan had no moon. The stars were clear but unfamiliar, so Nielson had to be very careful about his direction. And so they went down the ravine.

"Now here, you see, we have a clue. Why is it Wolke chose such an obvious, incautious way to go down into the valley? That is very odd. He had been hunting the Morgans for months now with very little success, yet he apparently had so little respect for them, for their cunning, that he chose the worst possible way to go in after them. Creeping over the sides of the ravine over rocks, rifle in hand, separated as they were, what position were they in to fight if they came across Morgans? Cramped and awkward they must have been, should have known they would be, yet that is the way they went in, and that was where the Morgans ambushed them. Maybe Wolke was so emboldened by Nielson's presence that he became overconfident. Or maybe, and this is likely, he did not want Nielson to see that he had so great a respect for the Morgans and therefore took the simplest, quickest way down. At any rate, there is something about it which looks almost *arranged*, and yet I know Wolke was not a man to commit suicide.

"Well, they had been moving down the gorge for maybe half an hour, and they had just crossed the ridge and were on their way down when Nielson became aware of something ahead of him in the woods—something quiet and still but alive, waiting. He did not see it or hear it or smell it, but he knew it was there. Take that as you will, this is the way he told it. It is a sense he had, an electric sensation, and it was his most valuable tool. That night he *knew* the thing was in front of him, did not doubt at all, and so he melted down into an alcove between a rock and a bush and waited without moving. He was sure the thing ahead was large and dangerous, because in the past these were the things his sense had warned him about. He was also sure that it did not know he was there.

"Now just faintly he heard the thing moving in the leaves, shifting its position. He could not hear any breathing but he began to be certain the thing was a Morgan. For a while he thought it was sleeping and was about to move toward it when he heard something else moving up above, another one, and then all at once he realized that there were a great many of them all around him in among the bushes and trees, spread out and waiting. It was possible that they already knew where he was so he began to move. There was nowhere to go but down, and in the bottom of the gorge there was no cover. Nielson stopped by the edge of the bushes, trying now to think his way out, beginning to understand that the position was very bad. He could not be sure whether to warn Wolke, to make a noise, because more of them were probably on the other side of the gorge, or maybe Wolke already knew, and maybe the ones above had not yet spotted him. But then in the next moment it made no difference.

"Suddenly, viciously, out of the blackness across the gorge came a quick whish and a cracking, horrible thump. Then there was a thrashing in the leaves, which was an enormous uproar in the night, and a terrible victorious inhuman scream from above, and Nielson knew that Wolke had been hit. They could kill you with a rock at fifty yards, Nielson knew, and then he heard the ones above him beginning to move down toward *him*, moving without caution or cries, rustling in the bush and leaping toward the place where Wolke lay.

Instantly Nielson lay down his rifle and drew his pistol and knife and crouched with both hands ready for close action, tensed and huge and vicious, overwhelmingly ready to kill—but then he heard them running down the gorge and up the other side, seven or eight of them, and they had not known where he was after all. But now they were going to Wolke, who might still be alive, to make sure that he died where he lay.

"And then all this in an instant: knowing he could escape now easily back up the ravine, knowing that there were at least a dozen of them ahead, knowing that Wolke was already probably dead or at the very least would die before he could fight them off and get him back across half a continent to the city, still Nielson leapt out of the spot where he crouched and screamed his own human scream that made the one Morgan who crouched over Wolke leap up in surprise; and then he flew straight up the side of the gorge, roared like a great black engine through bushes and over rocks to the spot where Wolke lay, knife in one hand and pistol in the other, lips drawn back like an ape, enormous body of flying steel running into and over one lone stunned Morgan, bursting through a thicket and snapping off dead tree limbs with his head and shoulders, moving all in one frantic moment to the leafy hollow where Wolke was hit, arriving before the one Morgan there knew what had happened, killing that one on the spot, to whirl then and crouch and wait for the others.

"Then they should have rushed him, of course, or at the very least turned their rocks upon him, but here now again the likely did not happen. In the dark they were none of them sure what had happened. But they had seen the flash of his gun and one or two had seen the huge flying form of him, and they had no idea how many men had really come, so they sank into the bush and waited. Therefore Nielson had time to pull Wolke with him into cover, and also to cool his rage enough to think and let his senses work, to tell him where they were.

"As it turned out, he was very lucky. The Morgans

had been upset, because they had learned by this time that their sense of smell was no good in hunting humans. And then Nielson saw one and killed him with a flash from the blaster, which made up the minds of the others. And then also the Morgans were thinking simply of self-preservation, for there were not many of them left, at this point only fifteen or twenty on the whole continent. Therefore most of them left.

"But still two remained, one on the rise above him and another on a level with him across the ravine. These two remained after the others left. Were they more bitter, these two, for private reasons, or simply more stubborn and courageous? Odd that they should stay, but you can see that the Morgans were in this at least unusual. Would two wolves remain if the rest had left?

"Well, there was a long time yet till morning. Nielson moved quickly to stop the flow of blood from Wolke's head, and at the same time watched and listened for the two Morgans. From time to time, with a terrible unseen violence, a sharp rock would rip the air above him, to tear with mortal rage through the leaves around him, to shatter on a boulder or plow its way into a tree. Then the Morgan above, seeing that Nielson was well hidden, began craftily to lob bigger rocks down, heavy jagged rocks, heaving them into the air on a high trajectory like a mortar shell, so that they came down on Nielson and Wolke directly from above. Immediately that was very bad, and so Nielson turned and concentrated his attention uphill, perilously ignoring the one across the way, and when the Morgan above heaved up another rock his long arm was briefly visible, flung out above the cliff like a snake, and Nielson shot it off.

"Then there was only the other one across the way, the last helpless, mad, indomitable savage who still would not move, who waited until the dawn, flinging rocks with a desperate, increasing frenzy. But now Nielson was safe and knew it, and turned his attention to Wolke.

"By that time, however, Wolke was dead. He bled to

death at approximately the same time as the Morgan in the rocks above, like the Morgan silently, like the Morgan a creature hunted in the dark.

"And so Nielson passed the night with Wolke soft and sleeping on the ground beside him. You wonder, don't you, what he thought of the Morgans then. And shortly before dawn the last Morgan left, for unlike Nielson he could not slip the night lenses from his eyes and see just as well, or better, in the daylight, and therefore even this last stubborn one saw that he was exposed and had to leave. When he was gone Nielson knew it, but remained where he was until the sun was fully up. Then he picked up little Wolke and set him gently across his shoulders, went down into the gorge and retrieved his rifle from where he had left it, and walked back to the camp.

The sun had lowered and the old man had gone into shadow, so he shifted himself out into the light. The psychologist continued to stare at him without moving.

"If you had known Wolke—" The old man stopped and shrugged, embarrassed, then looked at his watch. There was now about an hour until sundown.

"We had better get on," he said, now somewhat wearily. "Now I will have to tell you about Maas."

"But—"

"All right, I am no storyteller. But you see Maas is the next important thing, not Nielson. Eventually you will learn about Nielson. Don't get the idea—I see you already have it—that Maas is the villain of the piece. No, not any more than that this is the story of a noble wild man betrayed by a city slicker. Maas was a genuinely worthwhile man. For what he did no doubt he suffered, but still, he believed he was right. That's what makes it so difficult to judge, to understand.

"Maas, you see, was a man of substantial family and education, of all the best schools, the best breeding, the best of everything. And he turned out the way men like that rarely do, a really sincere idealist. He believed in Man, in the dignity and future of Man, with something like a small boy's faith. Perhaps he substituted Man for God. At any rate, he made his faith evident in his speeches and his behavior, and men found him an exceptionally good man to work for, even though he was very handsome and suave and clean cut. For cynical men he had a charm. They followed him because of his great desire to conquer all the planets for Man, to reach the farther stars, not because they also believed, but because they would have liked to believe, and at any rate, it was inspiring to be believed *in*. So Maas was a very effective man, a comer. He gained his directorship while quite young, and so came to Morgan, and so set in motion, because of his great faith, the dark damned flow which was to destroy Nielson.

"Yet blame? Where is there blame? Here was a man, Maas, who believed that Man was the purpose of the universe, that he would eventually reach out even further and eventually, perhaps, transmute himself into a finer, nobler thing. And then, of course, keeping with this philosophy in mind, you can see how he must have looked upon the Morgans. How easy it would have been for Maas, how right for him in the long run, to overlook a report on the Morgans. Not really falsify, perhaps just not press it, perhaps just approve it when it had not been thorough—for let us remember that the Morgans paid no attention to tests. And then, did it bother him, Maas, that he had done it? Did it weigh with him at all? Where really was the wrong in it? I mean ultimately, from the viewpoint of a thousand years?"

"And Nielson," the psychologist said. "I begin to see. Nielson was at the other extreme. 'I think I could go live with the animals, they are so clean and pure'—that sort of thing?"

"No. Not at all. I told you this was not the story of a noble savage. Exactly what Nielson was I am not sure, but he was not simply a nature lover, nor a man hater either. Even when you know the whole thing you may not be able to classify. Always behind it there is some dark point that eludes you . . . but we had better get on."

* * *

"When Nielson came back with dead Wolke over his shoulder, no doubt it was with certain questions in his mind. But of course he could not be sure. And anyway, he could do nothing immediately, for there remained the grave question of Jen Wolke and her two children. Wolke had no insurance, being a professional hunter, and for the same reason had little in the bank. What money she had, Jen Wolke, was barely enough to get her home to Earth. Many of us chipped in, of course, as we had done when the Morgans killed others, and yet in the long run the end was automatically that Nielson had to go back into the woods. Killing the last of the Morgans would complete Wolke's contract and earn a few thousand, and also, perhaps, there was for Nielson some primitive debt of honor besides, yet the end was that he who had come here to help through killing was forced almost, impelled, you see, to go on helping, and at the same time killing, and so forged on to the last inevitable moment.

"But he could not go right away. He saw Wolke into the ground—there was not money to send him home— and then for a while he moved in with Jen Wolke, who was a fine woman, tall and soft, with thick black hair, fiery at times but also very affectionate—perhaps a strange wife for Wolke but a good one, and Nielson knew it. And did tongues wag? Oh, yes, indeed. But not to Nielson. There were many very large and ominous men among us, but none to jest with Nielson, or argue with him, and perhaps even many understood. To the woman Nielson was a great help. Although he was not what you might call an overly domesticated and helpful man, still, he was beyond doubt a tower of strength, no matter which way you look at it, and he was very good with the children, what with tales of lions and tigers and so on, and there was much room on his shoulder for crying.

"But in this I ought not be ironic. I don't mean to be. I do it to hide. He was a good, sincere man, and a great help simply with his presence. And I suppose few peo-

ple had ever really needed him. Later I learned that he
was debating with himself whether or not to ask her to
marry him. He told me she was a hunter's wife and he
was ready now and he needed *her*, was not doing any
favors. But I am not sure he believed it, or knew really
what he believed. Up until then he had been a man
who went his own way.

"And so, as it turned out, he remained.

"Well, then, shortly after Wolke was in the ground
Nielson came to ask me for a look at the captured
Morgans. I was happy to allow it and went along with
him, and oddly enough, we were not at the tank very
long before Director Maas came in behind us and stood
in the doorway watching.

"Now here is the scene. In the Bio tank were eleven
Morgans—seven male, four female. The Bio tank was a
huge steel affair with plastic windows, a standardized
model built to hold any game yet known, with pressure, atmosphere, temperature all carefully controlled
from the outside. The windows were one-way—you
could see in without the things inside seeing out—and
that was Nielson's first real sight of the Morgans.

"Eleven of them sitting in the tank together, close
together, not moving, not scratching or picking at themselves, not even sleeping or resting, just sitting upright,
all of them, arms folded in various positions and eyes
partly closed, statuesque, alien even in a setting of their
natural bushes and trees. Occasionally one would stretch
slightly and a weird ripple would flip down its body,
but otherwise there was no movement at all. And even
at rest like that, perhaps because of it, they were distinctly ominous. The least of them was seven feet tall.
They weighed an average of two hundred pounds, lean
and whiplike with gray fur all over them. Short fur,
silvery in the light. Their arms were long, out of proportion and three-jointed, which was the only really
fundamental difference between their body structure
and ours. Their faces were flat nosed and round, the fur
on their heads was no longer or different than the rest
of their hair, and of course they had no eyebrows or

hairline. But what you noticed most, after the long flowing arms, was the eyes. Set deep in the silvery fur like black rubber balls, no pupil, just wide solid balls. A long time after you left you could see those eyes. A long time.

"When Nielson turned I saw he was smiling. Then he saw Maas and he broke into a grin. Maas smiled too, very nicely, the two stood smiling together, Maas cautious and perhaps even now a little worried, Nielson beginning to understand and also beginning to wonder whether or not this was intentional, and so going directly to the point.

" 'Where do they rate on the intelligence scale?' he said, gesturing at the Morgans and still grinning, and Maas said cheerfully, 'Higher than most animals,' although he should have known Nielson had some professional knowledge of animal intelligence, and then somewhat surprised when Nielson wanted to know the exact figure, but saying, still smiling, that the figure was approximately level with that of a dog. And then, as I recall, Nielson did not say anything, but just looked at him for a long while, wondering now for the first time seriously if someone here was trying to put something over on him, and wondering also at the same time if he should say anything about it, and possibly perhaps unable to keep himself from letting this character know that they might be kidding each other, but they weren't kidding him, because then he said, 'Somebody's been kidding you.' And he turned to go, but Maas was not smiling now and stopped him. 'Why, what do you mean?' Shocked, puzzled, wounded, and now also Nielson was not smiling, and he said, 'They're a hell of a lot smarter than dogs.'

"And Maas said, 'You think there's been a mistake?'

"And Nielson said, 'Can't you tell just by looking at them?' And Maas, recovering himself now, said a bit more suavely, 'No, I confess I cannot. But then, undoubtedly, I don't have your natural sensitivity to animals.'

"And Nielson shrugged, annoyed with himself now

for having brought up the obvious and become involved
in it, and glanced at me, wishing for me to say something, but until that moment I had been incurious, had
not thought, and was useless.

"So Maas said, 'The man who examined them was
quite reputable, Mr. Nielson.'

"To which Nielson said stiffly, 'Don't worry about it.
Forget I said anything.' And turned to go, but Maas
said, 'But this is a very serious business—' to which
Nielson replied, 'Not to me it isn't, just so long as it's
legal, that's all,' at which point, with a slight nod at me,
he went out the door and away, leaving Maas standing
somewhat stunned with one hand out like a man reaching for the keys of a piano.

" 'Well,' he said eventually, 'now what do you make
of that?' wondering, no doubt, just how much I really
did make of it. And I, fumbling, turned to look in at the
Morgans, not doubting Maas at all yet, but doubting
Nielson certainly, until I looked in and saw the black
rubber eyes, and so began the doubt which has lasted
from that moment until this day.

"Maas said then, feeling his way, because actually
you know he had not been very bright about this, that
he knew there were rumors going round, but had not
paid them any attention because everyone knew how
reports of animals are exaggerated, how just normal
cleverness in an animal often seems remarkable, and besides, there was the psychologist's report, and the psychologist was a reputable man. Testing me, you see,
and then looking into my eyes and intelligent enough
himself at least to see the vague doubt forming there,
so bringing himself to say that it was, after all, the
question of our right to an entire planet, 'Man's right,'
he said, and therefore we must, of course, have the
Morgans reexamined. He said that when the first
rocketload of immigrants landed next week perhaps
there would be a qualified man aboard, and if not we
would send for one. And I agreed, was wholly in favor,
still in no way suspecting Maas, my mind occupied now
with the last alarming question, which was, namely,

that Nielson thought the Morgans were intelligent and yet could apparently easily go on killing them."

"And so we entered upon the last few days, during which I found out all I was ever to find out about Nielson, and during which he also found out a great deal about himself. I went to him and got him to drink with me—no small feat since he was not a drinker—but he had seen the Mapping Command patch on my shoulder and had some small respect for Mapping Command men, and so came with me to learn a few things about the uncharted region of the Rim, although to end by doing most of the talking himself, under the influence of liquor he ought not hold but seemed, at that time, to accept with relish.

"First I wanted to know why he was willing to kill the Morgans if he thought they were intelligent, for though I am no moralist I still am curious what people think about things like that, and he told me without ceremony. Hell, he said, everything is eaten. Everything alive is sooner or later killed and eaten. The big animals are allowed to grow old first, but the end is the same. The only real difference between man and animal, Nielson said, was that man was eaten after he went into the ground, but the animal rarely got that far.

"So there we sat in the beery afternoon—you begin to see him now, yes, he so very grave and so young, so young, not a fool, but simply young. He had given the matter a great deal of thought, that I could see, for when I asked him if he really believed that he said, Well, partly anyway. The point is: sometimes a man can be a magnificent thing. But so also sometimes can an animal. Not all animals, not all men. But then a great many things can be magnificent in different ways, like a mountain is magnificent, or a waterfall, or a big wind. And if it all has no meaning, if there really is Nobody Above who really gives a damn, if there are really no rules, still, a man can make his own rules and with luck he can get by. 'What bothers me most though,' Nielson said, slightly drunk now and brooding, 'is the goddamn blindness of it. A big wind, you see, is not aware of the ships it wrecks, nor is a tiger aware of the body it eats, but you die all the same, and what bothers me most is that you are eventually killed by something that doesn't give a damn. What I would like is to know that when I die I get it from something that has a good reason for it and knows it's me he's killing.'

"And thus Nielson the philosopher. And if that is all nonsense, well, that was three years ago and I still remember it almost word for word, and I put it in here because you cannot understand him without it. And see, in the end, the strange twist we take. Nielson, the woodsman, becomes the cynic, and Maas, the city man, is the idealist. But again, too simple, too simple. For deep down in Nielson, under the fragile outward layer which reasoned and saw much too much hate and waste and injustice, much deeper down in the region which knew the beauty of a leaf and a stormy sky, down so deep that Nielson himself was not aware of it, was something . . ."

"But I philosophize," George said wearily. "Let me get on with it. Listen carefully now. The sun is going down and we'll kill him soon. I would like you to know before we kill him. Watch how the rest of it happens and tell me then why.

"The rocket came and Nielson went back into the woods. There was no qualified man on the rocket to examine the Morgans so Maas sent for one, yet also let Nielson go kill the few remaining.

"And then, when Nielson was gone a week, a strange thing happened, oh, an odd, unfortunate, annoying thing. Such a time for it to happen too, because Nielson had just sent in several bodies by plane and informed Maas that there were only two left, and that he had them pinned down and would get them certainly by the end of the week. On that same day, in the evening, new atmosphere was given to the eleven Morgans in the tank. Curiously, it turned out that by a rare error someone mistook a tank of chlorine for a tank of oxygen—it was lying in the same rack with all the other oxygen tanks—and this man did not notice and so fed chlorine to the Morgans, who all strangled in a very short time. All eleven. It was not noticed until the next morning, because the Morgans did not move much anyway, but by that time it was much too late and none of them ever moved again. And Maas was greatly shaken when he heard of it, was he not? because racial murder is a very serious thing, and immediately he sent out word to find Nielson before he killed the last two.

"But Nielson was half a continent away.

"That same evening Nielson shot one of them as it came down to the river to drink. He shot it from a perch in a thick thorn bush across the way, in which he had been sitting for almost three days. During all that time he had not moved out of the bush, but sat waiting with diabolical patience while the last two Morgans, undoubtedly in a state of panic now, tried to sense him or get some sign of him. At last they thought he was gone, or at least not in the area, and they came out of hiding to drink at the stream. That was when Nielson got one of them. But the shot was from a long way off, and the Morgan had been careful to drink from a sheltered place, so it was not immediately fatal. The Morgan moved away as quickly as it could, plainly hit. The other seemed to be helping it. Nielson left the thorn bush and began to track them.

"It kept coming into his mind then, as it had kept coming to him during the three days in the thorn bush, that if you thought about this in the right light it was a dirty business. The two Morgans were sticking together. For some reason that bothered him. The unwounded one could easily have gotten away while Nielson trailed the other, could even circle around behind and try to get him from the rear. Yet the two stuck together, making it easy for him. He found himself wishing they would break up.

"They were moving to the north. He wondered where they were heading. He was between them and the only real cover, a marsh to the west. He supposed that they would try to double back. It was already quite murky in the woods, so he slipped his night lenses on, pressing forward silently and cautiously but very quickly, keeping his mind clear of everything but the hunt. He wondered how badly the one was hit, then began finding blood and knew. Pretty bad. And moving like that the Morgan would keep bleeding. Well, by morning he should end it. And then get off this planet for good. Go somewhere else and hunt things with tentacles. Maybe not hunt at all for a while. Maybe marry Jen Wolke. Have a home to go to and someone to talk to at night . . .

"All night long the two Morgans dragged on into the north, with Nielson closing in steadily behind. Early in the morning they began to climb, reaching the first line of low mountains, and then Nielson knew they would try to find a high rocky place where he would have to come at them from below. He quickened his pace, slowly passed them in the night, knowing where they were by little far-off movements. When daylight came he was well ahead of them, up in the high cold country, beginning to feel unnaturally tired now and wondering how in hell the wounded Morgan could keep it up, looking for a good place from which to get them as they passed.

"By eight o'clock he had figured the path they would take. He found a dark narrow place on a ledge between two boulders and wedged himself in. It was very cold and he was not dressed for it. He sat for a long while with his hand tucked in his armpit to keep the trigger finger warm and supple. At last he heard them coming.

"The wounded Morgan was breathing heavily. Nielson heard it a long way off. Then he heard a clatter in the rocks and thought they'd seen him and were trying to run away, so he peered out.

"But the two of them were in the open, perhaps fifty yards away, and they had not seen him. The wounded one had fallen, which was what made the clatter, and lay now on its back while the other bent over, talking to it. Talking to it.

"Quickly, not thinking, making a special effort to

bring the rifle to his shoulder slowly, icily, Nielson aimed and sighted and pressed the trigger, but the trigger wouldn't pull. He was suddenly dizzy, swore at himself. He bore down on his hand, on his mind. The gun went off. The kneeling one jerked, then fell across the other one. Although Nielson's hands had been trembling the shot was clean. When he reached them both Morgans were dead.

"He stood for a long while looking down, feeling very odd, very quiet and dazed. The one underneath, which he had wounded the night before, was a female. Nielson felt a cold wind begin to blow in his brain. The female had been with child.

"He sat down on a rock, rested his head in his hands. He sat there for a long while. When it began to snow he put out his hand and watched the flakes melt on his palm.

"The snow began coating the dead Morgans. Eventually they were completely covered and Nielson was able to leave. He did not take them with him. He wanted to go somewhere quickly and take a bath . . ."

"Oh my Lord," the psychologist said.

"Yes," George said. "He came back and they were all dead. All the Morgans. All of them. Racial murder. But even before he knew that he was already damned. He told me all about it on the plane coming in. He did not blame himself, he said. How could you break the rules when there were no rules? He said what he was feeling now was probably something left over from his childhood, something childlike and virtuous they had put in him when he was young but which he knew amounted to nothing and which he would certainly easily get over. And then I had to tell him about the other Morgans, the dead Morgans, the last eleven all dead, and when he heard that he sat with his hands shaking until we got back to the city, and then he left me and went to Maas's office and killed him with his bare hands."

The psychologist bowed his head.

"So he put the blame on Maas. He had to put it somewhere. He knew that Maas and he had done it and in killing Maas unconsciously punished them both, for he made it necessary then, inevitable then, that we should come after him and kill him too. But he could not face his own guilt and his huge sad terrible pride would not let him quit, so he destroyed Maas, really destroyed him, and then went back into the woods. We came after him. He fought back. Maybe he thought that in this way he was for a while at least taking the Morgans' place. Or maybe after the event he was cold and realistic about it and realized there was nothing else to do. But the point was that he could not admit to himself what he had done. It was all his parents' fault, or Maas's, or God's, that such a rage should be in him, but not his own. And yet always, always, always running through the dark trees he knew, *he knew* it was wrong. And so will die knowing, God help him, unclean, unclean, and yet in the end of him somehow magnificent, if wrong before God and man then wrong all the way, all the last bloody way down to the futile tragic last second of his life—heroic, damn it, no matter which way you look at it, taking on a whole planet with no hope of winning, knowing the end is a bullet or a burn, a bullet or a burn . . ."

The two men sat silently in the hot red glare of the dying sun. A little while later there was a single shot from the rocks near them and someone cried exultantly, "Got him!" and there was a scramble down to the river.

George and the psychologist rose and went down, found Nielson lying face down in the water, the blond hair long and dirty and bloody. His back was pink and bare, because when he had come out into the open he had taken his shirt off before going into the water. He was already dead. Even in death he was still very big.

Some years ago I agreed to write a brief article on the fiction of Arthur Porges. I thought Porges had done only a few stories in the '50s and '60s, some of which were memorable.

Actually there are about seventy stories. Most of them are quite short; all of them are expertly crafted; and a very high percentage of them are memorable, though often for the gimmick on which the piece is hung rather than for the weight of the story.

"Priceless Possession" has no gimmick. It's about three perfectly decent people faced with a decision that's bigger than they are.

But they're the ones making it.

He heard the lieutenant whistle softly, and knew why.

In 1870, a whaler—or beachcomber—who found a large chunk of that mysterious substance, ambergris, was a fortunate fellow, sure to make a lot of money from his discovery. In 2270, a comparable but even rarer and more valuable windfall was the taking of an S-2, or Solar Sailor.

The first had been spotted in 2164. It knocked the world of science off balance for years to follow. The notion that any organism could live and grow in airless, irradiated, non-temperatured space was so novel and hard to accept that the crew of the *Hakluyt* were long called hoaxers, who with fake photos were amusing themselves at the public's expense.

However, after several more of the weird creatures had been seen, the evidence built up beyond doubting. It was no longer possible to deny the truth.

The S-2, like the Portuguese Man of War of Earth's seas, consists of a jelly-like body from which sprouts a sail that reacts to the pressure of light. The organism apparently lives by ingesting cosmic dust much as whales utilize plankton. It can furl or twist its sail—something never observed, but inferred—but quite slowly, having no muscles as such, and so guides its movement in space. Obviously, it must avoid getting trapped in a strong gravitational field, since it could never escape, and would either crash on a planet or be immolated in a sun. Of necessity, it cruises only where the impact of photons against the sail dominates the pull of matter.

Since all attempts to communicate with the organism were failures, the Galactic Council reluctantly classified it as a lower animal of inconsiderable consciousness, and lawful game.

As for the sail, the source of the creature's commercial value, it is the most remarkable fabric to be found in the whole galaxy, and almost beyond price. Thin and light as the finest spider-silk, it is stronger than the toughest synthetics, from nylon-gamma to durette; and can be cut only with power shears of concillium alloy. It is fireproof, waterproof and unaffected by any chemical reagent, however concentrated. It is also a near-perfect conductor of electricity, having a resistance close to zero at all temperatures. Finally, the material shimmers rainbowlike under radiation of every wavelength, from cosmic rays to the longest members of the AM band. Whether for the most precise instruments or the gowns of multimillionaire women, the fabric is so much in demand, and so scarce, that the price must be set by public auction.

Every attempt at duplication in the laboratory failed; and it is thought that the missing factor may be time. It might take an S-2 a thousand years to grow its sail, one molecule at a time, under the rays of many classes of stars, in the hard vacuum of space—and such conditions aren't to be simulated in any laboratory.

The note of excitement in Alvarez' voice was now accounted for. Aside from the basic drama of the find, the boy saw barriers dropping in all directions. He saw, too, in his mind's eye, the lovely face of Julia Marlowe, whose father was a senior member of the Galactic Council, and not likely to let his daughter marry a penniless ensign. She was fond enough of the boy, approving his darkly handsome face and muscular body; but she spent more on cosmetics and perfume than he earned. She was beautiful, gay, generous and sweet, but there was plenty of her father's iron in the girl, and she would never settle down to live on love alone.

But now that he was about to be one-third owner of a huge S-2 sail . . .

Garret had been studying the image on the screen, his pale, glittering eyes a glacial blue.

"You're right, by God—I didn't believe it until this minute! Luis, do you know what that lovely beastie out there means to us?"

The lieutenant knew what it meant to *him*, all right. He was over age in grade, and soon to be retired on the usual pittance. A first-rate fighting man, brave, quick-

witted and up to every dirty dodge of battle, it was only
his lack of self-control that kept him from climbing.
Thick-set, blocky, with hot, intolerant eyes, he always
preferred a blow to a word: tops in a messy brawl, but
never seeing more than ten minutes ahead.

"Do I?" the ensign replied to Garret's question. "It
means about a million credits, at least—a three-way
split. If the captain lives," he added quickly. "And then
I can ask Julia to marry me."

"Good for you," the lieutenant said, only half-hearing.
He was thinking what his own share would do. No
more worry about living on his retirement pay, or taking some job that exploited his former rank and cluster
of decorations. A life of luxury was now the prognosis:
wine, women—he could do without song; the rustle of
large-denomination bills was the most musical sound of
all.

"Well," Alvarez said, grinning hugely. "What are we
waiting for? They say a laser beam in that big bluish
spot just off center kills the thing dead. And no risk of
hurting the sail—as if anything could."

"Right. Move in now. We should be within range in
an hour. The first in fourteen years," he murmured
gloatingly. "They may be practically extinct, even with
the few taken. Or bunched up in some other galaxy; the
ones captured here might be real wanderers." He made
some careful measurements with the micrometers, and
said in an exultant voice: "I make the dimensions of this
sail as giving five hundred square feet. And it should
bring in a lot more than the last, because they've gone
without so long. Million credits, hell—if this doesn't
net us twice that at the auction, I'll eat the jelly part—no
bread!"

The ensign manipulated the controls, and the ship
began to converge on the S-2. Then the captain's voice,
weak but lucid, came over the intercom.

"Lieutenant Garret," it said. "Please come to my
quarters at once. Alvarez, too."

"Say," the boy said. "The new drug's working. He

sounds fine. Kill or cure, the medicos said, and they were right. He'd be dead without it—you saw how bad he was."

"This is a lucky day all around," the lieutenant said. "One quickie course in Medical Techniques, and you save the skipper's life; not bad. Well, put the ship on auto again, and let's go. This news ought to complete the cure."

When they came in, Captain Ling was struggling to a sitting position; his eyes were feverishly bright, and he panted.

"There's something outside," he gasped. "It's been communicating with me—mentally."

They gaped at him.

"What is?" the boy demanded.

"An S-2," the captain said. "Didn't you spot it? What kind of a watch you two keeping while I—never mind. Maybe it's still too far off. Anyhow, it was telling a friend: 'I'm going to die soon; the Killers are near, and must have detected me. We can't communicate with them, and they always destroy us; I don't know why. Good-by—' I didn't get the other's name, if it has one. It was so far away . . . another galaxy, I think. Yet they were in touch instantly."

"You're hallucinating, Captain," Garret said. "You know very well that nobody's ever talked to an S-2. They're just space jellyfish—lower animals. Weird and wonderful, but no more intelligent than a worm."

Ling propped himself up, lips narrowing.

"Is there an S-2 out there or not?"

"Yes, sir," the lieutenant admitted reluctantly. He gave the captain a lowering stare. "Telepathy is known to occur among humans. It's not subject to control, but does exist. You must have caught some of my thoughts —or Luis's. That has to be it."

Ling looked bewildered; he was still very ill, and not thinking clearly. He sank back in his bunk, breathing heavily.

"Maybe you're right, but we must be sure. Don't kill

it; you mustn't. That's an order," he said, his voice hardening.

"But, Captain," his exec protested. "The S-2 is officially classified as a lower animal, subject to capture—legitimate game. Your order is actually illegal. I don't have to remind you, sir, what such a find is worth. Your share would be at least—"

"Never mind that," Ling snapped. "I'm in command, Lieutenant. If an order's illegal, you know the regulations; obey it, and complain later. I shouldn't have to point that out to an officer of your experience."

"But we'll lose the thing!" Garret said angrily. "Maybe you don't care, but I'm not passing up a fortune—one of the few a serviceman can get. Everything else the civvies latch on to, while we must settle for wages!"

Ling's eyes widened at Garret's tone, but he merely said quietly: "You can follow it for a while. Maybe I can make contact again."

"I'm sure it was the new drug, Captain," Alvarez suggested. "You were so far gone we took a chance on that new stuff—the psychic energizer. It gave you hallucinations."

"But it was all so clear—and logical," Ling said, almost to himself. "They live very slowly compared to us, sailing from one universe to another—across those incredible gaps we haven't dared to tackle yet. They avoid matter; maybe that's why we've found so few. They daren't get trapped by a gravity field. That small mass of theirs—it takes millennia to build up from cosmic dust down into usable food. Their thoughts are too sluggish for us, and their motions, too. They just can't signal in time to ask our mercy. Helpless—it's a terrible thing. If only I could slow my thinking down to match . . . we can record speech, and run that at any speed, but thought . . ." He closed his eyes.

"Just how will you make contact, then?" Garret demanded sullenly. "We can't follow it forever; we have a deadline of our own. Rigel III by next month, remember?"

"I don't know," the captain admitted, without opening his eyes. "I'm all muddled up right now. Nothing's coming through at the moment." Then his lids snapped up. "There's only one way, but it's obvious enough. You'll have to give me more of the new drug."

"But, Captain," Alvarez objected. "That's risky. You were lucky once. Why push it?"

"I have to. If that's the stuff to stir up nerve endings or get them synchronized somehow with an S-2's thoughts, I have to try it. I won't have it on my conscience that I let a highly intelligent being get killed by my crew. And a noble being, too. If you could have felt its personality! No hatred of us; a pure spirit . . ."

"I'd be pure, too, just floating alone in space," Garret said sourly. "But I have to live on Earth, and that costs money."

"You don't know what you're saying," Ling said. "You're not that callous. And there's more. They can't *do* anything; no organs for manipulation, but what minds! I could hear this one; he was building up a mathematical system. My specialty—and he lost me after the first five postulates! Think what we could learn! The theorem he was working towards would have unified electricity, gravitation, magnetism, elasticity, the nucleus—sounds wild, but I believe. I really do believe!"

"Not all math has practical significance," Garret said.

"Granted. But consider this one point. They've licked the communications problem. By some kind of thought exchange they converse over distances we can hardly conceive. When one buds—that's how they reproduce—the two drift apart for maybe fifty thousand years. The acceleration may be only .000001 meters per second squared, but you know how that builds up the velocity in time—simple integration. Yet father—and—call it 'son'—have no trouble talking across the void. Think how we need such a technique. Light's too slow for anything out of the piddling solar system itself. And we're stymied with it." He sat up again, jaw out. "I don't have to convince you, damn it. Ensign—give me the drug again: that's an order!"

There was no resisting the command, not in this

navy. The boy looked at Garret, who scowled, then shrugged.

When the second dose had been injected, the two men waited impatiently for a reaction. It came more quickly this time.

As soon as the captain began to recover, he said: "I'll prove it to you. If I can receive from the S-2, it can receive from me. I'll—I'll ask it to signal."

"Captain, that's crazy," said Garret. "What kind of signal could it give? It can't talk. It can't shoot off flares . . ."

"I'll ask it to furl its sail."

Garret hesitated. "We'll watch," he promised.

And watch they did, for hours, while the prospect of the money began to grow larger in both their minds.

"A million credits," said Alvarez.

"More than that. Twice that much."

"And it's all out there waiting for us. Can't get away. Wonder if its smart enough to run anyway? Not that it could; you move pretty slow, sailing that way, with just a push from light-beams. It's as good as ours, no matter what. Two million credits—ooh!"

Then he gulped, staring at the micrometer dial, which was zeroed in on the sail's upper right-hand corner. "Oh, no!"

"What?" the lieutenant barked, bringing his thoughts back from a pleasure-palace on Rigel II, where a little money bought delights unknown on earth.

"It's furling! So help me God, it is—look! We'd better tell the captain right away."

He reached for the intercom, but Garret put a thick hand on his wrist.

"Hold it a minute. We need to make sure. Give it more time—while we talk."

But for many minutes they said nothing; just stared as the sail, curling very slowly, as a flower might, began to bring one corner down. After the motion left no doubt, Alvarez stirred restlessly; again the lieutenant restrained him.

"Listen," he said. "I'll make this linear—not a curve. And strictly negative on the memory-cube. I'll deny saying it, officially." His dark face was grim. "All right; the thing's signalling; it has some sense. But it's not human—not like us; just a damned jelly-fish. No matter what the Single Universe cloud-heads say, I don't call every weird blob my brother just because it knows the multiplication table! There's a fortune out there, a real life for us. Gonna let it get away?"

"B—but," the boy stammered. "What about communication? That's just as valuable. We could make a pile."

"We? Don't be stupid! The lab boys would have to work on the S-2 for years, maybe. And after they get the idea, how long to duplicate it? And who knows even if the drug would act the same on another guy? We could have long, gray beards before it's all worked out—and still have no claim, either." He gave the ensign a steady, cold stare. "I'll talk to the captain; you back me—okay?"

Alvarez hesitated briefly, then said: "Okay."

"Let's go down; we can talk some more on the way."

They entered the cabin, and Ling peered at them.

"Sick," he mumbled. "Damned stuff hits my guts now." He managed to sit up. "Well? What happened? You must have seen it. The S-2 told me it had furled."

"I'm sorry, Captain," Garret said, his face open and honest, gaze steady. "Nothing happened. We watched very closely. Not the slightest sign of a signal. In fact, the thing opened its sail further and was moving off our course—running away, obviously. Or trying to; but it's just too slow. An animal reaction, I'd say. Lower animal escaping instinctively. You had hallucinations from that drug. Right, Alvarez?"

His face pale, the boy said: "That's right, Captain. No sign of any intelligent response. You must have dreamed up the whole exchange. It's a pity," he sighed.

"I should have known," Ling said bitterly, settling

back in his bunk. "Some mighty good men tried to communicate—like Duclaux of the old *Josiah Willard Gibbs*—and couldn't get through. Just a drug, after all. Well," he said, looking at them owlishly, "I've held up your jackpot long enough. Go get your millions!"

"*Our* jackpot," Garret said. "And it's a big one, Captain. Your share will buy you that estate you've mentioned so often—that, and a whole lot more."

"I'd sooner have found what I thought was out there. But at least my conscience is clear."

Outside the cabin, the two officers exchanged glances.

"*His* conscience is clear," the lieutenant said. "And mine isn't worth two-thirds of a million credits." He put his hand on the boy's shoulder. "Your people have a saying I like: 'Take what you want—and pay for it.'"

"I know that one," Alvarez said wryly. "My father uses it quite a bit. And then Mother tells him: 'Ah, but when the bill finally comes, it may be too high.'" For a moment, as he spoke, his face, normally round and boyish, seemed old.

"On the other hand, sometimes the bill never comes," Garret said.

The stories in this collection are as much about moral decisions as they are about hunting; if you're reading straight through, you'll have noticed that. That's inevitable (at least given my personal outlook), because the question of whether or not to kill is as basic a moral decision as any a human being will make.

But there are other issues as well. "Good Night, Mr. James" involves a man who's treating as a personal problem an event which threatens to loose something very nasty on society as a whole.

And it involves something else as well.

GOOD NIGHT, MR. JAMES

Clifford D. Simak

He came alive from nothing. He became aware from unawareness.

He smelled the air of the night and heard the trees whispering on the embankment above him and the breeze that had set the trees to whispering came down to him and felt him over with soft and tender fingers, for all the world as if it were examining him for broken bones or contusions and abrasions.

He sat up and put both his palms down upon the ground beside him to help him sit erect and stared into the darkness. Memory came slowly and when it came it was incomplete and answered nothing.

His name was Henderson James and he was a human being and he was sitting somewhere on a planet that was called the Earth. He was thirty-six years old and he was, in his own way, famous, and comfortably well-off. He lived in an old ancestral home on Summit Avenue, which was a respectable address even if it had lost some of its smartness in the last twenty years or so.

On the road above the slope of the embankment a car

went past with its tires whining on the pavement and for a moment its headlights made the treetops glow. Far away, muted by the distance, a whistle cried out. And somewhere else a dog was barking with a flat viciousness.

His name was Henderson James and if that were true, why was he here? Why should Henderson James be sitting on the slope of an embankment, listening to the wind in the trees and to a wailing whistle and a barking dog? Something had gone wrong, some incident that, if he could but remember it, might answer all his questions.

There was a job to do.

He sat and stared into the night and found that he was shivering, although there was no reason why he should, for the night was not that cold. Beyond the embankment he heard the sounds of a city late at night, the distant whine of the speeding car and the far-off wind-broken screaming of a siren. Once a man walked along a street close by and James sat listening to his footsteps until they faded out of hearing.

Something had happened and there was a job to do, a job that he had been doing, a job that somehow had been strangely interrupted by the inexplicable incident which had left him lying here on this embankment.

He checked himself. Clothing . . . shorts and shirt, strong shoes, his wristwatch and the gun in the holster at his side.

A gun?

The job involved a gun.

He had been hunting in the city, hunting something that required a gun. Something that was prowling in the night and a thing that must be killed.

Then he knew the answer, but even as he knew it he sat for a moment wondering at the strange, methodical, step-by-step progression of reasoning that had brought him to the memory. First his name and the basic facts pertaining to himself, then the realization of where he was and the problem of why he happened to be there and finally the realization that he had a gun and that it was meant to be used. It was a logical way to think, a primer schoolbook way to work it out:

I am a man named Henderson James.

I live in a house on Summit Avenue.

Am I in the house on Summit Avenue?

No, I am not in the house on Summit Avenue.

I am on an embankment somewhere.

Why am I on the embankment?

But it wasn't the way a man thought, at least not the normal way a normal man would think. Man thought in shortcuts. He cut across the block and did not go all the way around.

It was a frightening thing, he told himself, this clear-around-the-block thinking. It wasn't normal and it wasn't right and it made no sense at all . . . no more sense than did the fact that he should find himself in a place with no memory of getting there.

He rose to his feet and ran his hands up and down his body. His clothes were neat, not rumpled. He hadn't been beaten up and he hadn't been thrown from a speeding car. There were no sore places on his body and his face was unbloody and whole and he felt all right.

He hooked his fingers in the holster belt and shucked it up so that it rode tightly on his hips. He pulled out the gun and checked it with expert and familiar fingers and the gun was ready.

He walked up the embankment and reached the road, went across it with a swinging stride to reach the sidewalk that fronted the row of new bungalows. He heard a car coming and stepped off the sidewalk to crouch in a clump of evergreens that landscaped one corner of a lawn. The move was instinctive and he crouched there, feeling just a little foolish at the thing he'd done.

The car went past and no one saw him. They would not, he now realized, have noticed him even if he had remained out on the sidewalk.

He was unsure of himself; that must be the reason for

his fear. There was a blank spot in his life, some mysterious incident that he did not know and the unknowing
of it had undermined the sure and solid foundation of
his own existence, had wrecked the basis of his motive
and had turned him, momentarily, into a furtive animal
that darted and hid at the approach of his fellow men.

That and something that had happened to him that
made him think clear around the block.

He remained crouching in the evergreens, watching
the street and the stretch of sidewalk, conscious of the
white-painted, ghostly bungalows squatting back in their
landscaped lots.

A word came into his mind. *Puudly*. An odd word,
unearthly, yet it held terror.

The *puudly* had escaped and that was why he was
here, hiding on the front lawn of some unsuspecting
and sleeping citizen, equipped with a gun and a determination to use it, ready to match his wits and the
quickness of brain and muscle against the most bloodthirsty, hate-filled thing yet found in the Galaxy.

The *puudly* was dangerous. It was not a thing to
harbor. In fact, there was a law against harboring not
only a *puudly*, but certain other alien beasties even less
lethal than a *puudly*. There was good reason for such a
law, reason which no one, much less himself, would
ever think to question.

And now the *puudly* was loose and somewhere in the
city.

James grew cold at the thought of it, his brain forming images of the things that might come to pass if he
did not hunt down the alien beast and put an end to it.

Although beast was not quite the word to use. The
puudly was more than a beast . . . just how much more
than a beast he once had hoped to learn. He had not
learned a lot, he now admitted to himself, not nearly all
there was to learn, but he had learned enough. More
than enough to frighten him.

For one thing, he had learned what hate could be
and how shallow an emotion human hate turned out

when measured against the depth and intensity and the ravening horror of the *puudly's* hate. Not unreasoning hate, for unreasoning hate defeats itself, but a rational, calculating, driving hate that motivated a clever and deadly killing machine which directed its rapacity and its cunning against every living thing that was not a *puudly*.

For the beast had a mind and a personality that operated upon the basic law of self-preservation against all comers, whoever they might be, extending that law to the interpretation that safety lay in one direction only . . . the death of every other living being. No other reason was needed for a *puudly's* killing. The fact that anything else lived and moved and was thus posing a threat, no matter how remote, against a *puudly*, was sufficient reason in itself.

It was psychotic, of course, some murderous instinct planted far back in time and deep in the creature's racial consciousness, but no more psychotic, perhaps, than many human instincts.

The *puudly* had been, and still was for that matter, a unique opportunity for a study in alien behaviorism. Given a permit, one could have studied them on their native planet. Refused a permit, one sometimes did a foolish thing, as James had.

And foolish acts backfire, as this one did.

James put down a hand and patted the gun at his side, as if by doing so he might derive some assurance that he was equal to the task. There was no question in his mind as to the thing that must be done. He must find the *puudly* and kill it and he must do that before the break of dawn. Anything less than that would be abject and horrifying failure.

For the *puudly* would bud. It was long past its time for the reproductive act and there were bare hours left to find it before it had loosed upon the Earth dozens of baby *puudlies*. They would not remain babies for long. A few hours after budding they would strike out on their own. To find one *puudly*, lost in the vastness of a sleeping city, seemed bad enough; to track down some dozens of them would be impossible.

So it was tonight or never.

Tonight there would be no killing on the *puudly's* part. Tonight the beast would be intent on one thing only, to find a place where it could rest in quiet, where it could give itself over wholeheartedly and with no interference, to the business of bringing other *puudlies* into being.

It was clever. It would have known where it was going before it had escaped. There would be, on its part, no time wasted in seeking or in doubling back. It would have known where it was going and already it was there, already the buds would be rising on its body, bursting forth and growing.

There was one place, and one place only, in the entire city where an alien beast would be safe from prying eyes. A man could figure that one out and so could a *puudly*. The question was: Would the *puudly* know that a man could figure it out? Would the *puudly* underestimate a man? Or, knowing that the man would know it, too, would it find another place of hiding?

James rose from the evergreens and went down the sidewalk. The street marker at the corner, standing underneath a swinging street light, told him where he was and it was closer to the place where he was going than he might have hoped.

II

The zoo was quiet for a while, and then something sent up a howl that raised James' hackles and made his blood stop in his veins.

James, having scaled the fence, stood tensely at its foot, trying to identify the howling animal. He was unable to place it. More than likely, he told himself, it was a new one. A person simply couldn't keep track of all the zoo's occupants. New ones were coming in all the time, strange, unheard of creatures from the distant stars.

Straight ahead lay the unoccupied moat cage that up until a day or two before had held an unbelievable

monstrosity from the jungles of one of the Arctian worlds.
James grimaced in the dark, remembering the thing.
They had finally had to kill it.

And now the *puudly* was there . . . well, maybe not
there, but one place that it could be, the one place in
the entire city where it might be seen and arouse no
comment, for the zoo was filled with animals that were
seldom seen and another strange one would arouse only
momentary wonder. One animal more would go unnoticed unless some zoo attendant should think to check
the records.

There, in that unoccupied cage area, the *puudly* would
be undisturbed, could quietly go about its business of
budding out more *puudlies*. No one would bother it, for
things like *puudlies* were the normal occupants of this
place set aside for the strangers brought to Earth to be
stared at and studied by that ferocious race, the humans.

James stood quietly beside the fence.

Henderson James. Thirty-six. Unmarried. Alien psychologist. An official of this zoo. And an offender against
the law for having secured and harbored an alien being
that was barred from Earth.

Why, he asked himself, did he think of himself in this
way? Why, standing here, did he catalogue himself? It
was instinctive to know one's self . . . there was no
need, no sense of setting up a mental outline of one's
self.

It had been foolish to go ahead with his *puudly*
business. He recalled how he had spent days fighting it
out with himself, reviewing all the disastrous possibilities
which might arise from it. If the old renegade spaceman
had not come to him and had not said, over a bottle of
most delicious Lupan wine, that he could deliver, for a
certain, rather staggering sum, one live *puudly*, in good
condition, it never would have happened.

James was sure that of himself he never would have
thought of it. But the old space captain was a man he
knew and admired from former dealings. He was a
man who was not adverse to turning either an honest or

a dishonest dollar, and yet he was a man, for all of that, that you could depend upon. He would do what you paid him for and keep his lip buttoned tight once the deed was done.

James had wanted a *puudly*, for it was a most engaging beast with certain little tricks that, once understood, might open up new avenues of speculation and approach, might write new chapters in the tortuous study of alien minds and manners.

But for all of that, it had been a terrifying thing to do and now that the beast was loose, the terror was compounded. For it was not wholly beyond speculation that the descendants of this one brood that the escaped *puudly* would spawn might wipe out the population of the Earth, or at the best, make the Earth untenable for its rightful dwellers.

A place like the Earth, with its teeming millions, would provide a field day for the fangs of the *puudlies*, and the minds that drove the fangs. They would not hunt for hunger, nor for the sheer madness of the kill, but because of the compelling conviction that no *puudly* would be safe until Earth was wiped clean of life. They would be killing for survival, as a cornered rat would kill . . . except that they would be cornered nowhere but in the murderous insecurity of their minds.

If the posses scoured the Earth to hunt them down, they would be found in all directions, for they would be shrewd enough to scatter. They would know the ways of guns and traps and poisons and there would be more and more of them as time went on. Each of them would accelerate their budding to replace with a dozen or a hundred the ones that might be killed.

James moved quietly forward to the edge of the moat and let himself down into the mud that covered the bottom. When the monstrosity had been killed, the moat had been drained and should long since have been cleaned, but the press of work, James thought, must have prevented its getting done.

Slowly he waded out into the mud, feeling his way, his feet making sucking noises as he pulled them through the slime. Finally he reached the rocky incline that led out of the moat to the island cage.

He stood for a moment, his hands on the great, wet boulders, listening, trying to hold his breath so the sound of it would not interfere with hearing. The thing that howled had quieted and the night was deathly quiet. Or seemed, at first, to be. Then he heard the little insect noises that ran through the grass and bushes and the whisper of the leaves in the trees across the moat and the far-off sound that was the hoarse breathing of a sleeping city.

Now, for the first time, he felt fear. Felt it in the silence that was not a silence, in the mud beneath his feet, in the upthrust boulders that rose out of the moat.

The *puudly* was a dangerous thing, not only because it was strong and quick, but because it was intelligent. Just how intelligent, he did not know. It reasoned and it planned and schemed. It could talk, though not as a human talks . . . probably better than a human ever could. For it not only could talk words, but it could talk emotions. It lured its victims to it by the thoughts it put into their minds; it held them entranced with dreams and illusion until it slit their throats. It could purr a man to sleep, could lull him to suicidal inaction. It could drive him crazy with a single flicking thought, hurling a perception so foul and alien that the mind recoiled deep inside itself and stayed there, coiled tight, like a watch that has been overwound and will not run.

It should have budded long ago, but it had fought off its budding, holding back against the day when it might escape, planning, he realized now, its fight to stay on Earth, which meant its conquest of Earth. It had planned, and planned well, against this very moment, and it would feel or show no mercy to anyone who interfered with it.

His hand went down and touched the gun and he felt the muscles in his jaw involuntarily tightening and suddenly there was at once a lightness and a hardness in him that had not been there before. He pulled himself up the boulder face, seeking cautious hand- and toe-holds, breathing shallowly, body pressed against the rock. Quickly, and surely, and no noise, for he must reach the top and be there before the *puudly* knew there was anyone around.

The *puudly* would be relaxed and intent upon its business, engrossed in the budding forth of that numerous family that in days to come would begin the grim and relentless crusade to make an alien planet safe for *puudlies* . . . and for *puudlies* alone.

That is, if the *puudly* were here and not somewhere else. James was only a human trying to think like a *puudly* and that was not an easy or a pleasant job and he had no way of knowing if he succeeded. He could only hope that his reasoning was vicious and crafty enough.

His clawing hand found grass and earth and he sank his fingers deep into the soil, hauling his body up the last few feet of the rock face above the pit.

He lay flat upon the gently sloping ground, listening, tensed for any danger. He studied the ground in front of him, probing every foot. Distant street lamps lighting the zoo walks threw back the total blackness that had engulfed him as he climbed out of the moat, but there still were areas of shadow that he had to study closely.

Inch by inch, he squirmed his way along, making sure of the terrain immediately ahead before he moved a muscle. He held the gun in a rock-hard fist, ready for instant action, watching for the faintest hint of motion, alert for any hump or irregularity that was not rock or bush or grass.

Minutes magnified themselves into hours, his eyes ached with staring and the lightness that had been in him drained away, leaving only the hardness, which was as tense as a drawn bowstring. A sense of failure began to seep into his mind and with it came the full-fledged, until now unadmitted, realization of what failure meant, not only for the world, but for the dignity and the pride that was Henderson James.

Now, faced with the possibility, he admitted to himself the action he must take if the *puudly* were not here, if he did not find it here and kill it. He would have to notify the authorities, would have to attempt to alert the police, must plead with newspapers and radio to warn the citizenry, must reveal himself as a man who, through pride and self-conceit, had exposed the people of the Earth to this threat against their hold upon their native planet.

They would not believe him. They would laugh at him until the laughter died in their torn throats, choked off with their blood. He sweated, thinking of it, thinking of the price this city, and the world, would pay before it learned the truth.

There was a whisper of sound, a movement of black against deeper black.

The *puudly* rose in front of him, not more than six feet away, from its bed beside a bush. He jerked the pistol up and his finger tightened on the trigger.

"Don't," the *puudly* said inside his mind. "I'll go along with you."

His finger strained with the careful slowness of the squeeze and the gun leaped in his hand, but even as it did he felt the whiplash of terror slash at his brain, caught for just a second the terrible import, the mind-shattering obscenity that glanced off his mind and ricocheted away.

"Too late," he told the *puudly*, with his voice and his mind and his body shaking. "You should have tried that first. You wasted precious seconds. You would have got me if you had done it first."

It had been easy, he assured himself, much easier than he had thought. The *puudly* was dead or dying and the Earth and its millions of unsuspecting citizens were safe and, best of all, Henderson James was safe . . . safe from indignity, safe from being stripped naked of the little defenses he had built up through the years to shield him against the public stare. He felt relief flood over him and it left him pulseless and breathless and feeling clean, but weak.

"You fool," the dying *puudly* said, death clouding its words as they built up in his mind. "You fool, you half-thing, you duplicate . . ."

It died then and he felt it die, felt the life go out of it and leave it empty.

He rose softly to his feet and he seemed stunned and at first he thought it was from knowing death, from having touched hands with death within the *puudly's* mind.

The *puudly* had tried to fool him. Faced with the pistol, it had tried to throw him off his balance to give it the second that it needed to hurl the mind-blasting thought that had caught at the edge of his brain. If he had hesitated for a moment, he knew, it would have been all over with him. If his finger had slackened for a moment, it would have been too late.

The *puudly* must have known that he would think of the zoo as the first logical place to look and, even knowing that, it had held him in enough contempt to come here, had not even bothered to try to watch for him, had not tried to stalk him, had waited until he was almost on top of it before it moved.

And that was queer, for the *puudly* must have known, with its uncanny mental powers, every move that he had made. It must have maintained a casual contact with his mind every second of the time since it had escaped. He had known that and . . . wait a minute, he hadn't known it until this very moment, although, knowing it now, it seemed as if he had always known it.

What is the matter with me? he thought. There's something wrong with me. I should have known I could not surprise the *puudly*, and yet I didn't know it. I must have surprised it, for otherwise it would have finished me off quite leisurely at any moment after I climbed out of the moat.

You fool, the *puudly* had said. You fool, you half-thing, you duplicate . . .

You duplicate!

He felt the strength and the personality and the

hard, unquestioned identity of himself as Henderson James, human being, drain out of him, as if someone had cut the puppet string and he, the puppet, had slumped supine upon the stage.

So that was why he had been able to surprise the *puudly!*

There were two Henderson Jameses. The *puudly* had been in contact with one of them, the original, the real Henderson James, had known every move he made, had known that it was safe so far as that Henderson James might be concerned. It had not known of the second Henderson James that had stalked it through the night.

Henderson James, duplicate.

Henderson James, temporary.

Henderson James, here tonight, gone tomorrow.

For they would not let him live. The original Henderson James would not allow him to continue living, and even if he did, the world would not allow it. Duplicates were made only for very temporary and very special reasons and it was always understood that once their purpose was accomplished they would be done away with.

Done away with . . . those were the words exactly. Gotten out of the way. Swept out of sight and mind. Killed as unconcernedly and emotionlessly as one chops off a chicken's head.

He walked forward and dropped on one knee beside the *puudly,* running his hand over its body in the darkness. Lumps stood out all over it, the swelling buds that now would never break to spew forth in a loathsome birth a brood of *puudly* pups.

He rose to his feet.

The job was done. The *puudly* had been killed—killed before it had given birth to a horde of horrors.

The job was done and he could go home.

Home?

Of course, that was the thing that had been planted in his mind, the thing they wanted him to do. To go home, to go back to the house on Summit Avenue, where his executioners would wait, to walk back deliberately and unsuspectingly to the death that waited.

The job was done and his usefulness was over. He had been created to perform a certain task and the task was now performed and while an hour ago he had been a factor in the plans of men, he was no longer wanted. He was an embarrassment and superfluous.

Now wait a minute, he told himself. You may not be a duplicate. You do not feel like one.

That was true. He felt like Henderson James. He was Henderson James. He lived on Summit Avenue and had illegally brought to Earth a beast known as a *puudly* in order that he might study it and talk to it and test its alien reactions, attempt to measure its intelligence and guess at the strength and depth and the direction of its non-humanity. He had been a fool, of course, to do it, and yet at the time it had seemed important to understand the deadly, alien mentality.

I am human, he said, and that was right, but even so the fact meant nothing. Of course he was human. Henderson James was human and his duplicate would be exactly as human as the original. For the duplicate, processed from the pattern that held every trait and characteristic of the man he was to become a copy of, would differ in not a single basic factor.

In not a single basic factor, perhaps, but in certain other things. For no matter how much the duplicate might be like his pattern, no matter how full-limbed he might spring from his creation, he still would be a new man. He would have the capacity for knowledge and for thought and in a little time he would have and know and be all the things that his original was . . .

But it would take some time, some short while to come to a full realization of all he knew and was, some time to coordinate and recognize all the knowledge and experience that lay within his mind. At first he'd grope and search until he came upon the things that he must know. Until he became acquainted with himself, with the sort of man he was, he could not reach out blindly in the dark and put his hand exactly and unerringly upon the thing he wished.

That had been exactly what he'd done. He had groped and searched. He had been compelled to think, at first, in simple basic truths and facts.

I am a man.

I am on a planet called Earth.

I am Henderson James.

I live on Summit Avenue.

There is a job to do.

It had been quite a while, he remembered now, before he had been able to dig out of his mind the nature of the job.

There is a *puudly* to hunt down and destroy.

Even now he could not find in the hidden, still-veiled recesses of his mind the many valid reasons why a man should run so grave a risk to study a thing so vicious as a *puudly*. There were reasons, he knew there were, and in a little time he would know them quite specifically.

The point was that if he were Henderson James, original, he would know them now, know them as a part of himself and his life, without laboriously searching for them.

The *puudly* had known, of course. It had known, beyond any chance of error, that there were two Henderson Jameses. It had been keeping tabs on one when another one showed up. A mentality far less astute than the *puudly's* would have had no trouble in figuring that one out.

If the *puudly* had not talked, he told himself, I never would have known. If it had died at once and not had a chance to taunt me, I would not have known. I would even now be walking to the house on Summit Avenue.

He stood lonely and naked of soul in the wind that swept across the moated island. There was a sour bitterness in his mouth.

He moved a foot and touched the dead *puudly*.

"I'm sorry," he told the stiffening body. "I'm sorry

now I did it. If I had known, I never would have killed you."

Stiffly erect, he moved away.

III

He stopped at the street corner, keeping well in the shadow. Halfway down the block, and on the other side, was the house. A light burned in one of the rooms upstairs and another on the post beside the gate that opened into the yard, lighting the walk up to the door.

Just as if, he told himself, the house were waiting for the master to come home. And that, of course, was exactly what it was doing. An old lady of a house, waiting, hands folded in its lap, rocking very gently in a squeaky chair . . . and with a gun beneath the folded shawl.

His lip lifted in half a snarl as he stood there, looking at the house. What do they take me for, he thought, putting out a trap in plain sight and one that's not even baited? Then he remembered. They would not know, of course, that he knew he was a duplicate. They would think that he would think that he was Henderson James, the one and only. They would expect him to come walking home, quite naturally, believing he belonged there. So far as they would know, there would be no possibility of his finding out the truth.

And now that he had? Now that he was here, across the street from the waiting house?

He had been brought into being, had been given life, to do a job that his original had not dared to do, or had not wanted to do. He had carried out a killing his original didn't want to dirty his hands with, or risk his neck in doing.

Or had it not been that at all, but the necessity of two men working on the job, the original serving as a focus for the *puudly's* watchful mind while the other man sneaked up to kill it while it watched?

No matter what, he had been created, at a good stiff price, from the pattern of the man that was Henderson

James. The wizardry of man's knowledge, the magic of machines, a deep understanding of organic chemistry, of human physiology, of the mystery of life, had made a second Henderson James. It was legal, of course, under certain circumstances . . . for example, in the case of public policy, and his own creation, he knew, might have been validated under such a heading. But there were conditions and one of these was that a duplicate not be allowed to continue living once it had served the specific purpose for which it had been created.

Usually such a condition was a simple one to carry out, for the duplicate was not meant to know he was a duplicate. So far as he was concerned, he was the original. There was no suspicion in him, no foreknowledge of the doom that was invariably ordered for him, no reason for him to be on guard against the death that waited.

The duplicate knitted his brow, trying to puzzle it out.

There was a strange set of ethics here.

He was alive and he wanted to stay alive. Life, once it had been tasted, was too sweet, too good, to go back to the nothingness from which he had come . . . or would it be nothingness? Now that he had known life, now that he was alive, might he not hope for a life after death, the same as any other human being? Might not he, too, have the same human right as any other human to grasp at the shadowy and glorious promises and assurances held out by religion and by faith?

He tried to marshal what he knew about those promises and assurances, but his knowledge was illusive. A little later he would remember more about it. A little later, when the neural bookkeeper in his mind had been able to coordinate and activate the knowledge that he had inherited from the pattern, he would know.

He felt a trace of anger stir deep inside of him, anger at the unfairness of allowing him only a few short hours of life, of allowing him to learn how wonderful a thing life was, only to snatch it from him. It was a cruelty that went beyond mere human cruelty. It was something that had been fashioned out of the distorted perspective of a machine society that measured existence only in terms of mechanical and physical worth, that discarded with a ruthless hand whatever part of that society had no specific purpose.

The cruelty, he told himself, was in ever giving life, not in taking it away.

His original, of course, was the one to blame. He was the one who had obtained the *puudly* and allowed it to escape. It was his fumbling and his inability to correct his error without help which had created the necessity of fashioning a duplicate.

And yet, could he blame him?

Perhaps, rather, he owed him gratitude for a few hours of life at least, gratitude for the privilege of knowing what life was like. Although he could not quite decide whether or not it was something which called for gratitude.

He stood there, staring at the house. That light in the upstairs room was in the study off the master bedroom. Up there Henderson James, original, was waiting for the word that the duplicate had come home to death. It was an easy thing to sit there and wait, to sit and wait for the word that was sure to come. An easy thing to sentence to death a man one had never seen, even if that man be the walking image of one's self.

It would be a harder decision to kill him if you stood face to face with him . . . harder to kill someone who would be, of necessity, closer than a brother, someone who would be, even literally, flesh of your flesh, blood of your blood, brain of your brain.

There would be a practical side as well, a great advantage to be able to work with a man who thought as you did, who would be almost a second self. It would be almost as if there were two of you.

A thing like that could be arranged. Plastic surgery and a price for secrecy could make your duplicate into an unrecognizable other person. A little red tape, some

finagling . . . but it could be done. It was a proposition
that Henderson James, duplicate, thought would interest
Henderson James, original. Or at least he hoped it
would.

The room with the light could be reached with a little
luck, with strength and agility and determination. The
brick expanse of a chimney, its base cloaked by shrubs,
its length masked by a closely growing tree, ran up the
wall. A man could climb its rough brick face, could
reach out and swing himself through the open window
into the lighted room.

And once Henderson James, original, stood face to
face with Henderson James, duplicate . . . well, it would
be less of a gamble. The duplicate then would no longer
be an impersonal factor. He would be a man and one
that was very close to his original.

There would be watchers, but they would be watching the front door. If he were quiet, if he could reach
and climb the chimney without making any noise, he'd
be in the room before anyone would notice.

He drew back deeper in the shadows and considered.
It was either get into the room and face his original,
hope to be able to strike a compromise with him, or
simply to light out . . . to run and hide and wait,
watching his chance to get completely away, perhaps to
some far planet in some other part of the Galaxy.

Both ways were a gamble, but one was quick, would
either succeed or fail within the hour; the other might
drag on for months with a man never knowing whether
he was safe, never being sure.

Something nagged at him, a persistent little fact that
skittered through his brain and eluded his efforts to pin
it down. It might be important and then again it might
be a random thing, simply a floating piece of information that was looking for its pigeonhole.

His mind shrugged it off.

The quick way or the long way?

He stood thinking for a moment and then moved
swiftly down the street, seeking a place where he could
cross in shadow.

He had chosen the short way.

IV

The room was empty.

He stood beside the window, quietly, only his eyes moving, searching every corner, checking against a situation that couldn't seem quite true . . . that Henderson James was not here, waiting for the word.

Then he strode swiftly to the bedroom door and swung it open. His finger found the switch and the lights went on. The bedroom was empty and so was the bath. He went back into the study.

He stood with his back against the wall, facing the door that led into the hallway, but his eyes went over the room, foot by foot, orienting himself, feeling himself flow into the shape and form of it, feeling familiarity creep in upon him and enfold him in its comfort of belonging.

Here were the books, the fireplace with its mantel loaded with souvenirs, the easy chairs, the liquor cabinet . . . and all were a part of him, a background that was as much a part of Henderson James as his body and his inner thoughts were a part of him.

This, he thought, is what I would have missed, the experience I never would have had if the *puudly* had not taunted me. I would have died an empty and unrelated body that had no actual place in the universe.

The phone purred at him and he stood there startled by it, as if some intruder from the outside had pushed its way into the room, shattering the sense of belonging that had come to him.

The phone rang again and he went across the room and picked it up.

"James speaking," he said.

"That you, Mr. James?"

The voice was that of Anderson, the gardener.

"Why, yes," said the duplicate. "Who did you think it was?"

"We got a fellow here who says he's you."

Henderson James, duplicate, stiffened with fright and his hand, suddenly, was grasping the phone so hard that he found the time to wonder why it did not pulverize to bits beneath his fingers.

"He's dressed like you," the gardener said, "and I knew you went out. Talked to you, remember? Told you that you shouldn't? Not with us waiting for that . . . that thing."

"Yes," said the duplicate, his voice so even that he could not believe it was he who spoke. "Yes, certainly I remember talking with you."

"But, sir, how did you get back?"

"I came in the back way," the even voice said into the phone. "Now what's holding you back?"

"He's dressed like you."

"Naturally. Of course he would be, Anderson."

And that, to be sure, didn't quite follow, but Anderson wasn't too bright to start with and now he was somewhat upset.

"You remember," the duplicate said. "that we talked about it."

"I guess I was excited and forgot," admitted Anderson. "You told me to call you, to make sure you were in your study, though. That's right, isn't it, sir?"

"You've called me," the duplicate said, "and I am here."

"Then the other one out here is him?"

"Of course," said the duplicate. "Who else could it be?"

He put the phone back into the cradle and stood waiting. It came a moment after, the dull, throaty cough of a gun.

He walked to a chair and sank into it, spent with the knowledge of how events had so been ordered that now, finally, he was safe, safe beyond all question.

Soon he would have to change into other clothes, hide the gun and the clothes that he was wearing. The staff would ask no questions, most likely, but it was best to let nothing arouse suspicion in their minds.

He felt his nerves quieting and he allowed himself to glance about the room, take in the books and furnishings, the soft and easy . . . and earned . . . comfort of a man solidly and unshakably established in the world.

He smiled softly.

"It will be nice," he said.

It had been easy. Now that it was over, it seemed ridiculously easy. Easy because he had never seen the man who had walked up to the door. It was easy to kill a man you had never seen.

With each passing hour he would slip deeper and deeper into the personality that was his by right of heritage. There would be no one to question, after a time not even himself, that he was Henderson James.

The phone rang again and he got up to answer it.

A pleasant voice told him, "This is Allen, over at the duplication lab. We've been waiting for a report from you."

"Well," said James, "I . . ."

"I just called," interrupted Allen, "to tell you not to worry. It slipped my mind before."

"I see," said James, though he didn't.

"We did this one a little differently," Allen explained. "An experiment that we thought we'd try out. Slow poison in his bloodstream. Just another precaution. Probably not necessary, but we like to be positive. In case he fails to show up, you needn't worry any."

"I am sure he will show up."

Allen chuckled. "Twenty-four hours. Like a time bomb. No antidote for it even if he found out somehow."

"It was good of you to let me know," said James.

"Glad to," said Allen. "Good night, Mr. James."

In the 1940s, Wilson Tucker (well, Bob Tucker, as his byline was at the time) rang changes on most of the standard plots of pulp science fiction. These pieces were collected under the perfectly accurate title of The Science Fiction Sub-Treasury—which unfortunately sounds like another of the hideously boring books-about-SF that have proliferated since academics discovered the field.

The stories aren't academic exercises, goodness knows; but they could only have been written by someone with a scholar's knowledge of the field.

And most of them are extremely funny. . . .

GENTLEMEN, THE QUEEN!

Wilson Tucker

The three of us, Koenig majoring in electrical engineering, Evans working along advanced lines in chemistry, and myself . . . oh, I beg your pardon; allow me to introduce myself. I'm Putnam, Rawleigh '03. I dabble a bit in astrogation. As I was saying, the three of us were just returned to classes from the Christmas holidays, all feeling a mere touch of nostalgia for the old home town. There had been snow for Christmas, the first since 1983, or so the old-timers insisted. We found it rather disheartening to leave the beautiful snow-covered countryside to return to Rawleigh.

We were attempting to drown the mere touch in several mugs of beer at a little place just off the campus, when Tobru joined us. Tobru is a Martian. He didn't know what homesickness was but he was well acquainted with beer. So it was that during the evening we heard for the first time in our lives the legend, that amazing narration, of the wild woman of the planet Mars! It irritated me to realize so much of my life had been wasted not knowing her.

Tobru is a rather amazing fellow, and damned puzzling, too. A gawky person like most young Martians, he has a spent nearly seven years at Rawleigh studying the ancient American Indian. What in the world he wanted to study Indians for no one knew; but all agreed there was no better place to study Indians, or any other subject under the sun, than here at Rawleigh. The famed seat of learning offers courses in every branch of knowledge existent!

After the ninth or tenth beer, Tobru leaned far over the table in a manner common to sinister plotters seen on the screen, and whispered,

"Listen! Would you hear of a wonderful story of my country?" He peered up and ogled the nearby tables owlishly, and we did likewise. Our four heads came together over the mugs.

"Have you heard of the Wild Woman of Mars?" he asked suddenly, dramatically. "The untamed Queen of the Koru Range?"

"No!" Koenig fell into a whisper. "Is she really wild?"

"How wild?" I asked.

"What made her wild?" Evans demanded.

"Sssshhhhh!" Tobru cautioned. "She is wild. Take my word. I have it on close authority."

"Straight from the horse's mouth, so to speak," suggested Koenig.

Tobru favored him with a puzzled glance. "I don't follow that."

"Never mind," I cut in. "A horse is an extinct animal. Let's hear the legend."

"Is it connected with the Indians?" Tobru persisted.

"Yes, yes," I hastened to add again. "Horses used to ride Indians to and from their war dances, or perhaps it was the other way around. But get on with your story." I threw a glance at Koenig. "And no more historical remarks, please."

Tobru first consumed another beer. "Very well," he said. "It seems, I am told, that many, many years ago, perhaps twenty-five or so, a small stratosphere rocket crashed somewhere in the lower end of the Koru Range. In this rocket were three people: an old and half-crazed miner searching for gold, his young and pretty wife, and their small daughter, age perhaps two or three years—earth years. These were earth people.

"Now, as you know, the Koru Range is pretty rugged mountain country, and sad to say, rescue parties never found them, nor even the remains of the ship. To this day their fate remains a mystery, one of the very few unsolved disappearances on Mars. It was assumed, after the passing of months, and then years, that all aboard the little craft had perished and the search was accordingly cancelled.

"And then, four or five years ago, an old prospector drifted in with some fanciful reports of seeing a wild woman hunting in the Koru Range. He claimed she had a pack of Martian rats with her. She was described to be a beautiful young woman, quite the prettiest creature the old miner had set eyes on in many a year. He trailed her for hours before she got down wind of him, saw him, and slipped away into the caves!"

Tobru paused, his gawky head bounced up from the huddle to sweep the nearer tables suspiciously. Before coming back down he paused to gulp another beer. We were too fascinated to protest.

"His story, of course, was scouted as a fantastic mirage. Nobody would believe such a tale from an old man who has lived for months in the wilderness!"

"No, nobody," Koenig agreed.

"Nobody," Evans seconded.

"Quiet!" I had to insist. "Continue, Tobru."

"The old miner's story was promptly discounted and forgotten. Until one day there came a government mapper with a startlingly similar report. He claimed to have seen her high in the mountains, many miles from the region in which the miner had found her. The pack of rats was not with her. The mapper had no chance to get nearer for she saw him almost instantly and whisked away.

"After that, stories began to appear with regularity.

First she was here, then she was there, always miles and miles apart. If one believed all the stories, the girl covered hundreds of miles a day, and sometimes managed to be in two places at the same time. For instance, one source claimed to have seen her just outside Packrat, which is a mining town near the equator, while a bare few minutes later the radio announced she was spotted wandering around naked in the polar regions.

"By then someone remembered the crash of the strato ship, twenty-five years before. It was first suggested the wild woman was the wife of the miner, but this was quickly discarded because of the time angle. She would have been much too old to be mountain hopping; and only in one detail did all the reports agree: the wild girl was young, lithe, and pretty."

"Pretty," Koenig commented.

"Beautiful!" Evans countered.

"Ravishing, no doubt, but stop interrupting!" I said.

"So it was decided," Tobru continued, "—among those who accepted the story, that it was the little daughter now grown to womanhood, grown to a mature wildness because of the isolation in that mountain fastness. She would be about the correct age to fit with the descriptions of her. It was quite natural, and most amazing, that she should grow up alone, or perhaps almost alone, in that untamed country!"

Tobru stopped and regarded us owlishly. We hung there over beer mugs, waiting.

"Well?" I demanded at last.

"That's all. No one has ever captured her. The authorities, of course, scout the tale, pointing to the obvious impossibilities to the entire legend. They claim it is impossible for anyone, much less a young woman, to exist in that country for any length of time unaided. And there is no use pushing them . . ." He spread his hands. ". . . you know how stubborn Martians are!"

We silently agreed. We knew of a Martian who spent seven years pursuing dead Indians.

"So she has become a legend, one that grows with each telling, added to now and then by a factual report of some old prospector claiming to have glimpsed her, her and her wild pack of rats!" He stopped and looked around for another full mug. "But this much is certain: she is wild, young, beautiful—Queen of the Koru Range!"

At our silent question then, he pounded his fist on the table top, glared around belligerently.

"Yes, gentlemen, I have seen her!"

"Marvellous!" I was the first to cry.

"Incredible!" Evans exclaimed.

"Romantic!" Koenig insisted.

"I want more beer!" Tobru shouted.

And at eleven that evening the campus police cleared the place of sophomores, there was naught else to do but return to our rooms and speculate on the legend and its million implications. We left Tobru quite drunk, conversing with imaginary Indians.

We cornered Tobru again before many days had passed. He was resting under a shady oak, the city officials having decided to cause Spring early this year to offset the snow, and it was quite warm.

"Just think! gentlemen," he greeted us as we walked up. "It is just possible that Indians once lolled about under this very tree. Perhaps even made love, or were killed here. Fascinating, isn't it?"

"Yes, definitely," Evans agreed. "I can think of nothing more fascinating than being killed under this tree."

Tobru reproached him. "Please! The sense of humor possessed by Earthlings is at times outrageous! The death of an Indian is no joking matter."

"Neither is mine for that matter," Evans said. "But Tobru, we have a proposition to offer you."

"A fascinating proposition," Koenig put in.

"Please, gentlemen," I protested. "We agreed that I should be spokesman." I turned to the Martian. "Tobru, we have been giving a lot of thought to your story of the other night. Frankly, the legend, ah . . . (I almost said fascinated) . . . interests us exceedingly. To the point, even, to, ah . . ." I hesitated. What would Tobru think?

"Yes?" that worthy prompted. There was warmth in his voice.

"Tobru, we three have decided to go to Mars. To search for the Wild Queen! We want you to go with us. You know the country!"

He pondered this, came up with the objection we were expecting. "What about my Indians? I take it, you plan on going this summer when the term is out? Gentlemen, I'd like to accommodate you, but I had planned on a trip West this year to investigate some mounds."

So we began to talk. I was well prepared for this. I knew in advance what his objections would be and primed myself for them. We sat there in the shade of the oak and argued for hours, at least, it seemed to be for hours. I used every trick I knew of to win him over short of promising him money; that would have been below our stations. In the end, he weakened, and by my managing to keep my two cronies silent at this crucial moment, I won him to the cause.

"Very well," he said at last. "I will accompany you. But mark you, gentlemen, we must be back early! I want to do some work out West before the Fall term commences." And Tobru laid plans to return to Rawleigh for the coming year.

We were jubilant. For a few weeks.

And then the newscasters announced a small tribal uprising had broken out on Mars. Visitors would be banned for the duration of the summer. The trouble was isolated to a few localities, but because of the nature of it, could easily spread to other uneducated localities and become a full-fledged uprising if the proper caution was not taken. We would not be allowed on the planet this year!

Koenig paced the room and engaged in some choice, but very gentlemanly swearing. Evans and I felt equally disheartened. It was maddening, this being so close to the end of the term, so near our goal, to have this happen. We fretted and fumed, planned to the point where it could have been called a plot.

And with the end of school, we decided to go anyway!

Our final plan was complicated but complete. Koenig furnished the most of it, he was the imaginative one. We would ship to Mars separately, by widely different routes and methods. There must be no possible suspicion thrown on us by our leaving together for a common destination.

Tobru, he planned, would simply return home. There could be nothing more natural, and the authorities could not forbid him. Once there, he would hire a small stratosphere ship capable of carrying five (but he must make sure not to mention any such figure!), load it with provisions, not so as to suggest rations for five, but to indicate the one man, Tobru, wished to be out all summer long; although the seasons wouldn't match with Earth, he being a Rawleigh student, the circumstances would be known. He was to pose as an archeologist, hunting fossils. The ship was to be hired for the season, paid for in advance as well as food and fuel bills. That would appear most natural to the people renting the ships and to the police in their monthly check-ups. Meanwhile I was to take passage on the same liner carrying Tobru home.

The how was left to me; I could bribe, stow away, hire out as a cabin boy, or any way I chose, just so I got to Mars. Once there, I was to jump ship when Tobru left it.

I was to make my way to Packrat, hire a cabin in the foothills, buy a small supply of food so as to suggest my staying there for a week or two, and simply vanish into the cabin and await the others.

Koenig and Evans were to hire themselves out on different ships putting off for Mars, freighters, liners or whatever they had the good fortune to find. Once there, they, too, were to jump ship, make their way by roundabout routes to my cabin in the foothills. By that time Tobru should have our strato ship there. Our search would be on!

It sounded . . . well, simply fascinating! My pulse

tingled in anticipation of the venture! In my imagination I painted the girl as most fiction accounts would have her: a wild, lithe, gorgeous creature with wonderful windblown hair, dark hair streaming in the wind as she flew over the ground, kissed by sunshine! Sparkling blue eyes devoid of all the tawdriness of civilization, full of carefree devilishness and eager life! Creamy white skin flashing in the sun, tall, dynamic, beautiful! A wonderful treasure of femininity to behold. It was then that the thought struck me.

We were meeting for the last time in that little spot just off the campus. Mugs filled our table. Most of the room was bare, many of the students having already departed for places elsewhere. The three of us sat in golden silence, the treasures of our thoughts shining in our eyes. I believe the power of it somewhat sobered us. And then, as I said, this thing occurred to me.

"Gentlemen," I broke the silence, "—for we are gentlemen. There is a rather delicate matter in connection with our quest to bring up at this time. I am rather mildly surprised one of us hasn't thought of it before. It is . . . ah, rather delicate."

"Do you mean," Koenig asked, "who is going to pay the check?"

"I only drank three!" Evans made haste to add.

"No, no, nothing like that! Gentlemen, consider our quest. Hold in your minds a picture of our goal, what we actually propose to do! Imagine her. Imagine further, picture our bringing her back to civilization! Now consider please the implications involved in our bringing her back with us! Do you begin to understand?"

They looked at me, startled. Evans opened his mouth to speak and couldn't trust himself, so closed it again.

"Do you mean . . . ?" Koenig whispered, tightly.

"Exactly!" I nodded, and swept a beer to my mouth. "Consider it, gentlemen. Here are three of us—I shan't count Tobru, being interested only in Indians—three of us about to set forth upon a common goal. We simply cannot bring back that goal to be the toy of civilization.

The question is: to whom belong the spoils? Which of us is to have the honor of marrying the girl?"

The problem lay like an unexploded bomb in the stunned silence.

" 'A student is forbidden to possess a wife'," Evans quoted quietly. "But I, for one, will be glad to sacrifice my career to make a home for her!"

"And I!" chimed in Koenig. "I am more than willing to protect her! I can always secure employment in any of the myriad laboratories in the city."

"Likewise I," I said calmly, determined. "I'll toss astrogation overboard for a chance of being the husband of the Wild Queen. But . . . that isn't the question, exactly. The thing to decide is, which of us is to do the honors?"

"We might toss a coin," Koenig suggested.

"I object!" snapped Evans. "The lady's honor is to be considered. We cannot lower her reputation by gambling for her possession!"

"Quite right," I agreed. "Some honorable, moral means must be found, something of which she would approve. For remember, we expect to be together afterwards. The lucky man wouldn't care to be embarrassed by her finding out how we chose him!"

"Well," Evans hazarded, ". . . we might duel."

I shuddered. "No!" The beer burned my throat. "I wouldn't care to marry her deformed, earless or something. She would want a whole man . . . something more than just his personality."

"Well, then, what do you suggest?"

"It has occurred to me," I said, "that while not necessarily gambling, we still might make a sporting chance of it. Supposing, say, that we cooperate fully— one hundred percent—on this quest, until we come in sight of our goal. Actual, physical sight. Once we have seen her for the first time, it is every man for himself! The first man to her side wins her hand!"

"Bravo!" from Koenig.

"Excellent!" Evans stood up.

"May the best man win!" I whispered, awed. We clicked mugs.

We were again to be disappointed. Tobru announced that he could not desert his Indian chase, his really fascinating Indian hunt, to accompany us!

He had, he said, learned of a new mound somewhere in the West, along the banks of the Mississippi, a mound heretofore undiscovered and therefore unopened. If true, this was indeed a rare find; secretly, I did not blame him for deserting us. To him, as this trip was to us, it was the chance of a lifetime.

However, he offered to do the right thing. He said he not only could, but would arrange everything on his home planet for us, short of going himself. A faithful friend of his would fulfil his part of the obligation and deliver the strato ship, with the required provisions, to the cabin at the appointed time. After that we were on our own. We decided to accept this; really, we could do nothing else. The vital ship would be there with the supplies. We must carry on!

But it would take weeks. He would have to write his friend, enclosing money, because the authorities would certainly question such a message by any other mode of communication. He suggested waiting a few weeks so as to allow the letter to reach its destination. We made up the money between us to enclose in Tobru's letter.

We bid good-bye to him the next day as he set out for the West. He wished us luck upon our quest, cautioned us, and was gone.

I hid among some boulders in the foothills outside Packrat, and in this security looked down upon the little town. It occurred to me that it would be necessary to alter our plans somewhat.

Packrat was a smouldering pile of wreckage. A visiting band of guerilla raiders had preceded me by a few hours.

As the thought came to me of the possibility of the Martians still being in the district, an odd little noise at my back bore the thought out. I whirled around. The gawky fellow crouched there, grinning at me. There was something shining in his hand.

"Peace!" I chanted hopefully in the only native dialect I knew. "Peace to my Martian brother!" I hoped he understood.

He grinned again. "Hello, Rawleigh," he answered.

To say I was taken aback would be an understatement. I had gone to great length to perfect my disguise, had even forebore washing the dirt and scum of the space liner from me to further it. I knew I presented a not pretty picture. And the beggar knew my school—!

"Hello, yourself," I came back somewhat timidly. "Who are you, and how did you know me?"

"Your haircut," he said simply.

Of course! All the clothes in the world short of a Hindu turban wouldn't hide my college haircut. I cursed my shortsightedness. But this beggar? I turned back to him.

"Tobru said I would find you here." He waved the shining object. "Here is the key to your strato. It's over there behind that hut."

"What hut?" I asked in surprise. I couldn't see any.

"Come with me." He arose and slipped away. Not a hundred feet away I almost fell over the most beautiful camouflage job I have ever seen. It was a long, low building large enough to house a dozen people comfortably.

"I never knew these tourist and miners' huts were like this!" I exclaimed in surprise.

"They aren't." He surprised me again. "This isn't a hut. This belonged to a Martian named Yngvi. He was district governor for Packrat."

"Oh, but won't he object to our barging in this way? After all, we are strangers to him, you know."

"Not now, you aren't," Tobru's friend said. "He is among the corpses down in Packrat."

I swallowed my tongue, fumbled with the proper words. They wouldn't come. I stared at him helplessly, and he must have interpreted my thoughts. He laughed merrily.

"Oh, don't mind that! Move in and make yourself at home. It's all right. He was a louse, anyway."

"But . . . about those raiders! Won't they come here looking for him, looting or something?"

"Not now," he assured me. "They will sack every hut in the district but this one. They know he is dead. There is no point to bothering him or his belongings further. You'll be safe here. The ship is in the rocks out back." He handed me the key and walked to the door. "Tell Tobru hello for me!" and he was gone.

I stared at the door stupidly for a second, then thought to ask him something. When I opened it and looked out he had vanished.

The ship was as he said and Tobru had promised. It was well hidden among the boulders and small hills. I had trouble finding it myself. The supplies were adequate for our needs. I felt entirely familiar with the controls, they being quite similar to the dummy ships in the labs at Rawleigh.

Koenig and Evans put in an appearance together later in the week. We were well ahead of schedule, making allowances for the delay of Tobru's letter. It was quite funny to watch them hunting for the place. They had imagined, of course, I would be in one of the little huts dotting the hills, and had examined one after another of these, only to find each sacked, sometimes razed, and now and then bearing a corpse. They claimed they were not worried about me, nevertheless I detected unhidden relief in their manner when at last we met.

Like myself, earlier, they nearly stumbled over the governor's house before they found it. Evans almost fell in the door. It was then necessary for me to repeat to them the story of my being there, the wrecking of the town, and the present circumstances of the last owner.

"And," I finished up, "it's about time we were getting out of here. The authorities will be here any day checking into the governor's last days and his belongings. They mustn't find us here!"

"Correct," echoed Koenig. "Let's go."

"Check!" cried Evans. "To the Queen!"

I led the way out to the ship.

How we so calmly and unconsciously ambled through the picket line to the ship, I don't know. I only know that the three of us were at the ship's side when a sudden shout behind us caused us to turn. There around us was the ugliest ring of Martians, drunk apparently, I've laid eyes on. And we had walked right through them without seeing them!

"Back to the house!" Evans cried, and attempted to run.

"No!" I shouted. "Into the ship." I never saw a weapon raised, but something spanged on the hull and caromed away.

We climbed up and tumbled in with the howling madmen at our heels. Koenig slammed the lock shut. There were more shouts from without, dimmed by the walls, and a great number of guns were fired.

"You don't suppose they can puncture the hull?" Evans asked.

"I don't know," I said truthfully. "I'm not familiar with the structure of these ships. I certainly hope not!"

"Has it occurred to you, if I may be so bold as to question," Koenig put in, "that they cannot harm us if we take off?"

I inserted the key in the control panel and lifted the ship. The shouting and the shots died away below.

Koenig came back from a trip of inspection.

"Guess what? We have a passenger."

"One of the fools grabbed a rung below the lock and hung on. He's hanging out there now. Appears rather ill, too."

"I don't blame him," Evans said feelingly. "I rather think I would be ill myself."

We were flying over rugged terrain, the beginning of the mountain range. "Might as well set down," I offered. "We're getting into the mountains. We can drop him somewhere and begin our search from there. What say, gentlemen?"

The gentlemen agreed. I slanted rapidly towards the surface, while Koenig went to the lock in an attempt at communication with the uninvited guest. He was back almost at once.

"He's gone!"

"Who's gone?"

"Our passenger. The chap hanging outside!"

"Well, the rum!" Evans declared indignantly. "And he didn't even say thank you for the lift."

I glared at him, half sick, and turned my attention to landing the ship.

"Well, gentlemen—" I paused and swept their faces. We were standing on a rocky ledge that fell away before us in three directions. The ship was behind us. "Gentlemen, our quest is begun! Who knows but that before the sun has set one of us will possess her. The Wild Queen!"

The nearness of the adventure sparkled in our eyes. We stood there, solemnly, and clasped hands. On rough maps Koenig outlined our search for that day. We were to meet at opportune places every few hours. Once again we clasped hands, and broke up. I took the slope away to the left.

I would rather not go into detail on the following, heart-breaking three weeks. We did not discover the beautiful Queen of the Koru Range before sunset that day; and some twenty-odd other sunsets followed just as fruitlessly for us. Each night we returned to the ship empty-handed, empty-hearted, tired, forlorn. Courage waned. More than once I knew it wouldn't have taken much to decide me to abandon the search. It was logical to believe my companions felt likewise.

One morning . . . I forget how many days it was after we first set down in the mountains . . . Koenig came into possession of an idea.

"Putnam! Can you find that spot again where we first landed?"

"Easily," I affirmed. "But what for?"

"I suddenly thought of something. We have been dunces not to think of it before! Not far from that spot should be the body of the Martian who fell from the ship. We must find that body."

"I can do better than that," I interrupted. "Better than just the spot where we landed, I mean. I think I can get pretty near to where he fell. I seem to recall the terrain we were passing over at the time. Why?"

"Don't you see?" he was impatient. "That body will draw mountain rats. And where a pack is, is apt to be our Queen!"

"Brilliant thinking!" Evans exclaimed.

Next morning we hovered over the approximate spot where the Martian brigand fell. "It's about here," I called out. "We were between that jutting ledge over there—" I pointed it out, "—and those rocks here."

"I think I see something!" Evans cried. "Set her down!"

Silently I dropped the ship down to the ledge we had seen from the air. The three of us clambered out, awed. We stood by the ship and gazed down into the rock-strewn valley. Evans indicated a pile of huge boulders, behind which he believed was the scene he had seen from the air. Together we set out.

As quietly as we could, we scrambled across the rocks and around the jutting ledges towards the spot. We stopped just this side of the boulders we were making for.

Koenig motioned for quiet as sounds of gnawing came from the rocks. Silently we faced one another. Koenig put out his hand. We clasped. He didn't speak, but looked into our eyes, and we knew what he was thinking:

"Gentlemen—around these rocks probably lies our goal! The Wild Queen of the Koru Range! We have made the bargain, sealed it. The first man to her side wins her hand! Are we ready, gentlemen?"

And as if he had asked the question aloud, we nodded. Again we shook hands. I straightened my clothes, rearranged my tie and helmet. The sounds of definite activity on the farther side of the cluster of boulders activated us.

Together we sprang around the rocks, shouting!

Koenig somehow managed the lead before we had gone ten feet, Evans followed hard on his heels. I had the ill luck to twist my ankle on a stone and lost several steps as a result; was five to ten feet behind Evans. Koenig rounded the last rock in front, was lost to my sight. Instantly Evans followed. Cursing, casting caution to the wind, I sped on, ignoring the bounding pain in my ankle. I rounded the last rock at full speed, crashed head-on into Evans who stopped still. It wasn't his fault, he had crashed likewise into Koenig, in the lead. Koenig stood where he stopped, braced against the shock of our crashing into him from behind. I caught a glimpse of thousands of frightened rats scurrying away over the boulders.

The three of us were face to face with the Wild Queen of the Koru Range!

It was an electric moment. The rats had deserted us. On the ground between us lay the ravaged skeleton of the misguided Martian. Koenig, Evans and I were lined up on one side, while not ten feet away across the skeleton was the Queen. The Wild Queen! Koenig looked at Evans, Evans passed the stare on to me, and I looked back to the Queen.

In her hand was a parcel of flesh; torn, I knew, from the body of the unfortunate Martian. Strangely unafraid, she stood her ground and glared at us. Stupefied we stared back.

I looked at her hair. Witch's hair; it hung almost to her knees and of course never knew a comb. Tangled, matted and ratted, it hung in knots and lumps, nested with burrs and weeds; further decorated by some small human bones she had woven into the dirty strands.

The left eye was missing. Gouged out in some manner unknown, the gaping hole it had left so long ago stared redly at us, sickening to the sight.

She opened her mouth, and I knew the consequences of an Earthling torn from the little necessities of civilization. But few teeth graced her mouth. These few were browned, rotting, pointed fangs. Needle-sharp and needle-thin, employed for ripping meat from bone.

One arm hung askew at a crazy, impossible angle and I looked to see the cause. The arm had been broken long ago and never reset. It grew and continued to grow in the fashion it found itself. The dislodged bone in the arm caused the whole to jut sidewise at an ugly angle. Monstrous.

She was naked, having never known clothes. And dirty; her only baths must have been accidental falls into small bodies of water, or when caught in a mountain storm. And it rains seldom on Mars. The corresponding odor of her was overpowering. Her feet were hardened and black from mountain travelling, her legs bare, of course. Upon her ankles were hundreds and hundreds of vicious red marks. Rat bites. Covering her skin.

And then the electric moment was broken. Like a flash she turned and sped away after her rats. Before our startled eyes she streaked across a boulder and vanished into a cave mouth. A dislodged bone came rattling out in our faces.

With one accord we turned and ran the other way. My throbbing ankle was never thought of as I sprinted for the ship. I heard Koenig.

"I'm looking for a Martian!" he hissed, actually hissed. "I'm looking for a Martian who dotes on Indians. Someday soon I shall meet that Martian!"

We sped away from the Koru Range.

Maurice G. Hugi was (and perhaps still is) a real person; but he didn't write this story, which appeared under his name in Astounding and in some later reprints, or any other science fiction.

The real author, Eric Frank Russell, was a friend of Hugi's and used his name for a pseudonym only this once. My British agent (who knew both men well) can't suggest any reason for the pseudonym; and, though Russell was selling regularly to Astounding at the time under his own name, there wasn't another story by him in that issue.

So much for my hunting. "Mechanical Mice" is about men looking for one thing and finding another.

A thing that was looking for people like them.

MECHANICAL MICE

Eric Frank Russell

It's asking for trouble to fool around with the un-known. Burman did it! Now there are quite a lot of people who hate like the very devil anything that clicks, ticks, emits whirring sounds, or generally behaves like an asthmatic alarm clock. They've got mechanophobia. Dan Burman gave it to them.

Who hasn't heard of the Burman Bullfrog Battery? The same chap! He puzzled it out from first to last and topped it with his now world-famous slogan: "Power in Your Pocket " It was no mean feat to concoct a thing the size of a cigarette packet that would pour out a hundred times as much energy as its most efficient competitor. Burman differed from everyone else in thinking it a mean feat.

Burman looked me over very carefully, then said, "When that technical journal sent you around to see me twelve years ago, you listened sympathetically. You didn't treat me as if I were an idle dreamer or a congenital idiot. You gave me a decent write-up, and started all the publicity that eventually made me much money."

"Not because I loved you," I assured him, "but because I was honestly convinced that your battery was good."

"Maybe." He studied me in a way that conveyed he was anxious to get something off his chest. "We've been pretty pally since that time. We've filled in some idle hours together, and I feel that you're the one of my few friends to whom I can make a seemingly silly confession."

"Go ahead," I encouraged. We had been pretty pally, as he'd said. It was merely that we liked each other, found each other congenial. He was a clever chap, Burman, but there was nothing of the pedantic professor about him. Fortyish, normal, neat, he might have been a fashionable dentist to judge by appearances.

"Bill," he said, very seriously, "I didn't invent that damn battery."

"No?"

"No!" he confirmed. "I pinched the idea. What makes it madder is that I wasn't quite sure of what I was stealing and, crazier still, I don't know from whence I stole it."

"Which is as plain as a pikestaff," I commented.

"That's nothing. After twelve years of careful, exacting work I've built something else. It must be the most complicated thing in creation." He banged a fist on his knee, and his voice rose complainingly. "And now that I've done it, I don't know what I've done."

"Surely when an inventor experiments he knows what he's doing?"

"Not me!" Burman was amusingly lugubrious. "I've invented only one thing in my life, and that was more by accident than by good judgment." He perked up. "But that one thing was the key to a million notions. It gave me the battery. It has nearly given me things of greater importance. On several occasions it has nearly, but not quite, placed within my inadequate hands and half-understanding mind plans that would alter this world far beyond your conception." Leaning forward to lend emphasis to his speech, he said, "Now it has given me a mystery that has cost me twelve years of work and a nice sum of money. I finished it last night. I don't know what the devil it is."

"Perhaps if I had a look at it—"

"Just what I'd like you to do." He switched rapidly to mounting enthusiasm. "It's a beautiful job of work, even though I say so myself. Bet you that you can't say what it is, or what it's supposed to do."

"Assuming it can do something," I put in.

"Yes," he agreed. "But I'm positive it has a function of some sort." Getting up, he opened a door. "Come along."

It was a stunner. The thing was a metal box with a glossy, rhodium-plated surface. In general size and shape it bore a faint resemblance to an upended coffin, and had the same, brooding, ominous air of a casket waiting for its owner to give up the ghost.

There were a couple of small glass windows in its front through which could be seen a multitude of wheels as beautifully finished as those in a first-class watch. Elsewhere, several tiny lenses stared with sphinx-like indifference. There were three small trapdoors in one side, two in the other, and a large one in the front. From the top, two knobbed rods of metal stuck up like goat's horns, adding a satanic touch to the thing's vague air of yearning for midnight burial.

"It's an automatic layer-outer," I suggested, regarding the contraption with frank dislike. I pointed to one of the trapdoors. "You shove the shroud in there, and the corpse comes out the other side reverently composed and ready wrapped."

"So you don't like its air, either," Burman commented. He lugged open a drawer in a nearby tier, hauled out a mass of drawings. "These are its innards. It has an electric circuit, valves, condensers, and something that I can't quite understand, but which I suspect to be a tiny, extremely efficient electric furnace. It has parts I recognize as cog-cutters and pinion-shapers. It embodies several small-scale multiple stampers, apparently for dealing with sheet metal. There are vague suggestions of an assembly line ending in that large compartment shielded by the door in front. Have a look at the drawings yourself. You can see it's an extremely complicated device for manufacturing something only a little less complicated."

The drawings showed him to be right. But they didn't show everything. An efficient machine designer could correctly have deduced the gadget's function if given complete details. Burman admitted this, saying that some parts he had made "on the spur of the moment," while others he had been "impelled to draw." Short of pulling the machine to pieces, there was enough data to whet the curiosity, but not enough to satisfy it.

"Start the damn thing and see what it does."

"I've tried," said Burman. "It won't start. There's no starting handle, nothing to suggest how it can be started. I tried everything I could think of, without result. The electric circuit ends in those antennae at the top, and I even sent current through those, but nothing happened."

"Maybe it's a self-starter," I ventured. Staring at it, a thought struck me. "Timed," I added.

"Eh?"

"Set for an especial time. When the dread hour strikes, it'll go off of its own accord, like a bomb."

"Don't be so melodramatic," said Burman, uneasily.

Bending down, he peered into one of the tiny lenses.

"*Bz-z-z!*" murmured the contraption in a faint undertone that was almost inaudible.

Burman jumped a foot. Then he backed away, eyed the thing warily, turned his glance at me.

"Did you hear that?"

"Sure!" Getting the drawings, I mauled them around. That little lens took some finding, but it was there all right. It had a selenium cell behind it. "An eye," I said. "It saw you, and reacted. So it isn't dead even if it does just stand there seeing no evil, hearing no evil, speaking no evil." I put a white handkerchief against the lens.

"*Bz-z-z!*" repeated the coffin, emphatically.

Taking the handkerchief, Burman put it against the

other lenses. Nothing happened. Not a sound was heard, not a funeral note. Just nothing.

"It beats me," he confessed.

I'd got pretty fed up by this time. If the crazy article had performed, I'd have written it up and maybe I'd have started another financial snowball rolling for Burman's benefit. But you can't do anything with a box that buzzes whenever it feels temperamental. Firm treatment was required, I decided.

"You've been all nice and mysterious about how you got hold of this brain wave," I said. "Why can't you go to the same source for information about what it's supposed to be?"

"I'll tell you—or, rather, I'll show you."

From his safe, Burman dragged out a box, and from the box he produced a gadget. This one was far simpler than the useless mass of works over by the wall. It looked just like one of those old-fashioned crystal sets, except that the crystal was very big, very shiny, and was set in a horizontal vacuum tube. There was the same single dial, the same cat's whisker. Attached to the lot by a length of flex was what might have been a pair of headphones, except in place of the phones were a pair of polished, smoothly rounded copper circles shaped to fit outside the ears and close against the skull.

"My one and only invention," said Burman, not without a justifiable touch of pride.

"What is it?"

"A time-traveling device."

"Ha, ha!" My laugh was very sour. I'd read about such things. In fact, I'd written about them. They were buncombe. Nobody could travel through time, either backward or forward. "Let me see you grow hazy and vanish into the future."

"I'll show you something very soon." Burman said it with assurance I didn't like. He said it with the positive air of a man who knows darned well that he can do something that everybody else knows darned well can't be done. He pointed to the crystal set. "It wasn't discovered at the first attempt. Thousands must have tried and failed. I was the lucky one. I must have picked a peculiarly individualistic crystal; I still don't know how it does what it does; I've never been able to repeat its performance even with a crystal apparently identical."

"And it enables you to travel in time?"

"Only forward. It won't take me backward, not even as much as one day. But it can carry me forward an immense distance, perhaps to the very crack of doom, perhaps everlastingly through infinity."

I had him now! I'd got him firmly entangled in his own absurdities. My loud chuckle was something I couldn't control.

"You can travel forward, but not backward, not even one day back. Then how the devil can you return to the present once you've gone into the future?"

"Because I never leave the present," he replied, evenly. "I don't partake of the future. I merely survey it from the vantage point of the present. All the same, it is time-traveling in the correct sense of the term." He seated himself. "Look here, Bill, what are you?"

"Who, me?"

"Yes, what are you?" He went on to provide the answer. "Your name is Bill. You're a body and a mind. Which of them is Bill?"

"Both," I said, positively.

"True—but they're different parts of you. They're not the same even though they go around like Siamese twins." His voice grew serious. "Your body moves always in the present, the dividing line between the past and the future. But your mind is more free. It can think, and is in the present. It can remember, and at once is in the past. It can imagine, and at once is in the future, in its own choice of all the possible futures. *Your mind can travel through time!*"

He'd outwitted me. I could find points to pick upon and argue about, but I knew that fundamentally he was right. I'd not looked at it from this angle before, but he was correct in saying that anyone could travel through time within the limits of his own memory and imagination. At that very moment I could go back twelve years and see him in my mind's eye as a younger man, paler, thinner, more excitable, not so cool and self-possessed. The picture was as perfect as my memory was excellent. For that brief spell I was twelve years back in all but the flesh.

"I call this thing a psychophone," Burman went on. "When you imagine what the future will be like, you make a characteristic choice of all the logical possibilities, you pick your favorite from a multitude of likely futures. The psychophone, somehow—the Lord alone knows how—tunes you into future *reality*. It makes you depict within your mind the future as it will be shaped in actuality, eliminating all the alternatives that will not occur."

"An imagination-stimulator, a dream-machine," I scoffed, not feeling as sure of myself as I sounded. "How do you know it's giving you the McCoy?"

"Consistency," he answered, gravely. "It repeats the same features and the same trends far too often for the phenomena to be explained as mere coincidence. Besides," he waved a persuasive hand, "I got the battery from the future. It works, doesn't it?"

"It does," I agreed, reluctantly. I pointed to his psychophone. "I, too, may travel in time. How about letting me have a try? Maybe I'll solve your mystery for you."

"You can try if you wish," he replied, quite willingly. He pulled a chair into position. "Sit here, and I'll let you peer into the future."

Clipping the headband over my cranium, and fitting the copper rings against my skull where it sprouted ears, Burman connected his psychophone to the mains, switched it on; or rather he did some twiddling that I assumed was a mode of switching on.

"All you have to do," he said, "is to close your eyes, compose yourself, then try and permit your imagination to wander into the future."

He meddled with the cat's whisker. A couple of times he said, "Ah!" And each time he said it I got a peculiar dithery feeling around my unfortunate ears. After a few seconds of this, he drew it out to, "A-a-ah!" I played unfair, and peeped beneath lowered lids. The crystal was glowing like rats' eyes in a forgotten cellar. A furtive crimson.

Closing my own optics, I let my mind wander. Something was flowing between those copper electrodes, a queer, indescribable something that felt with stealthy fingers at some secret portion of my brain. I got the asinine notion that they were the dexterous digits of a yet-to-be-born magician who was going to shout, "Presto!" and pull my abused lump of think-meat out of a thirtieth century hat—assuming they'd wear hats in the thirtieth century.

What was it like, or, rather, what would it be like in the thirtieth century? Would there be retrogression? Would humanity again be composed of scowling, fur-kilted creatures lurking in caves? Or had progress continued—perhaps even to the development of men like gods?

Then it happened! I swear it! I pictured, quite voluntarily, a savage, and then a huge-domed individual with glittering eyes—the latter being my version of the ugliness we hope to attain. Right in the middle of this erratic dreaming, those weird fingers warped my brain, dissolved my phantoms, and replaced them with a dictated picture which I witnessed with all the helplessness and clarity of a nightmare.

I saw a fat man spouting. He was quite an ordinary man as far as looks went. In fact, he was so normal that he looked henpecked. But he was attired in a Roman toga, and he wore a small, black box where his laurel wreath ought to have been. His audience was similarly dressed, and all were balancing their boxes like a convention of fish porters. What Fatty was orating sounded gabble to me, but he said his piece as if he meant it.

The crowd was in the open air, with great, curved rows of seats visible in the background. Presumably an outside auditorium of some sort. Judging by the distance of the back rows, it must have been a devil of a size. Far behind its sweeping ridge a great edifice jutted into the sky, a cubical erection with walls of glossy squares, like an immense glasshouse.

"F'wot?" bellowed Fatty, with obvious heat. "Wuk, wuk, wuk, mor, noon'n'ni'! Bok onned, ord this, ord that." He stuck in indignant finger against the mysterious object on his cranium. "Bok onned, wuk, wuk, wuk. F'wot?" he glared around. "F'nix!" The crowd murmured approval somewhat timidly. But it was enough for Fatty. Making up his mind, he flourished a plump fist and shouted, "Th'ell wit'm!" Then he tore his box from his pate.

Nobody said anything, nobody moved. Dumb and wide-eyed, the crowd just stood and stared as if paralyzed by the sight of a human being sans box. Something with a long, slender streamlined body and broad wings soared gracefully upward in the distance, swooped over the auditorium, but still the crowd neither moved nor uttered a sound.

A smile of triumph upon his broad face, Fatty bawled, "Lem see'm make wuk now! Lem see'm—"

He got no further. With a rush of mistiness from its tail, but in perfect silence, the soaring thing hovered and sent down a spear of faint, silvery light. The light touched Fatty. He rotted where he stood, like a victim of ultra-rapid leprosy. He rotted, collapsed, crumbled within his sagging clothes, became dust as once he had been dust. It was horrible.

The watchers did not flee in utter panic; not one expression of fear, hatred or disgust came from their tightly closed lips. In perfect silence they stood there, staring, just staring, like a horde of wooden soldiers. The thing in the sky circled to survey its handiwork, then dived low over the mob, a stubby antenna in its prow sparking furiously. As one man, the crowd turned left. As one man it commenced to march, left, right, left, right.

*   *   *

Tearing off the headband, I told Burman what I'd seen, or what his contraption had persuaded me to think that I'd seen. "What the deuce did it mean?"

"Automatons," he murmured. "Glasshouses and re-action ships." He thumbed through a big diary filled with notations in his own hand. "Ah, yes, looks like you were very early in the thirtieth century. Unrest was persistent for twenty years prior to the Antibox Rebellion."

"What rebellion?"

"The Antibox—the revolt of the automatons against the thirty-first century Technocrats. Jackson-Dkj-99717, a successful and cunning schemer with a warped box, secretly warped hundreds of other boxes, and eventually led the rebels to victory in 3047. His great-grandson, a greedy, thick-headed individual, caused the rebellion of the Boxless Freemen against his own clique of Jacksocrats."

I gaped at this recital, then said, "The way you tell it makes it sound like history."

"Of course it's history," he asserted. "History that is yet to be." He was pensive for a while. "Studying the future will seem a weird process to you, but it appears quite a normal procedure to me. I've done it for years, and maybe familiarity has bred contempt. Trouble is though, that selectivity is poor. You can pick on some especial period twenty times in succession, but you'll never find yourself in the same month, or even the same year. In fact, you're fortunate if you strike twice in the same decade. Result is that my data is very erratic."

"I can imagine that," I told him. "A good guesser can guess the correct time to within a minute or two, but never to within ten or even fifty seconds."

"Quite!" he responded. "So the hell of it has been that mine was the privilege of watching the panorama of the future, but in a manner so sketchy that I could not grasp its prizes. Once I was lucky enough to watch a twenty-fifth century power pack assembled from first to last. I got every detail before I lost the scene which I've never managed to hit upon again. But I made that power pack—and you know the result."

"So that's how you concocted your famous battery!"

"It is! But mine, good as it may be, isn't as good as the one I saw. Some slight factor is missing." His voice was suddenly tight when he added, "I missed something because I had to miss it!"

"Why?" I asked, completely puzzled.

"Because history, past or future, permits no glaring paradox. Because, having snatched this battery from the twenty-fifth century, I am recorded in that age as the twentieth-century inventor of the thing. They've made a mild improvement to it in those five centuries, but that improvement was automatically withheld from me. Future history is as fixed and unalterable by those of the present time as is the history of the past."

"Then," I demanded, "explain to me that complicated contraption which does nothing but say *bz-z-z*."

"Damn it!" he said, with open ire, "that's just what's making me crazy! It can't be a paradox, it just can't." Then, more carefully, "So it must be a seeming paradox."

"O. K. You tell me how to market a seeming paradox, and the commercial uses thereof, and I'll give it a first-class write-up."

Ignoring my sarcasm, he went on, "I tried to probe the future as far as human minds can probe. I saw nothing, nothing but the vastness of a sterile floor upon which sat a queer machine, gleaming there in silent, solitary majesty. Somehow, it seemed aware of my scrutiny across the gulf of countless ages. It held my attention with a power almost hypnotic. For more than a day, for a full thirty hours, I kept that vision without losing it—the longest time I have ever kept a future scene."

"Well?"

"I drew it. I made complete drawings of it, performing the task with all the easy confidence of a trained machine draughtsman. Its insides could not be seen, but somehow they came to me, somehow I knew them.

I lost the scene at four o'clock in the morning, finding myself with masses of very complicated drawings, a thumping head, heavy-lidded eyes, and a half-scared feeling in my heart." He was silent for a short time. "A year later I plucked up courage and started to build the thing I had drawn. It cost me a hell of a lot of time and a hell of a lot of money. But I did it—it's finished."

"And all it does is buzz," I remarked, with genuine sympathy.

"Yes," he sighed, doubtfully.

There was nothing more to be said. Burman gazed moodily at the wall, his mind far, far away. I fiddled aimlessly with the copper earpieces of the psychophone. My imagination, I reckoned, was as good as anyone's, but for the life of me I could neither imagine nor suggest a profitable market for a metal coffin filled with watchmaker's junk. No, not even if it did make odd noises.

A faint, smooth *whir* came from the coffin. It was a new sound that swung us round to face it pop-eyed. *Whir-r-r!* it went again. I saw finely machined wheels spin behind the window in its front.

"Good heavens!" said Burman.

Bz-z-z! Whir-r! Click! The whole affair suddenly slid sidewise on its hidden castors.

The devil you know isn't half so frightening as the devil you don't. I don't mean that this sudden demonstration of life and motion got us scared, but it certainly made us leery, and our hearts put in an extra dozen bumps a minute. This coffin-thing was, or might be, a devil we didn't know. So we stood there, side by side, gazing at it fascinatedly, feeling apprehensive of we knew not what.

Motion ceased after the thing had slid two feet. It stood there, silent, imperturbable, its front lenses eyeing us with glassy lack of expression. Then it slid another two feet. Another stop. More meaningless contemplation. After that, a swifter and farther slide that brought it right up to the laboratory table. At that point it ceased moving, began to emit varied but synchronized ticks like those of a couple of sympathetic grandfather clocks.

Burman said, quietly, "Something's going to happen!"

If the machine could have spoken it would have taken the words right out of his mouth. He'd hardly uttered the sentence when a trapdoor in the machine's side fell open, a jointed, metallic arm snaked cautiously through the opening and reached for a marine chronometer standing on the table.

With a surprised oath, Burman dashed forward to rescue the chronometer. He was too late. The arm grabbed it, whisked it into the machine, the trapdoor shut with a hard snap, like the vicious clash of a sprung bear trap. Simultaneously, another trapdoor in the front flipped open, another jointed arm shot out and in again, spearing with ultra-rapid motion too fast to follow. That trapdoor also snapped shut, leaving Burman gaping down at his torn clothing from which his expensive watch and equally expensive gold chain had been ripped away.

"Good heavens!" said Burman, backing from the machine.

We stood looking at it a while. It didn't move again, just posed there ticking steadily as if ruminating upon its welcome meal. Its lenses looked at us with all the tranquil lack of interest of a well-fed cow. I got the idiotic notion that it was happily digesting a mess of cogs, pinions and wheels.

Because its subtle air of menace seemed to have faded away, or maybe because we sensed its entire preoccupation with the task in hand, we made an effort to rescue Burman's valuable timepiece. Burman tugged mightily at the trapdoor through which his watch had gone, but failed to move it. I tugged with him, without result. The thing was sealed as solidly as if welded in. A large screwdriver failed to pry it open. A crowbar, or a good jimmy would have done the job, but at that point Burman decided that he didn't want to damage the machine which had cost him more than the watch.

Tick-tick-tick! went the coffin, stolidly. We were back where we'd started, playing with our fingers, and no wiser than before. There was nothing to be done, and I felt that the accursed contraption knew it. So it stood there, gaping through its lenses, and jeered *tick-tick-tick*. From its belly, or where its belly would have been if it'd had one, a slow warmth radiated. According to Burman's drawings, that was the location of the tiny electric furnace.

The thing was functioning; there could be no doubt about that! If Burman felt the same way as I did, he must have been pretty mad. There we stood, like a couple of prize boobs, not knowing what the machine was supposed to do, and all the time it was doing under our very eyes whatever it was designed to do.

From where was it drawing its power? Were those antennae sticking like horns from its head busily sucking current from the atmosphere? Or was it, perhaps, absorbing radio power? Or did it have internal energy of its own? All the evidence suggested that it was making something, giving birth to something, but giving birth to what?

Tick-tick-tick! was the only reply.

Our questions were still unanswered, our curiosity was still unsatisfied, and the machine was still ticking industriously at the hour of midnight. We surrendered the problem until next morning. Burman locked and double-locked his laboratory before we left.

Police Officer Burke's job was a very simple one. All he had to do was walk round and round the block, keeping a wary eye on the stores in general and the big jewel depot in particular, phoning headquarters once per hour from the post at the corner.

Night work suited Burke's taciturn disposition. He could wander along, communing with himself, with nothing to bother him or divert him from his inward ruminations. In that particular section nothing ever happened at night, nothing.

Stopping outside the gem-bedecked window, he gazed through the glass and the heavy grille behind it to where a low-power bulb shed light over the massive

safe. There was a rajah's ransom in there. The guard,
the grille, the automatic alarms and sundry ingenious
traps preserved it from the adventurous fingers of anyone who wanted to ransom a rajah. Nobody had made
the brash attempt in twenty years. Nobody had even
made a try for the contents of the grille-protected
window.

He glanced upward at a faintly luminescent path of
cloud behind which lay the hidden moon. Turning, he
strolled on. A cat sneaked past him, treading cautiously,
silently, and hugging the angle of the wall. His sharp
eyes detected its slinking shape even in the nighttime
gloom, but he ignored it and progressed to the corner.

Back of him, the cat came below the window through
which he just had stared. It stopped, one forefoot half-
raised, its ears cocked forward. Then it flattened belly-
low against the concrete, its burning orbs wide, alert,
intent. Its tail waved slowly from side to side.

Something small and bright came skittering toward
it, moving with mouselike speed and agility close in the
angle of the wall. The cat tensed as the object came
nearer. Suddenly, the thing was within range, and the
cat pounced with lithe eagerness. Hungry paws dug at a
surface that was not soft and furry, but hard, bright and
slippery. The thing darted around like a clockwork toy
as the cat vainly tried to hold it. Finally, with an angry
snarl, the cat swiped it viciously, knocking it a couple of
yards where it rolled onto its back and emitted softly
protesting clicks and tiny, urgent impulses that its feline attacker could not sense.

Gaining the gutter with a single leap, the cat crouched
again. Something else was coming. The cat muscled, its
eyes glowed. Another object slightly similar to the curious thing it had just captured, but a little bit bigger, a
fraction noisier, and much different in shape. It resembled a small, gold-plated cylinder with a conical front
from which projected a slender blade, and it slid along
swiftly on invisible wheels.

Again the cat leaped. Down on the corner, Burke
heard its brief shriek and following gurgle. The sound

didn't bother Burke—he'd heard cats and rats and other vermin make all sorts of queer noises in the night. Phlegmatically, he continued on his beat.

Three quarters of an hour later, Police Officer Burke had worked his way around to the fatal spot. Putting his flash on the body, he rolled the supine animal over with his foot. Its throat was cut. Its throat had been cut with an utter savagery that had half-severed its head from its body. Burke scowled down at it. He was no lover of cats himself, but he found difficulty in imagining anyone hating like that!

"Somebody," he muttered, "wants flaying alive."

His big foot shoved the dead cat back into the gutter where street cleaners could cart it away in the morning. He turned his attention to the window, saw the light still glowing upon the untouched safe. His mind was still on the cat while his eyes looked in and said that something was wrong. Then he dragged his attention back to business, realized what was wrong, and sweated at every pore. It wasn't the safe, it was the window.

In front of the window the serried trays of valuable rings still gleamed undisturbed. To the right, the silverware still shone untouched. But on the left had been a small display of delicate and extremely expensive watches. They were no longer there, not one of them. He remembered that right in front had rested a neat, beautiful calendar-chronometer priced at a year's salary. That, too, was gone.

The beam of his flash trembled as he tried the gate, found it fast, secure. The door behind it was firmly locked. The transom was closed, its heavy wire guard still securely fixed. He went over the window, eventually found a small, neat hole, about two inches in diameter, down in the corner on the side nearest the missing display.

Burke's curse was explosive as he turned and ran to the corner. His hand shook with indignation while it grabbed the telephone from its box. Getting headquarters, he recited his story. He thought he'd a good idea of what had happened, fancied he'd read once of a similar stunt being pulled elsewhere.

"Looks like they cut a disk with a rotary diamond, lifted it out with a suction cup, then fished through the hole with a telescopic rod." He listened a moment, then said, "Yes, yes. That's just what gets me—the rings are worth ten times as much."

His still-startled eyes looked down the street while he paid attention to the voice at the other end of the line. The eyes wandered slowly, descended, found the gutter, remained fixed on the dim shape lying therein. Another dead cat! Still clinging to his phone, Burke moved out as far as the cord would allow, extended a boot, rolled the cat away from the curb. The flash settled on it. Just like the other—ear to ear!

"And listen," he shouted into the phone, "some maniac's wandering around slaughtering cats."

Replacing the phone, he hurried back to the maltreated window, stood guard in front of it until the police car rolled up. Four piled out.

The first said, "Cats! I'll say somebody's got it in for cats! We passed two a couple of blocks away. They were bang in the middle of the street, flat in the headlights, and had been damn near guillotined. Their bodies were still warm."

The second grunted, approached the window, stared at the small, neat hole, and said, "The mob that did this would be too cute to leave a print."

"They weren't too cute to leave the rings," growled Burke.

"Maybe you've got something there," conceded the other. "If they've left the one, they might have left the other. We'll test for prints, anyway."

A taxi swung into the dark street, pulled up behind the police car. An elegantly dressed, fussy, and very agitated individual got out, rushed up to the waiting group. Keys jangled in his pale, moist hand.

"Maley, the manager—you phoned me," he explained, breathlessly. "Gentlemen, this is terrible, terrible! The

window show is worth thousands, thousands! What a
loss, what a loss!"

"How about letting us in?" asked one of the policemen, calmly.

"Of course, of course."

Jerkily, he opened the gate, unlocked the door, using
about six keys for the job. They walked inside. Maley
switched on the lights, stuck his head between the
plateglass shelves, surveyed the depleted window.

"My watches, my watches," he groaned.

"It's awful, it's awful!" said one of the policemen,
speaking with beautiful solemnity. He favored his companions with a sly wink.

Maley leaned farther over, the better to inspect an
empty corner. "All gone, all gone," he moaned, "all my
show of the finest makes in—*Yeeouw!*" His yelp made
them jump. Maley bucked as he tried to force himself
through the obstructing shelves toward the grille and
the window beyond it. "My watch! My own watch!"

The others tiptoed, stared over his shoulders, saw
the gold buckle of a black velvet fob go through the
hole in the window. Burke was the first outside, his
ready flash searching the concrete. Then he spotted the
watch. It was moving rapidly along, hugging the angle of
the wall, but it stopped dead as his beam settled upon
it. He fancied he saw something else, equally bright
and metallic, scoot swiftly into the darkness beyond the
circle of his beam.

Picking up the watch, Burke stood and listened. The
noises of the others coming out prevented him from
hearing clearly, but he could have sworn he'd heard a
tiny whirring noise, and a swift, juicy ticking that was
not coming from the instrument in his hand. Must have
been only his worried fancy. Frowning deeply, he returned to his companions.

"There was nobody," he asserted. "It must have
dropped out of your pocket and rolled."

Damn it, he thought, could a watch roll that far?
What the devil was happening this night? Far up the
street, something screeched, then it bubbled. Burke

shuddered—he could make a shrewd guess at that! He looked at the others, but apparently they hadn't heard the noise.

The papers gave it space in the morning. The total was sixty watches and eight cats, also some oddments from the small stock of a local scientific instrument maker. I read about it on my way down to Burman's place. The details were fairly lavish, but not complete. I got them completely at a later time when we discovered the true significance of what had occurred.

Burman was waiting for me when I arrived. He appeared both annoyed and bothered. Over in the corner, the coffin was ticking away steadily, its noise much louder than it had been the previous day. The thing sounded a veritable hive of industry.

"Well?" I asked.

"It's moved around a lot during the night," said Burman. "It's smashed a couple of thermometers and taken the mercury out of them. I found some drawers and cupboards shut, some open, but I've an uneasy feeling that it's made a thorough search through the lot. A packet of nickel foil has vanished, a coil of copper wire has gone with it." He pointed an angry finger at the bottom of the door through which I'd just entered. "And I blame it for gnawing rat holes in that. They weren't there yesterday."

Sure enough, there were a couple of holes in the bottom of that door. But no rat made those—they were neat and smooth and round, almost as if a carpenter had cut them with a keyhole saw.

"Where's the sense in it making those?" I questioned. "It can't crawl through apertures that size."

"Where's the sense in the whole affair?" Burman countered. He glowered at the busy machine which stared back at him with its expressionless lenses and churned steadily on. *Tick-tick-tick!* persisted the confounded thing. Then, *whir-thump-click!*

I opened my mouth intending to voice a nice, sarcastic comment at the machine's expense when there came

a very tiny, very subtle and extremely high-pitched
whine. Something small, metallic, glittering shot through
one of the rat holes, fled across the floor toward the
churning monstrosity. A trapdoor opened and swallowed it with such swiftness that it had disappeared
before I realized what I'd seen. The thing had been a
cylindrical, polished object resembling the shuttle of a
sewing machine, but about four times the size. And it
had been dragging something also small and metallic.

Burman stared at me; I stared at Burman. Then he
foraged around the laboratory, found a three-foot length
of half-inch steel pipe. Dragging a chair to the door, he
seated himself, gripped the pipe like a bludgeon, and
watched the rat holes. Imperturbably, the machine
watched him and continued to *tick-tick-tick*.

Ten minutes later, there came a sudden click and
another tiny whine. Nothing darted inward through the
holes, but the curious object we'd already seen—or
another one exactly like it—dropped out of the trap,
scooted to the door by which we were waiting. It caught
Burman by surprise. He made a mad swipe with the
steel as the thing skittered elusively past his feet and
through a hole. It had gone even as the weapon walloped
the floor.

"Damn!" said Burman, heartily. He held the pipe
loosely in his grip while he glared at the industrious
coffin. "I'd smash it to bits except that I'd like to catch
one of these small gadgets first."

"Look out!" I yelled.

He was too late. He ripped his attention away from
the coffin toward the holes, swinging up the heavy
length of pipe, a startled look on his face. But his
reaction was far too slow. Three of the little mysteries
were through the holes and halfway across the floor
before his weapon was ready to swing. The coffin swallowed them with the crash of a trapdoor.

The invading trio had rushed through in single file,
and I'd got a better picture of them this time. The first
two were golden shuttles, much like the one we'd already seen. The third was bigger, speedier, and gave

me the notion that it could dodge around more dexterously. It had a long, sharp projection in front, a wicked, ominous thing like a surgeon's scalpel. Sheer speed deprived me of a good look at it, but I fancied that the tip of the scalpel had been tinged with red. My spine exuded perspiration.

Came an irritated scratching upon the outside of the door and a white-tipped paw poked tentatively through one of the holes. The cat backed to a safe distance when Burman opened the door, but looked lingeringly toward the laboratory. Its presence needed no explaining— the alert animal must have caught a glimpse of those infernal little whizzers. The same thought struck both of us; cats are quick on the pounce, very quick. Given a chance, maybe this one could make a catch for us.

We enticed it in with fair words and soothing noises. Its eagerness overcame its normal caution toward strangers, and it entered. We closed the door behind it; Burman got his length of pipe, sat by the door, tried to keep one eye on the holes and the other on the cat. He couldn't do both, but he tried. The cat sniffed and prowled around, mewed defeatedly. Its behavior suggested that it was seeking by sight rather than scent. There wasn't any scent.

With feline persistence, the animal searched the whole laboratory. It passed the buzzing coffin several times, but ignored it completely. In the end, the cat gave it up, sat on the corner of the laboratory table and started to wash its face.

Tick-tick-tick! went the big machine. Then *whir-thump!* A trap popped open, a shuttle fell out and raced for the door. A second one followed it. The first was too fast even for the cat, too fast for the surprised Burman as well. *Bang!* The length of steel tube came down viciously as the leading shuttle bulleted triumphantly through a hole.

But the cat got the second one. With a mighty leap, paws extended claws out, it caught its victim one foot from the door. It tried to handle the slippery thing, failed, lost it for an instant. The shuttle whisked around in a crazy loop. The cat got it again, lost it again, emitted an angry snarl, batted it against the skirting board. The shuttle lay there, upside down, four midget wheels in its underside spinning madly with a high, almost inaudible whine.

Eyes alight with excitement, Burman put down his weapon, went to pick up the shuttle. At the same time, the cat slunk toward it ready to play with it. The shuttle lay there, helplessly functioning upon its back. Before either could reach it the big machine across the room went *clunk!*, opened a trap and ejected another gadget.

With astounding swiftness, the cat turned and pounced upon the newcomer. Then followed pandemonium. Its prey swerved agilely with a fitful gleam of gold; the cat swerved with it, cursed and spat. Black-and-white fur whirled around in a fighting haze in which gold occasionally glowed; the cat's hissings and spittings overlay a persistent whine that swelled and sank in the manner of accelerating or decelerating gears.

A peculiar gasp came from the cat, and blood spotted the floor. The animal clawed wildly, emitted another gasp followed by a gurgle. It shivered and flopped, a stream of crimson pouring from the great gash in its gullet.

We'd hardly time to appreciate the full significance of the ghastly scene when the victor made for Burman. He was standing by the skirting board, the still-buzzing shuttle in his hand. His eyes were sticking out with utter horror, but he retained enough presence of mind to make a frantic jump a second before the bulleting menace reached his feet.

He landed behind the thing, but it reversed in its own length and came for him again. I saw the mirror-like sheen of its scalpel as it banked at terrific speed, and the sheen was drowned in sticky crimson two inches along the blade. Burman jumped over it again, reached the lab table, got up on that.

"Lord!" he breathed.

By this time I'd got the piece of pipe which he'd

discarded. I hefted it, feeling its comforting weight,
then did my best to bat the buzzing lump of wickedness
through the window and over the roofs. It was too agile
for me. It whirled, accelerated, dodged the very tip of
the descending steel, and flashed twice around the
table upon which Burman had taken refuge. It ignored
me completely. Somehow, I felt that it was responding
entirely to some mysterious call from the shuttle Burman
had captured.

I swiped desperately, missed it again, though I swear
I missed by no more than a millimeter. Something
whipped through the holes in the door, fled past me
into the big machine. Dimly, I heard traps opening and
closing, and beyond all other sounds that steady, persistent *tick-tick-tick*. Another furious blow that accomplished no more than to dent the floor and jar my arm
to the shoulder.

Unexpectedly, unbelievably, the golden curse ceased
its insane gyrations on the floor and around the table.
With a hard click, and a whir much louder than before,
it raced easily up one leg of the table and reached the
top.

Burman left his sanctuary in one jump. He was still
clinging to the shuttle. I'd never seen his face so white.

"The machine!" he said, hoarsely. "Bash it to hell!"

Thunk! went the machine. A trap gaped, released
another demon with a scalpel. *Tzz-z-z!* a third shot in
through the holes in the door. Four shuttles skimmed
through behind it, made for the machine, reached it
safely. A fifth came through more slowly. It was dragging an automobile valve spring. I kicked the thing
against the wall even as I struck a vain blow at one with
a scalpel.

With another jump, Burman cleared an attacker. A
second sheared off the toe of his right shoe as he
landed. Again he reached the table from which his first
foe had departed. All three things with scalpels made
for the table with a reckless vim that was frightening.

"Drop that damned shuttle," I yelled.

He didn't drop it. As the fighting trio whirred up the legs, he flung the shuttle with all his might at the coffin that had given it birth. It struck, dented the casing, fell to the floor. Burman was off the table again. The thrown shuttle lay battered and noiseless, its small motive wheels stilled.

The armed contraptions scooting around the table seemed to change their purpose coincidently with the captured shuttle's smashing. Together, they dived off the table, sped through the holes in the door. A fourth came out of the machine, escorting two shuttles, and those two vanished beyond the door. A second or two later, a new thing, different from the rest, came in through one of the holes. It was long, round-bodied, snub-nosed, about half the length of a policeman's nightstick, had six wheels beneath, and a double row of peculiar serrations in front. It almost sauntered across the room while we watched it fascinatedly. I saw the serrations jerk and shift when it climbed the lowered trap into the machine. They were midget caterpillar tracks!

Burman had had enough. He made up his mind. Finding the steel pipe, he gripped it firmly, approached the coffin. Its lenses seemed to leer at him as he stood before it. Twelve years of intensive work to be destroyed at a blow. Endless days and nights of effort to be undone at one stroke. But Burman was past caring. With a ferocious swing he demolished the glass, with a fierce thrust he shattered the assembly of wheels and cogs behind.

The coffin shuddered and slid beneath his increasingly angry blows. Trapdoors dropped open, spilled out lifeless samples of the thing's metallic brood. Grindings and raspings came from the accursed object while Burman battered it to pieces. Then it was silent, stilled, a shapeless, useless mass of twisted and broken parts.

I picked up the dented shape of the object that had sauntered in. It was heavy, astonishingly heavy, and even after partial destruction its workmanship looked wonderful. It had a tiny, almost unnoticeable eye in front, but the minature lens was cracked. Had it returned for repairs and overhaul?

"That," said Burman, breathing audibly, "is that!"

I opened the door to see if the noise had attracted attention. It hadn't. There was a lifeless shuttle outside the door, a second a yard behind it. The first had a short length of brass chain attached to a tiny hook projecting from its rear. The nose cap of the second had opened fanwise, like an iris diaphragm, and a pair of jointed metal arms were folded inside, hugging a medium-sized diamond. It looked as if they'd been about to enter when Burman destroyed the big machine.

Picking them up, I brought them in. Their complete inactivity, though they were undamaged, suggested that they had been controlled by the big machine and had drawn their motive power from it. If so, then we'd solved our problem simply, and by destroying the one had destroyed the lot.

Burman got his breath back and began to talk.

He said, "The Robot Mother! That's what I made—a duplicate of the Robot Mother. I didn't realize it, but I was patiently building the most dangerous thing in creation, a thing that is a terrible menace because it shares with mankind the ability to propagate. Thank Heaven we stopped it in time!"

"So," I remarked, remembering that he claimed to have got it from the extreme future, "that's the eventual master, or mistress, of Earth. A dismal prospect for humanity, eh?"

"Not necessarily. I don't know just how far I got, but I've an idea it was so tremendously distant in the future that Earth had become sterile from humanity's viewpoint. Maybe we'd emigrated to somewhere else in the cosmos, leaving our semi-intelligent slave machines to fight for existence or die. They fought—and survived."

"And then wangled things to try and alter the past in their favor," I suggested.

"No, I don't think so," Burman had become much calmer by now. "I don't think it was a dastardly attempt so much as an interesting experiment. The whole affair was damned in advance because success would have meant an impossible paradox. There are no robots in the next century, nor any knowledge of them. Therefore the intruders in this time must have been wiped out and forgotten."

"Which means," I pointed out, "that you must not only have destroyed the machine, but also all your drawings, all your notes, as well as the psychophone, leaving nothing but a few strange events and a story for me to tell."

"Exactly—I shall destroy everything. I've been thinking over the whole affair, and it's not until now I've understood that the psychophone can never be of the slightest use to me. It permits me to discover or invent only those things that history has decreed I shall invent, and which, therefore, I shall find with or without the contraption. I can't play tricks with history, past or future."

"Humph!" I couldn't find any flaw in his reasoning. "Did you notice," I went on, "the touch of bee-psychology in our antagonists? You built the hive, and from it emerged workers, warriors, and"—I indicated the dead saunterer—"one drone."

"Yes," he said, lugubriously. "And I'm thinking of the honey—eighty watches! Not to mention any other items the late papers may report, plus any claims for slaughtered cats. Good thing I'm wealthy."

"Nobody knows you've anything to do with those incidents. You can pay secretly if you wish."

"I shall," he declared.

"Well," I went on, cheerfully, "all's well that ends well. Thank goodness we've got rid of what we brought upon ourselves."

With a sigh of relief, I strolled toward the door. A high whine of midget motors drew my startled attention downward. While Burman and I stared aghast, a golden shuttle slid easily through one of the rat holes, sensed the death of the Robot Mother and scooted back through the other hole before I could stop it.

If Burman had been shaken before, he was doubly so now. He came over to the door, stared incredulously at the little exit just used by the shuttle, then at the couple of other undamaged but lifeless shuttles lying about the room.

"Bill," he mouthed, "your bee analogy was perfect. Don't you understand? There's another swarm! A queen got loose!"

There was another swarm all right. For the next forty-eight hours it played merry hell. Burman spent the whole time down at headquarters trying to convince them that his evidence wasn't just a fantastic story, but what helped him to persuade the police of his veracity were the equally fantastic reports that came rolling in.

To start with, old Gildersome heard a crash in his shop at midnight, thought of his valuable stock of cameras and miniature movie projectors, pulled on his pants and rushed downstairs. A razor-sharp instrument stabbed him through the right instep when halfway down, and he fell the rest of the way. He lay there, badly bruised and partly stunned, while things clicked, ticked and whirred in the darkness and the gloom. One by one, all the contents of his box of expensive lenses went through a hole in the door. A quantity of projector cogs and wheels went with them.

Ten people complained of being robbed in the night of watches and alarm clocks. Two were hysterical. One swore that the bandit was "a six-inch cockroach" which purred like a toy dynamo. Getting out of bed, he'd put his foot upon it and felt its cold hardness wriggle away from beneath him. Filled with revulsion, he'd whipped his foot back into bed "just as another cockroach scuttled toward me." Burman did not tell that agitated complainant how near he had come to losing his foot.

Thirty more reports rolled in next day. A score of houses had been entered and four shops robbed by things that had the agility and furtiveness of rats—except that they emitted tiny ticks and buzzing noises. One was seen racing along the road by a homing railway worker. He tried to pick it up, lost his forefinger and thumb, stood nursing the stumps until an ambulance rushed him away.

Rare metals and fine parts were the prey of these ticking marauders. I couldn't see how Burman or anyone else could wipe them out once and for all, but he did it. He did it by baiting them like rats. I went around with him, helping him on the job, while he consulted a map.

"Every report," said Burman, "leads to this street. An alarm clock that suddenly sounded was abandoned near here. Two automobiles were robbed of small parts near here. Shuttles have been seen going to or from this area. Five cats were dealt with practically on this spot. Every other incident has taken place within easy reach."

"Which means," I guessed, "that the queen is somewhere near this point?"

"Yes." He stared up and down the quiet empty street over which the crescent moon shed a sickly light. It was two o'clock in the morning. "We'll settle this matter pretty soon!"

He attached the end of a reel of firm cotton to a small piece of silver chain, nailed the reel to the wall, dropped the chain on the concrete. I did the same with the movement of a broken watch. We distributed several small cogs, a few clock wheels, several camera fitments, some small, tangled bunches of copper wire, and other attractive oddments.

Three hours later, we returned accompanied by the police. They had mallets and hammers with them. All of us were wearing steel leg-and-foot shields knocked up at short notice by a handy sheet-metal worker.

The bait had been taken! Several cotton strands had broken after being unreeled a short distance, but others were intact. All of them either led to or pointed to a steel grating leading to a cellar below an abandoned warehouse. Looking down, we could see a few telltale strands running through the window frame beneath.

Burman said, "Now!" and we went in with a rush.

Rusty locks snapped, rotten doors collapsed, we poured through the warehouse and into the cellar.

There was a small, coffin-shaped thing against one wall, a thing that ticked steadily away while its lenses stared at us with ghastly lack of emotion. It was very similar to the Robot Mother, but only a quarter of the size. In the light of a police torch, it was a brooding, ominous thing of dreadful significance. Around it, an active clan swarmed over the floor, buzzing and ticking in metallic fury.

Amid angry whirs and the crack of snapping scalpels on steel, we waded headlong through the lot. Burman reached the coffin first, crashing it with one mighty blow of his twelve-pound hammer, then bashing it to utter ruin with a rapid succession of blows. He finished exhausted. The daughter of the Robot Mother was no more, nor did her alien tribe move or stir.

Sitting down on a rickety wooden case, Burman mopped his brow and said, "Thank heavens that's done!"

Tick-tick-tick!

He shot up, snatched his hammer, a wild look in his eyes.

"Only my watch," apologized one of the policemen. "It's a cheap one, and it makes a hell of a noise." He pulled it out to show the worried Burman.

"Tick! tick!" said the watch, with mechanical aplomb.

Bob Silverberg wrote extensively for the digest magazines of the '50s (my phrasing; his is "about a jillion stories"). Competent writing wasn't general then, any more than it is today; and Bob was always competent.

He was usually more than that, because he understood the economic underpinning that's basic to most human interactions—and is generally ignored in fiction. "The Day the Monsters Broke Loose" involves the business of capturing alien monsters.

And the business of the games which the capture teams serve.

THE DAY THE MONSTERS BROKE LOOSE

Robert Silverberg

Next week they'll be holding the Big Show, the Spectacular of Spectaculars, in Chicago. One hundred and fifty-thousand people will be packed into Soldier Field to watch a couple of alien monsters rip each other to shreds.

Well, I'm not going to be there, for once. I'm going to be a couple of thousand miles away, in Los Angeles, sitting in a little bar off Wilshire where they *don't* have video, and I'll be guzzling syntho-scotch and trying to forget all about my part in next week's show.

I'm the guy who caught the creatures that are going to perform next Fiveday night. I'm Jim Barstow of Barstow Expediters, Incorporated. *We Bring 'em Back Alive* is our motto, shamefully stolen from a great hunter of a couple of centuries ago, and right up until our last trip we were considered the top outfit in our line. But now I want to sell my share and get out of the filthy business while I still have a little piece of my soul left.

We made our first trip to World Twelve of Star System DA-7116 exactly two years ago. Herschel, my booking agent, gave me a buzz on the telestat one morning and said he had landed a fat contract for us. Barstow Expediters happened to be between jobs at the moment, and I was enjoying the pleasant layoff, but I obediently came shuttling across the country to New York for the contract interview.

We were being hired by J. Franklin Magnus of Magnus Promotions—the number one spectacle-producer of the twenty-second century. Magnus was famous for the way he threw money around. I flew to New York determined to soak him for all he would part with.

We met in his office on the 180th floor of the Universe Building in uptown Manhattan. Magnus was a small, roly-poly man with a deep and probably phoney suntan and a thick, stubby mustache dyed blue according to the latest fashion. He was wearing a blue-white Sirian diamond the size of a peach. He reeked of wealth.

He offered me some hundred-year-old brandy and said, "Sit down, Barstow."

I sat. He pulled out photographs in tridim solido and shoved them across the desk at me.

"Know what they are, Barstow?"

The tridims showed an animal. A big animal. Somebody had parked a two-man jetflitter in the picture to provide comparison, and I figured the beast was at least eighty feet high. It stood on two legs the size of tree trunks, only thicker, ending in flat pads. There were four more limbs, but these were made for grabbing and tearing.

The creature's head looked like it was all teeth, except for a trio of eyes the size of platters, mounted to swivel in all directions.

I nodded and said, "Sure I know what it is. It's a beastie called by a Latin name two yards long. It lives on—let me think—World Twelve of Star System DA-7116."

"Right!" Magnus exclaimed, as if I'd just answered the million-ruble question on a quiz program. Of course, it's my job to know where the really fierce creatures of the galaxy can be found.

Magnus went on, "I want you to catch me one of

those things, Barstow. I'm going to match it in the arena with a pair of knifeleg killersaurs from Procyon Eight." His eyes were glittering with delight.

"Nobody's ever brought a World Twelve monster back to Earth alive before. Think you can do it?"

"Yes," I said. "For a price."

"Name it!"

"How soon do you need the animal?"

"Tomorrow. Next week. Next month. Anytime!"

I thought for a moment. "The round trip to Star System DA-7116 takes nine weeks. Allow two weeks more for catching the beast. I can deliver within twelve weeks, Magnus. Is that good enough?"

"Splendid!"

"And the price," I added casually. "I've got to figure on the cost of shipping out a three-month expedition. Insurance, food, fuel, payroll. Plus margin of profit. I'd say I could supply you with your animal for—oh, in the neighborhood of $750,000. If that sounds okay, I can give you a detailed estimate later in the day—"

"Make it $800,000," he said buoyantly, "and don't worry about counting the nickels. Just get me that creature, Barstow!"

So we signed the contract right then and there. I got $250,000 as an advance, the rest to be paid on delivery. Delivery to be made in three months or less, of one adult and healthy creature.

I picked my crew out of the pool of thirty or forty men I use on such expeditions. Seven men, hand-picked, went along with me when we blasted off for Star System DA-7116 four days later.

I don't think historians of the future are going to be very kind to the twenty-second century. It was a century of peace, sure—harmony prevailed on Earth and for the first time in aeons no war even loomed on the distant horizon. Earth knew peace.

But, sad to say, there are various instincts of aggres-

sion and hostility bound up in the human psyche, unhappy remnants of our caveman past. And with no war
to release these dark emotions, they manifested themselves in other ways. It was a bloody century for the
entertainment industry. First there was the bullfight
craze sweeping the world, but that soon bored everyone. And then the human gladiators, the Roman Re-
vival period, only that was on the shocking side, and
the United States finally banned it.

There were steeplechases and jet races and all sorts
of other hazardous exhibitions. The populace loved the
sight of blood. They loved to feel vicarious pain.

Then along came Magnus and the others of his ilk,
the monster merchandisers. It seemed that the universe was full of ferocious and ghastly creatures, many
of them formidable in size. Why not, reasoned these
promoters, hire explorers to bring back alien creatures
and pit them against each other in the arenas?

So the spectacular contests began. My outfit and a
dozen others began to roam the stars, bringing back the
wildlife of a thousand worlds. The arenas reeked with
alien blood. Green blood, yellow blood. The crowds
loved it. They paid ten bucks a seat to watch a giant
octopus from Bellatrix VII go at a land-whale from Rigel
III.

The monsters really packed them in. Guys like J.
Franklin Magnus became billionaires promoting the monster contests, and guys like me built up comfortable
bank accounts by supplying the raw material for these
bloodfests.

This was my fortieth collecting trip. I didn't want to
think about the tons and tons of monsterflesh I had
ferried back to Earth to be ripped apart in the arenas,
while a hundred thousand screaming maniacs yelled
encouragement from the sidelines and a hundred million more sat on the edges of their seats and drooled
into their video sets.

We made the thirty-two-day outbound trip without

any complications, shuttling into spacewarp on schedule and shuttling out at the proper time.

"There she is," said Mickey Delacorte, our navigator, as Star System DA-7116 burst into view on our screens. It was a yellow Sol-type sun, young and hot, orbited by seventeen worlds. The first nine or ten planets of the system had never been explored; they were too hot, with temperatures up around three hundred plus, and obviously life had not yet appeared on them.

World Twelve was our baby—Earthtype, though a little bigger, and still in its infancy as planets go. An exploring team had visited the place five years back; I had a copy of the report. They described the planet as "primitive," still in the era of giant plants and big animals.

We landed and set up camp next to the ship. The ship was a big one—it had to be, if we were going to transport an eighty-foot-long monster back to Earth in it—but most of the ship was given up to cargo space and fuel storage, and living quarters were on the cramped side. So we were glad to get out and stretch.

The air was fresh and reasonably breathable—a little high on carbon dioxide, but still within our tolerance levels. The sun was up on the side of the planet where we had landed, and it was *hot*; temperature was around 112, the humidity was tremendous, and sweat poured down our sides in waves.

We didn't say much. We had worked together a long time, and we knew our jobs. We were here to catch an animal and get it home, not to see the sights or to collect souvenirs for the museum. So we set about our jobs.

Delacorte and I did the scouting work. We broke out the collapsible two-man jetflitter and took off, making a quick reconnaissance tour of the area to find out if any of our quarry happened to be in the vicinity.

Abrams, the signalman, remained in the ship to monitor our dispatches and keep track of us. McDonnell and Webster checked through our hunting equipment, making sure that the force-field projectors were in working order and the blaster charges renewed. Crosley and Manners busied themselves with the receiving chamber for the big beastie, when we caught him—we would virtually split the ship in half the long way, hoist the trussed-up animal into his berth, and close up the ship again. Anderson, the final man, scouted the area to see how edible the local food was.

Delacorte and I covered about three hundred square miles that afternoon in the flitter before we saw what we were looking for. We had spied plenty of other nasties—a snake that must have been a hundred fifty feet long, sunning itself by the bank of a river; crocodiles with snouts like boxcars shuttling under the surface of the water; flying creatures with leathery wings that opened out wider than the wingspread of our plane; lots of stuff like that. But so far as we were concerned these were just small fry.

We were after bigger game. We found it a little while after we saw the snake.

Delacorte, with his quick eyes, spotted it first. He sucked in his breath and pointed.

"There!"

I looked down. The creature had emerged into a little clearing in the thick jungle, and he had heard the sound of our engines as we circled five hundred to a thousand feet above him.

He was glaring up at us and snarling. I estimated that he was close to a hundred feet tall. He was waving his upper set of arms at us as if wishing we would come within reach so he could rip us apart and stuff us down that yawning mouth. His teeth were like shining swords in the bright sun.

Delacorte scribbled our coordinates down on a piece of paper and shoved them over to me. I clicked on the radio and said, "Abrams, are you getting me?"

"Clear as a bell, Jim."

"Okay. We've found one of Magnus' little pets." I gave him the coordinates. "He's big and he looks mean—

just the kind we want. Alert the men. I'm going to start driving him toward the ship."

We had caught plenty of big boys before, though never quite such a behemoth as this. The procedure was the same as always, though. First find your prey, then drive it toward the ship, then immobilize and capture. There was no sense slapping the monster down with a force-field way out here, and then having to transport a couple of dozen tons of flesh overland for fifty or a hundred miles. We couldn't bring the ship to the monster; the next best thing was to bring the monster to the ship.

Delacorte got on the controls of the jetflitter, and I handled the artillery. This part of the operation was always tricky, and I liked to take care of it personally.

One thing I *didn't* want to do was dump a bomb right onto the beast and kill or maim it. I just wanted to attract its attention, that was all.

I racked the implosion bombs out over the dropping bay and squeezed the first one down. I wanted to put it just back of the big boy, and I succeeded. It landed two hundred yards behind the monster, in some thick shrubbery, and detonated with a quick inward swooshing sound followed by a loud clap.

The monster jumped forward cagily and snarled at our flitter above him. I had Delacorte take another swoop around behind the beast and I dropped two more bombs in quick succession.

Then we lit out shipward, and the thoroughly angry monster followed us.

"Cut the altitude to three hundred feet," I ordered. "Just skim the treetops."

The flitter dropped. I looked through the rear windows and saw the beast bashing along through the underbrush on our tail. We hovered in place with the rotors until the animal had caught up with us. We hung, no more than a couple of hundred feet above that yawning mouthful of yellowish swords, while the beast bellowed and clawed at the sky and implored us to come within reach.

I gave it a little peppering with our light machine-gun—solid pellets, strong enough to tickle and annoy him without messing up his hide. The creature howled and ripped up a couple of tree trunks to wave at us.

"Okay," I told Delacorte. "Start heading toward the ship again."

And so it went, over the twenty miles that separated us from the landing area. Our little jetflitter danced in and out of the monster's path while I dropped implosion bombs, fired guns, and otherwise worked hard to distract and enrage the beast. He followed along, getting angrier and angrier, probably thinking he was pursuing some new and troublesome kind of insect. He didn't know it, but we were leading him right into the jaws of a trap.

When we were a couple of miles from the ship I radioed ahead, warning the men to get ready. By this time I hoped McDonnell and Webster had checked out all the force-field projectors and had them set up ready for use. If this baby burst onto the clearing before they were prepared to nail him, our expedition would come crashing down into ignominious fiascohood.

I got confirmation from Abrams: everything was set and in readiness. They were on their toes and waiting for our pet to appear.

As we approached the ship area, with the creature in anxious pursuit, I racked in the remaining implosion bombs and brought our secondary weapon into use: gas bombs. We had devised these bombs specially for use against creatures of this size.

The gas was a light one that never got closer to the ground than forty or fifty feet. It hung in a thick cloud around the monster's head, generally slowing him down considerably, but left the operators on ground-side with free and unhindered vision so they could carry out the trapping job.

* * *

As Delacorte piloted us into the clearing where we had set up our camp, I nudged the ejector and a gas bomb went through the bay. I scored a direct hit; the bomb landed athwart the monster's skull, and a moment later a blinding cloud of dense, oily gas swirled around him. Above the noise of the jetflitter's engines I could hear the anguished roar of the maddened beast. I saw mighty arms threshing as he tried fruitlessly to sweep away the gas that clung to him.

The beast stumbled around in confused circles. I signalled Delacorte and he lifted the flitter up to the thousand-foot level, where we ran no risk of getting ourselves entangled in groundside activities. I saw our men running around near the ship, manning the force-field projectors.

Then they came into play. Four projectors at once when into operation, and green beams of light converged on the monster, wrapping him in an impenetrable cocoon of neutronic force. We were bagging the ninety-foot giant as simply as if we were out netting butterflies on a balmy summer day.

Within minutes the confused and baffled beast was utterly and hopelessly bottled up. He came toppling down to the ground, falling like a mighty oak, and I knew the worst was over.

"Bring us down," I told Delacorte.

By the time I leaped from the hatch of the jetflitter's cockpit, ten minutes later, my team had already done a quite efficient job. The monster lay prostrate, totally hemmed in by the force-field. We could glimpse his blazing, furious eyes through the mistiness of the neutronic field that bound him.

Anderson and Webster were busily rigging the hoist, while the others were occupied in opening the ship and preparing the hold to receive its burden. The entire operation took no more than two hours.

The crane creaked and complained, but got the beast off the ground and into the waiting chamber. Manners supervised the closing of the ship after the atmospheric pumps had done their job. The monster was locked up in the heart of our ship. We had taken less than a day of our scheduled two weeks for the catch.

The next morning we blasted off for Earth, having taken aboard in the meanwhile enough raw meat to content the pinioned and imprisoned monster for the four-and-a-half-week journey home. We didn't congratulate each other on a job well done. We had been together too long for stuff like that.

One thing we knew, and knew silently: we had captured a jungle monarch and we were taking him trussed back to Earth to meet a grisly fate in a public arena. We had captured a lord of a primitive world, and we were fetching him to satisfy the blood-lust of a bunch of over-fed, over-civilized Earthmen.

It wasn't a pretty thing we had done. But what the hell, we each told ourselves in silent rationalization. If we hadn't done it, someone else would have. It wasn't much of an excuse, but we tried to satisfy our consciences with it.

The monster caused a stir when we landed it on Earth, naturally. It was the biggest alien being ever transported alive from its home world to the Solar System.

It measured 92 feet from the flaming red crest at the top of its skull to its flat pads. We didn't have any way of determining its weight, but we estimated something in the neighborhood of twenty tons. It gobbled up a ton of fresh meat a day by way of food.

Magnus gave us the big welcome—and the big check, too. Much fuss was made. As arranged, we delivered the monster to Magnus' animal ranch in Nevada; the show itself was to be held at the Rose Bowl in Pasadena.

The advertising splash was colossal. Two bloodthirsty knifeleg killersaurs were being groomed to fight our boy. The killersaurs, which came from Procyon Eight, grew to about thirty feet in height, and the lower halves of their bodies were studded with razor-keen spines. They were considered the most ferocious creatures in the galaxy, and my outfit had imported fifteen or twenty of them for various promoters. They were automatic smash hits whenever they fought.

Magnus was putting two of them up against the beast from World Twelve—which might result in a collaborative effort that would bring the huge animal down, or which might turn into a tremendous free-for-all with no holds barred and all three beasts out for blood.

Magnus had the best public-relations men in the trade, and he succeeded in getting the public worked up about the contest to such an extent that hardly anyone talked about anything else for the month between the time of our arrival and the day of the fight.

The Rose Bowl's 110,000 seats were booked solid; Magnus had peddled the seats at twenty bucks a throw, and word was getting around that some of the tickets had been changing hands privately for as much as three and four hundred dollars. He sold the world video rights for a sum way up in the millions. Oh, Magnus was getting a good return on his $800,000 investment, that was for sure!

The day of the fight was typical Southern California weather: dry, sunny, beautiful. Pasadena and Los Angeles were mobbed. The special convoy of armored trucks had fetched the animals in from Magnus' Nevada ranch the night before. They weren't being fed at all the day of the fight, to sharpen their appetites.

Magnus provided me with a good seat, midway up the Bowl where I could get a good view of what was going on. I had been tempted to sell my ticket, in view of the current going price for them, but decided against it. It would have looked bad.

Custom dictated that the promoter set aside a certain number of seats for the intrepid trappers who supplied him with his animals, and I knew I was supposed to be there to give the event a little extra twist, as if anything extra was needed.

McDonnell drove me out to the Bowl from his place in Santa Monica. We were all seated in the same section that afternoon, Crosley and Manners and Anderson and Delacorte and Webster and McDonnell and Abrams and me, the men who had brought the big beast back. Marty Beaumont was the hunter who had caught the killersaurs for Magnus. Marty and I shook hands for the benefit of the video camera before the show began, and exchanged a couple of insincere words about the production.

At two o'clock the show got under way with the prelim. It was an encounter between a Martian sandbat and a maneater cat from Venus, just something to whip up some excitement and put the smell of blood in the air. It lasted ten minutes. The maneater cat, which looked like a tiger with horns, did its best to claw the sandbat to shreds, but the bat managed to flutter out of harm's way—the heavier gravitation of Earth kept it from getting actually off the ground—and finally it opened its wings, folded them like a shroud around the cat, and made the kill.

When the arena was cleared, there was a fanfare and a gasp from the crowd, and the east gate was pulled open. A long moment of anxiety. Then one of the killersaurs came bounding out into the arena.

The audience shrieked with delight and horror. An invisible barrier of neutronic force surrounded the combat area to prevent any rambunctious beast from hopping into the audience—but because the barrier *is* invisible, the people down in the front rows often get qualms when they see something hopping around not very far from them and with no apparent restraining wall.

The killersaur was a real horror. It was a thirty-footer, with a full set of claws, spines, horns, and other implements for cutting, rending, and tearing. It galloped around the empty arena, snorting, pawing dirt, and just about doing everything but breathing fire.

The audience watched it for a while. Magnus had timed it just right. As soon as the audience had decided that there couldn't be anything in the universe more terrifying than a killersaur, the west gate swung open and out came the monster of World Twelve.

God, it looked big in that arena! It stood up to its full ninety-foot height and roared in anger and hatred, and you could hear the hush of horror that passed through the 110,000 onlookers and the hundreds of millions around the world who were viewing this scene on their video screens.

It caught sight of the killersaur. The killersaur glared back. The killersaur was big and mean-looking, but it looked like a puppy-dog next to our boy.

Then the east gate opened. The second killersaur came prancing out. Someone in the crowd screamed. The trumpets went off like the last call of Gabriel, and the battle was on.

The killersaurs didn't seem certain whether to make for each other or for the big fellow. The monster of World Twelve hit out for them both, though.

All three came together in the center of the arena. The killersaurs realized where their danger lay, and set about trying to slash the legs of the giant. For a moment I figured it would be all over in a few minutes: I saw the giant form of our monster towering up in the middle of the field, with the two killersaurs burrowing away at his legs with their tusks.

Then the monster reached down, picked up one of the killersaurs—picked up a beast weighing *five tons!* —and started to rip it to chunks.

It had to give up that idea when the other killersaur clamped its teeth on a huge leg and started gnawing. But I realized with some relief that those killersaurs weren't going to last long.

It was all over in fifteen minutes. The monster from World Twelve was just too big and too smart for the killersaurs. It got its hands into their mouths and split their jaws open; then it lifted them and crashed them down a few times on the ground.

There was blood everywhere, and most of it was thick black killersaur blood. The crowd screamed in delight as the monster relentlessly massacred two of the fiercest beasts in the universe. They were really getting their money's worth.

And then they got something that they weren't expecting for the price of admission.

The monster got tired of kicking the pieces of killersaur around the arena. He had eaten all he wanted, and the show had degenerated into a bloodbath. I figured that any minute Magnus' attendants would come out with the force-field projectors and recapture the monster for use some other time.

But the monster picked up and headed for the audience. It charged the far section down near the end of the field. I watched, confident that the force-field barriers would bounce it back. Then I gasped as the monster went ploughing through the place where the force-field barrier was supposed to be, and plunged on over the embankment into the bleachers, climbing merrily toward the rim of the Rose Bowl and crushing half a dozen people underfoot with each stride!

I've never heard such a wail of horror as went up when that beast broke loose in the Bowl. I got up and started running for the exit, and a hundred thousand other people got the same idea. The band tried to play to calm people down, but it was no good. There was a mass exodus. I was swept out with all the others. Once I looked back and saw the monster poised at the edge of the Bowl, peering down into the parking lot.

Then the force-field projectors were wheeled out, and green flares of neutronic force burst over the field, and the beast was immobilized before it could get out of the Rose Bowl. A plane standing by flew over and blasted the monster's head off. By that time I was outside the Rose Bowl, part of the swirling, hysterical mob that had fled when the creature broke loose.

The people sitting at home at their video sets saw a sight that afternoon that they won't ever forget. Two hundred people died before the monster was brought under control. Ten thousand suffered injuries in the mad rush of panic that followed.

It was quite a finale. What I couldn't understand was how the creature had gotten through the barriers in the first place.

A month later, when everything had calmed down and sanity had returned, I got another call from my agent, telling me to come to New York and talk contract with Magnus.

Magnus had survived the debacle of his Rose Bowl show. There had been loud talk of a Congressional investigation of the tragedy, but the promoters got together and smeared enough money around to quiet things down. Word went forth that there had been a once-in-a-lifetime failure of the force-field just at the moment when our monster decided to go rampaging through the crowd. It could never happen again, the public was told.

And the public listened. Two weeks after the Rose Bowl affair, another spectacular was staged at the Indianapolis Speedway by one of Magnus' competitors, and two hundred thousand people turned out to watch a couple of Arcturan centipedes fifty feet long slug it out.

I flew to Magnus' place and Magnus had a check waiting for me, all made out. He handed it to me. I looked at it. It was for $1,500,000.

"What's this?" I asked.

He smiled smugly. "I want you to go back to World Twelve of Star System DA-7116, Barstow. I want you to bring me *two* of those beasts. I'm planning to match them against each other in the show of the century!"

"Two of them?"

"That's right." His eyes were gleaming with excitement. "It'll be fantastic. We've booked Soldier Field in Chicago already. Can you do it?"

"The price is right," I said. "I won't disappoint you."

So we outfitted another expedition, *two* ships this time, and trundled off to Star System DA-7116 once again. I couldn't argue with a million and a half bucks. We caught the two beasts after some minor complications. They were smaller than the first one—only about seventy-five feet high, though that was enough—and two of my men got killed in the hunt. But we stuck to our motto, and we brought 'em back alive.

Two of them.

I delivered them to Magnus amid much fanfare and hoopla, and he paid as agreed. The promotion got under way immediately. The show of shows, he proclaimed. A fight to the death by the biggest creatures of the galaxy!

There was one thing I wanted to know, though. I asked Magnus about it the week before the show.

I said, "These tickets you gave me—they're pretty close to the arena, Magnus."

"So? Are you afraid? Barstow, the intrepid hunter, afraid?"

"I was in the Rose Bowl when that other beast broke out," I told him. "I don't mind hunting down monsters on alien worlds. But I don't like fighting for my life in a panicky mob. If those force-fields happen to give way again—"

"Oh, they won't," Magnus assured me. "Not this time. We don't want that happening too often or it'll give the sport a bad name."

"What do you mean—not *too* often?"

He had made a slip, and he knew it. "Well—that is—"

"You mean to say, Magnus, that you can let something like that happen again?"

*   *   *

That was when he gave me the spiel. He told me all about it, the new concept in public entertainment that he had worked out.

It seemed, according to Magnus, that the public was losing its interest in great spectacles. That the novelty had worn off, and within another couple of years or maybe less the entire kick would be gone.

So J. Franklin Magnus had thought up a new kick, all by himself.

Make the show risky. Scare the spectators. They won't be spectators any more; they'll sit in their seats wondering when the monsters are going to get tired of battering each other and decide to light out after the onlookers. It took the vicarious element out of the game. Now, every man took his life in his hands when he plunked down his money and bought a seat.

Yes, that's right. Magnus *deliberately* permitted the Monster of World Twelve to get out into the audience. The invisible force-barriers had been shut off the moment the killersaurs were dead.

"What do you think of it?" he finished up. "The spectators will never know whether they're protected or not. They experience constant anxiety. How's that for a kick? It's something the ancient Romans never thought of!"

I looked coldly at him. I realized it didn't make any sense saying anything, screaming to the authorities, raising any fuss at all. Magnus knew what he was doing. The public wanted this kind of entertainment nowadays. They would pay and pay through the nose for the chance to sit in a stadium and possibly be trampled down or slashed by a runaway killersaur. Maybe eventually they would shut off the force-barriers all the time, and make no pretense about anything.

I shook my head and took the block of tickets Magnus had given me out of my pocket. I handed them back to him.

"Here," I said. "Take them."

"What's the matter? Don't you want them?"

"I'm not going to be there," I said.

"Now hold on! I told you there wouldn't be any danger this time, and—"

I didn't listen. I got up and walked out, and I flew back across the country to Los Angeles, and now I'm trying to sell my share in Barstow Expediters and get the hell out of the monster-catching business while my soul is intact. I see the direction we're travelling in, and I don't like it. The next step is just to turn monsters loose in big cities, for kicks. For laughs.

So here I am. Next week they'll be holding the Big Show, the Spectacular of Spectaculars, out in Chicago. I won't be there. I'll be sitting in a little bar off Wilshire where video isn't allowed, and I'll be sipping synthoscotch and trying to forget. While halfway across the continent two seventy-five-foot monsters will kill each other.

"I give the public what it wants," Magnus says. Maybe he's right. But I hope to hell that he's the first to get ripped apart, the next time a monster busts loose.

Alister McAllister served in World War One as a machine gunner, which was not uncommon; and survived, which was very uncommon indeed.

Later, and until his death in 1943, McAllister wrote plays and mysteries with considerable success. He used a variety of pseudonyms: often Anthony Wharton, as with this story; and as Lynn Brock, Dorothy Sayers praises his mysteries highly.

I ran across "The Hunting on the Doonagh Bog" through a 1928 reprint anthology (Gruesome Cargoes, one of the Not At Night series); but the story was, from internal evidence, originally published in 1919.

It's about human beings. And it might be well to remember that until shortly before he wrote the story, the author had been observing human beings in the muddy killing grounds of the trenches.

THE HUNTING ON THE DOONAGH BOG

Alister McAllister

I

The inhabitants of the town of Ballaclare—there are some twelve hundred of them—accept the fact of its existence with the placid and unquestioning submission to the dispensations of an inexplicable and obviously unfriendly Providence which the faith of their fathers dictates. And indeed only to a heretic and rebellious and otherwise uncomfortable kind of mind could any doubt as to the reasons for that existence suggest itself.

From it diverge five railroad lines—single lines, it is true, and traversed more often by foot-passengers than by trains—but none the less five authentic railroad lines leading eventually, according to the Midland Great Western Company's time-tables, to any particular spot upon the habitable globe to which any reasonable person may desire to proceed. It holds fairs, frequent and flourishing; horse, pig, cow and sheep fairs, which block its central street with noisy and odorous merchandise and yet more noisy and odorous merchants. It contains a

chapel, a church, a Court-house, a Town Hall, a Post
Office, a Constabulary Station, three hotels, thirty-four
establishments licensed for the consumption upon their
premises of alcoholic refreshment, and—in its outskirts—a
workhouse. It bears upon its face self-justification, plain,
satisfactorily and complete. Sometimes even, in this
year of Grace, 1919, the unmoved buyers and sellers of
pigs in the main street, pausing a moment in their
prolonged and delicate negotiations, may lift their eyes
skywards to the drone of a 'plane. So conclusively is
Ballaclare a part, and a necessary part, of Civilisation
and Progress and all the other workings of that obscure
but at least plainly persevering Planner, who has not, it
appears, forgotten even the county of Mayo.

Possibly, however, it may occur to the pilots of those
occasional 'planes—heretics probably, Englishmen certainly, from the aerodrome twenty miles away at
Castlebar—to wonder a little as to how and why a town
should have grown where Ballaclare now stands. To
them the place must present itself as a little straggling
cluster of houses, from which run out ten tentacles—
five ribands of railroad and five of highway—that twist
and coil from their centre in a haphazard way across a
vast plain of bog-land. For this is a world of bog-land,
flat, desolate and dreary, stretching North and East and
South as far as the eye can see, bounded Westwards by
a wall of stark, cloud-capped mountains, that come and
go in the mist incessantly. Water everywhere—lakes,
pools, streams, ditches, drains; the whole landscape is
water-logged. Save for a wooded ridge to the South-
West of the town, all those miles of treacherous brown
and black and green are sodden with moisture. Here
and there across the plain, on isolated dry patches,
stand lonely little white-washed cabins, about which
graze a few desolate cattle. And upon this forsaken
prospect falls without ceasing the soft, misting drizzle of
the West. It is perhaps not surprising that the folk of
such a country-side should look upon life through somewhat dispirited eyes; which may perhaps account for
Ballaclare's thirty-four licensed establishments.

A mile or so out from the town along the Ballinrobe Road two moss-grown gate pillars, surmounted by mutilated stags' heads and supporting heavy iron-work gates, rusted and lichen-stained, mark the entrance to the avenue of Hartstown House. The avenue, a mile in length, climbs the ridge in a gentle serpentine cut through the belt of timber that encircles the house, a grass-grown, lonely track leading up to the big, barrack-like building which has lain untenanted ever since Colonel Harte shot himself in his bedroom on a June night in the late nineties.

The house itself is square and unlovely; the view from its many windows monotonous and depressing. Only the avenue, with its fine old trees and glimpses of bracken-covered slopes, redeems the place from absolute ugliness. And it was for that reason, on a June afternoon just forty years ago, that Mrs. Harte, armed with a sunshade and a novel, and accompanied by her little daughter, Norah, then three years of age, and a nursemaid bearing rugs and cushions, set out down its shady length towards a certain fallen tree upon which she proposed, with the aid of Miss Braddon, to beguile the tedium of the long hot hours that yawned between luncheon and tea-time.

She appears to have been an extremely pretty, clever, accomplished, and—but for one failing—altogether blameless young woman. The one failing, however, seems to have been a serious one. No servant could be induced to remain at Hartstown House for longer than a month; Mrs. Harte's temper was, by common agreement of the successive local Hebes who had experienced it, unbearable. It was known that she had come to Ballaclare straight from India, where her husband had served with distinction; doubtless her methods of asserting household authority had been contracted in her dealings with "the niggers." One unlucky housemaid had fled down that mile of avenue half-blind from a blow dealt her by her mistress's hunting-crop. In all the country-side no one had a good word to say for Mrs. Harte, and Mrs. Harte knew it; knew it by the black looks that followed her from the doors of roadside cabins as she passed, by the scarcely-veiled impertinence of the Ballaclare shopkeepers, by the embarrassed politeness of the few distant neighbours with whom she judged social relations possible. Matters indeed seem to have reached such a pass that she seldom left the grounds of Hartstown House; indeed for many months before that June afternoon she had not been seen in Ballaclare. Her household supplies were now imported from Castlebar, her maids from England. Her husband, who was passionately fond of her, gave way to her in these matters, as in all others. He was a pleasant, cheerful man, twenty years his wife's senior, an enthusiastic sportsman, a popular landlord and a lenient magistrate. Also there had been Hartes in Hartstown House since the days of George the First. More active unpleasantnesses, doubtless, were spared to his wife for the sake of his genial, handsome face, his knowledge of a "baste" and the fact that his name was Ulick Harte.

There was another reason, too, why Mrs. Harte preferred at this time the privacy of her own grounds. She expected to become a mother again, much, it was rumoured, to her dismay, and the hour of her trial was now close at hand. Her step as she strolled along the shadow-chequered avenue, a little way behind the nursemaid and her charge, was slow and languid, her expression one of listless and rather anxious dejection.

You may picture her under her pink silk sunshade, a dark, tall, rather stately young woman, with small, clear-cut features, a somewhat pallid colour, and very fine, very haughty brown eyes that had broken many questing hearts in the far-off Simla to which her brooding memory returned with insistent regret. Ireland and everything Irish she regarded with a contemptuous and openly-expressed dislike bordering upon hatred.

I have not been able to ascertain what business, lawful or unlawful, accounted for Mrs. Garraty's appearance that afternoon in the avenue of Hartstown House. That she was trespassing may be admitted; that her intentions were any but the most harmless can scarcely be believed. She was a very aged, decrepit old woman who lived alone in a miserable hovel on the Ballincar Road—the widow of a long deceased herd in the employment of Colonel Harte's father—a very ugly, very dirty, and very bitter-tongued old woman whom the small boys of the neighbourhood, from a safe distance, were accustomed to assail with unkind personalities, provoked by the futile malevolence of her little blood-shot eyes and slobbering, toothless mouth. Their elders, with the dubious caution of a country-side where mysterious evils fall without reasonable explanation upon man and beast, contented themselves with having nothing whatever to do with her. It was known that Larry Hennessy's son, Paddy, who had struck her on the leg with a too skillfully-thrown stone, had on the very same day been kicked by his father's mare with a justice so uncomfortably apt that he had ever thereafter walked with a limp. And there had been various inexplicable misfortunes connected with sundry local calvings and foalings and churnings and other more intimate activities of Mrs. Garraty's neighbours. Some there were, of the younger generation these, fortified by the training of the National School and the enlightenment of a prosaic Press, who affected to deride the notion that Mrs. Garraty was responsible for these manifestations. But the older folk shook their heads and averted their eyes when these things were spoken of. With very ugly and very dirty old women it is best to be on the safe side.

But when Mrs. Harte, seated on the fallen trunk beneath the shade of her elms, raised her eyes from her novel and beheld Mrs. Garraty hobbling slowly and audaciously along the avenue, her emotion appears to have been one of anger untempered by any restraining caution.

"What is that horrible old creature doing here?" she demanded of the nursemaid in her clear, high-pitched voice. "Send her away at once!"

Doubtless Mrs. Garraty, halted now upon her stick a few yards away, heard the words. At all events she left the avenue and came hobbling across the grass towards the little group seated under the trees. The nursemaid, struck by the intruder's age and perhaps by her excessive ugliness, hesitated, looked at the old woman, looked at her mistress, took an uncertain step forward, hesitated again. Mrs. Harte's little daughter, frightened by the fierce little red-rimmed eyes that had fixed themselves intently upon her, shrank up against her mother's side and buried her face in her sleeve as if to shut out the unlovely apparition that stood blinking and mumbling in the hot sunshine.

"What are you doing here?" asked Mrs. Harte imperiously. "You have no business to be in these grounds. Go away at once!"

The old woman made no reply. She had ceased to mumble now and her eyes travelled slowly over Mrs. Harte from head to foot. The child, venturing to peep at her, uttered a little cry to find her still there, and buried her face again in her mother's sleeve. Mrs. Harte rose in uncontrolled anger.

"Do you hear?" she repeated vehemently. "Go away at once, you dirty old creature. You are frightening my little girl. I insist upon your going at once!"

Mrs. Garraty hobbled a step nearer, her little eyes malevolent and threatening.

"Frightenin' your child, am I? Frightenin' her, am I, me fine lady? An' what's she frightened of then, will you tell me? Will you tell me that, me fine lady?"

"Tell you?" repeated Mrs. Harte, indignant at the unabashed impertinence of the old harridan's look and tone. "I *will* tell you. She's frightened by your horrible, wicked old face." She patted the little girl's head reassuringly. "It's all right, darling," she said soothingly. "It isn't really a monkey. It's only a dirty old beggar-woman."

She turned upon the nursemaid, standing openmouthed and round-eyed beside her. "*Will* you put her away, Baillie? Don't stand there like a fool! Drive her away!"

The nursemaid, spurred thus to action, made as if to catch the old woman's arm and received upon her lower limbs a blow from the intruder's stick delivered with such shrewd venom that she thereupon abandoned all further attempt at aggression. For a moment Mrs. Garraty glared menacingly at Mrs. Harte, twitching her stick up and down as if she meditated more audacious violence. Then she spat upon the grass before her and looked Mrs. Harte once more from head to foot and spat again. Then she said, slowly and deliberately, speaking, the nursemaid afterwards reported, as if she had an evil spirit within her.

"The curse o' God be upon you an' upon your's, livin' an' to live, born an' unborn. May you live in fear an' sorrow, may you die in fear an' pain. May the child that is in your body never see the light o' the day, nor use the speech of his tongue. May he run from men an' the ways o' men all his days. May he die in fear and agony. May the child that holds to your skirt die in the fear an' the smother o' the black wather. May the man that is your husband die in blood and shame. The curse o' God be upon you an' upon your's, livin' an' to live, born an' unborn."

She spat once more upon the sunlit grass, turned and hobbled away down the avenue. Mrs. Harte's eyes watched the slowly moving figure until it disappeared around a distant bend. Then she shivered slightly.

"It has grown chilly, Baillie," she said abruptly. "I am going back to the house."

In the small hours of the following morning a son was born to Ulick Harte. The child was born blind, and coated from head to foot with a thick brownish-red pelt. In addition to the fact that it was ugly beyond the ordinary ugliness of the new-born young of man, it possessed other physical peculiarities which seriously perturbed the worthy young local practitioner who was hastily summoned to usher it into a dismayed world. It was he who attended Mrs. Harte during the few hours of sick raving for which she survived its birth; it was he who personally undertook and carried out the task of procuring a foster-mother; it was he who, forty years later, told me this story.

The four English maids received a month's wages, packed their trunks and departed from Hartstown House;

so did the English coachman, an English groom, Colonel Harte's English body-servant and the Scotch gardener. A month after Mrs. Harte's death there were, besides Colonel Harte and the doctor, but two people in the neighbourhood who knew that she had given birth to a son.

II

The Ballincar Road runs South-West from Ballaclare; the Ballinrobe Road nearly due South. The two roads diverge, not in direct spoke-like lines from their hub at Ballaclare, but with re-approachings and retreatings, as if unwillingly meandering in wide curves across the bog. Some three miles from the town, a grass-grown cross-track, a narrow causeway of stone and earth built up upon the underlying turf, unites them, forming thus, roughly, the base of a triangle of which Ballaclare is the apex. From road to road along the causeway is a good two miles, Irish. But if you had walked those two miles with Colonel Harte one grey, blowy afternoon in the December following his wife's death, you would have seen but three cottages along the way, each of them standing some two hundred yards back from the causeway and each approached by its own narrow side-track, built up, like the causeway itself, to a level of eight or nine feet above the surrounding ground. All around, beneath a lowering, steel-grey sky, the brown-green of the Doonagh Bog, scarred and gashed with the wet black of the countless turf-cuts, blacker still in that fading light by contrast with the pale gleam of the water-filled trenches.

Northwards, to Colonel Harte's left hand as he walked, rose the timbered ridge upon the farther side of which lay Hartstown House. He saw, without seeing, a flock of gulls, wheeling whitely against the darkness of the sky, rise suddenly and disappear over the tree-tops. A drop of rain caught his cheek. No cheerful afternoon this, for a walk across the bog.

The middle cottage of the three along the causeway, separated from its fellows by a distance of half-a-mile on either hand, was at that time occupied by a farmer named Mellish. His household consisted of his wife, a child born in the preceding summer, and his wife's mother. Mellish himself was then a man of over fifty, a surly, quarrelsome fellow, for ever at feud with one or other of his neighbours; his wife, a hard-featured woman a few years his junior, a "stranger" from Donegal; her mother a bed-ridden crazy old creature, whom it was well known her daughter and her son-in-law ill-treated persistently and brutally. The old woman had some money, and her reluctance to die appears to have exasperated Mellish and his wife at times to the point of savagery. Their avarice in money matters was notorious and seems to have formed the one link which kept them together, since it was common knowledge that from morning to night they quarrelled with bitter and foul-tongued animosity. The birth of a child—or perhaps, as malicious tongues suggested, its death when a few weeks old—had, however, apparently, improved the relations of man and wife, aided by the fact that Mellish had, it was supposed, at last gained control over his mother-in-law's coveted hoardings. During the Autumn and Winter of that year he had made frequent visits to the Ballaclare fairs and had laid out a sum considerable for his position upon the purchase of pigs and cattle. Also he had bought, second-hand, a double-barrelled gun, and a silver watch—the latter designed, he was at pains to inform all and sundry—as a present to his wife. His acquaintances—he had no friends—wondered a little; then, as his extravagances ceased no less abruptly than they had begun, dismissed them and him from their minds.

In the length of a summer's day not half-a-dozen people passed along the causeway; in a month of days not half a dozen used the side-track that led from it to Bernard Mellish's cottage. On that darkening, blustery afternoon, as Colonel Harte strode up it with a sharp, quick step that brought a snarling collie to meet him with vicious hostility, not a living soul was in sight—a fact of which he had assured himself with some deliberation before turning off the causeway.

At the sound of the dog's continued growling, Mellish appeared, hastily, in the doorway of the cabin, a thickset, low-browed peasant, with a jutting under-jaw and cunning, evasive eyes. He removed a blackened clay pipe from his mouth and greeted his visitor with a familiar nod.

"I thought it'd be yerself," he said laconically. "Not many visithors throubles this house. An' so much the bether for both of us, Colonel. Will yeh come inside?"

Colonel Harte shook his head.

"No," he replied curtly. "I prefer to say what I've got to say to you out here in the light." He took from his pocket a small sheet of paper, soiled and creased and written upon in a sprawling hand. "You recognise this?" He held it up for the other to see.

Mellish grinned feebly.

"Yes. I recognise it shure enough," he said calmly. "An' what about it?"

"You're a cunning fellow, Mellish—and this is a cunning letter of yours. But I understand what this letter means—and anyone could understand what it means, cunning as it is. I tell you what you have written here is enough to put the walls of a gaol about you for the rest of your life. You understand?"

"Understand?" snarled Mellish, dropping the pretence of amity which he had maintained so far with obvious difficulty. "Then I'm damned if I understand. I understand nothin' except that I was fool enough to let me take your . . . your . . . well, God knows what it is . . . your child if you like to call it. Aye! A fool I was . . . but that's another thing. None o' yer threats to me! Mind you that! None o' yer threats to me!" His voice rose angrily; his chin thrust forward towards the erect, unmoved figure that fronted him.

"I am not threatening you, Mellish," said Colonel Harte with studied quietness. "I am merely warning you. If you repent of your agreement—well, I must only make other arrangements and there's an end to it. I have paid you well. You had thirty pounds in July, and two pounds a week since August. I am quite willing to pay you well to look after this unfortunate child of mine. That is not what I have come to talk to you about. But I want you to understand this clearly." He raised his voice, aware now of a woman's figure lurking in the darkness of the cabin. "You and your wife. If it is God's will that this poor little creature shall live, it must live. I am an unhappy man. God has laid this burden upon me. But I am not a murderer."

He tore the scrap of paper into minute fragments and scattered them in the wind that blew them gustily across the bog. For a moment his eyes followed their flight broodily, then he turned again to Mellish.

"Yes or no?" he demanded sharply. "Are you willing to keep the child and care for it properly?"

Mellish, with averted eyes, considered a space before replying.

"Make it two pound ten a week then," he said at length.

"Very well," said Colonel Harte. "You shall have your two pounds ten. Good evening to you."

He turned upon his heel and walked rapidly away from the lounging figure in the doorway. He had reached the causeway and had set his face towards the Ballincar Road when he heard Mellish's voice call his name, and saw that worthy hastening down the side-track towards him.

"Make it three pound, Colonel. I'll keep it for three pound a week. An' that's the las' I'll say about it. You won't find many willin' to keep it undher their roof for twice the money. Make it three pound. An' you know you can thrust me, when all's said an' done."

"Very well," said Colonel Harte, with weary impatience. "Three pounds. But not a penny more. Remember that. Not a penny more will I pay you."

Mellish lingered a little while in the fading light, looking after his visitor's receding figure with a grin upon his unprepossessing countenance. Then he went back slowly towards his cottage, whistling softly through his teeth. His wife met him on the doorstep.

"Well?" she asked expectantly.

"I've riz him to three pound a week," said her husband, elbowing her unceremoniously from his path. He threw his caubeen on a chair.

"I'll rise him to five before I've done with him," he added pleasantly. "Gimme me tea."

A few weeks later Colonel Harte left Ballaclare; it was seventeen years before he returned to it. After some months his agent, a cheerful young man, with a cheerful young wife, and several cheerful children, installed himself in Hartstown House. Colonel Harte it was learned had gone back to India, taking with him his little daughter Norah. Seventeen times with unmoved regularity the elms in the avenue covered with a carpet of russet and gold the spot where Mrs. Garraty had stood and spat and called down evil. And for seventeen years, with a regularity that grew to appear no less inevitable, did Bernard Mellish every Monday morning walk into the office of Messrs. Hughes and Lalor, solicitors, in the main street of Ballaclare, and emerging therefrom some quarter of an hour later, drive back the way he had come, whistling softly through his teeth.

III

And so this narrative passes on to another afternoon in June, the June of 1896, the afternoon on which Colonel Harte returned to Hartstown House.

In and about the town of Ballaclare, during those seventeen years, things had gone on very much as they had always gone, expectedly and undramatically. Every year had held its usual quota of fair-days and court-days, of christenings and weddings in the big new chapel, of buryings in the little lonely churchyard out at Ballismalla. Some old shops had closed, some new ones had opened; some old faces had disappeared, some young ones had staled gradually to middle-age. The boys that had shouted injurious gibings at old Mrs.

Garraty had passed, most of them, through the railway station and so out of this story. For in the eighties and nineties America was still for the youth of the West the Promised Land. Mrs. Garraty herself had been laid to rest in Ballismalla, with all seemly rites, on the very day that brought to Ballaclare the news of the Phœnix Park murders. Her grave, as you may see to-day, lies by curious chance beside that which contains what is left of Bernard Mellish and Bernard Mellish's wife. Mrs. McGovern, Mrs. Mellish's obstinate old mother, died very shortly after Colonel Harte's visit to her son-in-law's cottage, and her grave, too, lies in Ballismalla, under the ruined Eastern wall of the old chapel.

The cheerful young agent had become a grandfather and his cheerful young wife a grandmother without losing much of their cheerfulness or their reputation as formidable performers in mixed doubles. Of the three cheerful children, a boy had gone to Sandhurst, a girl had married, another girl remained, a jolly, freckled hoyden of eighteen who, astride a big, wicked-eyed chestnut, came cantering down the avenue to meet the trap that bore Colonel Harte and his luggage from the station. His manner as he returned her rather boisterous greeting was chillingly reserved. On arriving at the house, he went almost immediately to his room, bathed and changed hurriedly and, pleading a headache as an excuse to his hostess for his absence from the dinner-table, left the house alone about a quarter-past seven. He was seen by various people in the course of the following three hours, and there is little doubt, though no evidence to this direct effect transpired at the inquest, that he visited the cabin of Bernard Mellish that evening. Mellish and his wife, for reasons of their own, did not appear as witnesses at the inquest, though Mellish it was afterwards recalled by both the doctor and Mr. Hughes—of Messrs. Hughes and Lalor—was present and listened with marked attention to the evidence.

About ten o'clock Colonel Harte returned to Hartstown House, chatted for a few minutes with his host and

hostess, drank a whiskey-and-soda, declared that his
headache had disappeared, and, bidding them good-
night, as they agreed, quite cheerfully, retired to his
bedroom. There, about half-an-hour later, he blew his
brains out.

The affair created naturally, in that uneventful neighborhood, a profound sensation. But as the inquest failed
to elicit any satisfactory explanation of the tragedy, it
was generally believed that some lingering traces of
sunstroke—an explanation plausible and probable—had
revived suddenly in the guise of an impulse to self-
destruction. The funeral—by common agreement the
finest that had been seen in the district since that of the
dead man's father—was attended, at least for part of its
course, by every farmer for five miles around—with
one exception. Bernard Mellish's trap remained in its
shed behind the cabin that day.

Beside the shed which sheltered the trap and the cart
and the plough, stood a small stone outhouse, with two
narrow slits of windows, securely boarded up, and a
padlocked door. About the time that Ulick Harte's coffin was being lowered into the newly-dug grave in
Crossgar Cemetery—for the dead Hartes were buried
by the parson at Crossgar and not by the priest at
Ballismalla—Mellish was standing just outside this outhouse, his hands deep in the pockets of his corduroys,
his eyes fixed on the padlocked door, whistling softly
through such yellow ruins of teeth as his seventy-odd
years had spared to him. Beside him a collie growled
uneasily. Behind the padlocked door something was
stirring stealthily, something that brushed along the
walls of the outhouse, as it moved, and uttered at
moments a little odd chattering sound. Presently the
chattering and the brushing ceased, and there was the
soft thud of a heavy body falling upon loose straw.
When Mellish had turned away and gone into the cottage to seat himself by the fire that burned in its one
living-room, winter's day and summer's day alike, the
dog crept cautiously up to the outhouse door, and blew
and sniffed for a while with surly suspicion, and barked

once challengingly with uplifted muzzle, before it trotted away, stiff-legged and bristling, to join its master by the fireside.

IV

On the Monday following the funeral Mellish presented himself at Messrs. Hughes and Lalor's office in Ballaclare and was ushered, as usual, into the little musty back room in which Mr. Hughes interviewed his clients. But on this occasion the customary formalities of Mellish's weekly visit were replaced by a conversation of a nature disappointing and disconcerting in the extreme. Colonel Harte, so far as could be ascertained, had died without making a will—certainly without making any provision for the payment to Bernard Mellish by Messrs. Hughes and Lalor of three pounds on that or any following Monday.

"You must understand, Mellish," said Mr. Hughes, balancing his gold-rimmed glasses carefully upon his sharp-bridged nose, and then surveying his visitor over them with some intentness. "You must understand that we have not, in any general sense, acted as the late Colonel Harte's solicitors."

"What's the use o' tellin' me all that?" interrupted Mellish, irritably, "y'acted as his 'torney in this business an' that's enough for me."

"Will you allow me to finish, please," said Mr. Hughes, coldly. "This payment to you—Colonel Harte, I may say, now, never intimated to us for what reason this payment was made to you. Doubtless he had good grounds for not doing so."

The solicitor paused a moment and brushed an imaginary speck of dust from his coat lapel. But Mellish merely stared stolidly at the litter of dusty papers on the table at which he sat.

"I am bound to say," continued Mr. Hughes, concealing his disappointment creditably, "that I think Colonel Harte displayed an unnecessary lack of confidence in us in the matter . . . however . . . such is the fact. Our instructions were simply to pay to you at the office the sum of three pounds every Monday, to obtain a receipt and a certificate that the money had, each week, been expended upon the purpose for which Colonel Harte had agreed to pay it to you, and to present to Colonel Harte our bill of costs in the usual course and at the usual times. Those instructions we have carried out during the life-time of Colonel Harte. And of course, we may receive instructions from Colonel Harte's heir or heirs to continue them in the future. Until we receive such instructions, however, I'm afraid we must hold our hands. You understand the position, I hope?"

But Mellish, it was plain, was not disposed to understand the position so easily as all that. He argued the matter doggedly for the best part of an hour, without displaying any symptoms of understanding it in the least. Finally Mr. Hughes' clerk, summoned to his employer's assistance, ejected him, blasphemous and unconvinced, into the main street. He returned next day, and during the following months almost daily. But on each occasion the clerk barred his progress to the little inner room and with a curt intimation that Mr. Hughes had and desired to have, nothing to say to him, expelled him from the office. Never again, it became clear to him, would he draw from Messrs. Hughes and Lalor those three weekly sovereigns—he had always insisted that the payment should be made in gold. Never again would he drop them with a clink into his capacious breeches pocket and button its flap and smack it finally and reassuringly before he signed the weekly receipt. His visits grew rarer and irregular. Finally they ceased altogether. So did his trick of whistling through his teeth.

With his immediate neighbours, Martin Brett and Martin Heneghan, the occupants of the other two cottages along the causeway, Mellish still waged the bitter feud the first battles of which had been fought twenty years back. One or other of them—he had never learned which—had left open a gate leading from the causeway down to a small patch of grazing on to which, at that time, Mellish was accustomed to turn two bullocks. The bullocks had strayed out on to the causeway and from thence on to the bog; one had been rescued with considerable difficulty, the other had been drowned. For twenty years the loss of that bullock had filled Mellish's heart with a rancorous hatred almost murderous, a hate renewed in latter years by the contemptuous pretence of indifference which the younger generation of Bretts and Heneghans returned to his scowlings and glarings when they encountered him along the road. And so it was perhaps with a natural hesitation that young Owen Brett and his sister, Maggie, returning late one dark night from a dance at Ballaclare, in the week before the Christmas of 1896, came to a sudden halt by the side-track leading to Mellish's cottage, on perceiving, standing in the middle of the causeway, a figure which they recognised as that of Mellish, holding what they believed to be a gun in front of his body and pointed towards them.

"Is that you, Mr. Mellish?" called out young Brett, cautiously.

Mellish made some unintelligible reply, and stumbled away in the darkness towards his cottage. For a little while the Bretts listened to the retreating crackle of his footsteps crunching through the then thin ice coating of frozen pools. Then they proceeded on their way, in silence, and I fancy rather hurriedly, until a remark of Maggie Brett's brought them to a stop again, listening in the darkness.

"What's all the dogs barkin' at, Owen, I wondher?" she said. "Listen."

It was a still, frosty night—a night on which, in that flat country-side, one might hear a dog barking three miles away across the bog. And as they listened, it seemed to them that every dog for miles around was barking. From the direction of the two little red-blinded squares of light ahead of them, the windows of their father's farmhouse, came a furious uproar, in the inter-

vals of which they could hear distinctly a faint answer-
ing clamour northwards, where the nearest house was a
mile away as the crow flies. And between these nearest
and most remote sounds a running fire of warnings
unmistakably angry ran round them through the encircling blackness. Suddenly it occurred to Owen Brett
that it was a curious thing, since there was no moon,
that the dogs should bark so. He turned to make some
remark to this effect to his sister, yawning and shivering
beside him, and as he did so they both saw, some
twenty yards from where they stood, what they afterwards described as an animal like a man on his hands
and knees, clambering up the sloping side of the causeway out of the darkness of the bog. It halted for a few
moments on reaching the level of the causeway and sat
there, as they related, "squatting on its hunkers," looking in their direction. Though in this last particular they
were not quite accurate. Finally it began to move slowly
towards them. They had time to discern a hideous,
whitey face, with a huge mouth, no nose and two black
hollow places where eyes should have been, before
panic seized them and deprived them of all consciousness save the instinct to blind flight. For a little while
the horror followed them, but apparently for a little
while only, since it was on a patch of grass but twenty
or thirty yards from where they had seen it, that they
found next morning the dead and horribly mauled body
of an aged donkey, the property of Bernard Mellish,
lying with its four hoofs pointing miserably to heaven,
its carcase frozen hard to earth.

V

As the Bretts, father and son, stood gazing down at
the slain animal, speculating indecisively as to the connection between the wanton savagery of its injuries
and the apparition of the preceding night—a connection
which appeared to them inevitable—Mellish appeared

at the gate leading into the little field in which they stood, and seeing them there came angrily towards them. They noticed at once that his left hand was bandaged, and that his left cheek bore a long, fresh scar from which blood was still oozing.

"What the hell are yeh doin' here, the two o' yeh?" he demanded bellicosely, and then caught sight of the donkey's upturned belly.

He went close to the animal and examined it with a calmness in such contrast with his previous excitement that Martin Brett's curiosity, already aroused by the bandaged hand and scarred cheek, provoked him to blunt interrogation.

"What hurted yer hand, Mellish?" he enquired. "An' yer face, too. Yer face is all scraubed an' tore."

"Never you mind me face, Brett," retorted Mellish, surlily, "me face is me own business."

"Mebbe it is an' mebbe it isn't, then," returned the other. "There's somethin' dam quare about them cuts on that donkey, I know that. An' I'd like to know what you were doin' las' night at one o'clock in the mornin', walkin' about with a gun in yer han's. It's a dam quare business altogether. P'raps *you* met somethin' on the road too, las' night, as well as Owen here?"

But Mellish refused to be drawn.

"If I did," he said slowly, still eyeing the donkey, "I'd have faced it, old as I am. An' that's more than some I know of has the guts in them to do. Get on, now, the two o' yeh, about yer business! Get off my land an' keep off it. That's all I've got to say to yeh."

Now if Martin Brett had carried out the intention with which he left Mellish's field—which was to proceed straight away to the Constabulary Barracks at Ballaclare in company with his son and to seek the counsel of that sagacious and experienced person, Head Constable Leahy, this story would have ended differently. But the Mayo-man, however stainless his dealings, shrinks instinctively from relations of any kind with the "polis," and father and son, in the clear, secure brilliance of a sunlit winter's day, began to perceive with increasing distinctness that Owen Brett's behaviour in face of a danger which might, after all, be capable of simple explanation, had been sufficiently unheroic to excite derisive comment if the story of his adventure spread abroad. After some discussion they decided to say nothing of the matter to anyone, and having enjoined upon Mrs. Brett and her daughter Maggie a like reticence, started off for the Christmas poultry market in Ballaclare with a cart-load of protesting turkeys and geese.

It was close on five o'clock in the afternoon when they returned to find the two women standing at the corner where the causeway joins the Ballinrobe Road, awaiting their coming with anxious impatience.

"What kep' yeh so long, Martin?" complained Mrs. Brett, as she appeared suddenly in the light of the cart-lamp. "I thought yeh were never comin'. The life's frightened out o' me an' Maggie. There's been murdher goin' on up at Mellish's place."

Brett and his son got out of the cart and came to stand by the lamp. For a few moments there was a silence, broken only by the snorting of the horse. Westwards, towards the mountains, a faint line of light lingered in the sky. The frost had broken; the air was moist and heavy.

"I hear nothin'," said Brett, at length.

"It's quiet now," said his wife. "It's been quiet this last hour an' more. But if yeh heard the screamin' before that—I think it must have been herself that was screamin'. Like as if she was bein' murdhered."

Another silence followed.

"I'll unyoke the horse anyhow," said Brett. "There's no use our standin' here in the cowld."

When the horse had been fed, and the doors of the stable and the cowhouse carefully pulled to and wedged, father and son consumed in unusual silence the meal which their womenfolk prepared for them, and then lighting their respective pipes, drew their chairs up to the fire. For a little time the conversation ran upon their doings at the market, but declined soon to an oddly apprehensive silence. The two collies, which as a rule welcomed the return of their masters with demonstrative noisiness, had this evening been with difficulty induced by prolonged whistlings to return to the house, and now continued to wander restlessly between the fire and the closed front door. At length Owen Brett rose irritably, opened the door and let them out. They darted through the doorway like arrows released from the bow and disappeared into the darkness. As he stood there, still holding the door open, young Brett heard, some distance away and, as he judged on the Ballincar Road, the shouting of several voices and a babel of baying and barking like that of a pack of hounds. After a few moments his father joined him, followed presently by his mother and sister; for a long time all four stood hushed and motionless, their faces turned towards that distant tumult, receding from them towards the town. It was then a little after six o'clock. At that hour on any other winter's evening, two lights would have been visible to them, looking eastward from where they stood. To-night, between them and the little distant gleam of the Heneghan's living-room window, the darkness stretched unbroken. There was no light in Mellish's cottage to-night. Instinctively and surely those four people sensed calamity in the shivering, clammy air that hung above the Doonagh Bog.

"I wondher had we bether go an' see what's up at Mellish's," said the elder Brett, at length.

But, for that time his wife, without much difficulty, dissuaded him, and as everything had now grown still once more, the four chilled listeners retreated to the comfortable warmth of their blazing turf-fire, leaving, however, the door of the cottage ajar.

Now about that time Martin Heneghan's son, Larry, a reckless-eyed, red-haired young man, built of whipcord and steel, and a runner and jumper of fame all over the West of Ireland, was returning from Ballaclare along the Ballincar Road, in the joyous company of one Jack McNally, a well known horse-blocker, and his two cousins, Tom and Dermod Crowley. In honour of the

fact that Christmas was but three days distant they
were all four, if not drunk, at any rate "with dhrink
taken." That is to say, they sang and shouted as they
walked and repeated a great many times over mutual
assurances of esteem and affection, punctuated by frequent and prolonged pauses to re-light their pipes and
in other ways refresh their several comforts. So jour-
neying, a little unsteadily, they had reached the brow
of the hill outside Ballaclare, where the road passes
between two up-jutting, timbered hummocks, when they
heard on their left hand a savage growling and worrying, followed by an outburst of dolorous yelping from a
dog grievously hurt. A bulky, hunched black shape
came lumbering suddenly over the top of the left-hand
hummock, descended its slope, rolled rather than jumped
over the low stone wall bordering the road, and charged
into the very midst of the surprised and startled revel-
lers before they had time to collect their wits sufficiently to avoid its headlong course. Behind it came a
rabble of dogs of all sizes, shapes and breeds, yapping
and snarling and growling excitedly; yet sufficiently cautious to check their pursuit on the road in a circle well
outside the reach of their quarry. The four men, recovering from the confusion of its first onset, grappled with
it wildly and at the hazard of the darkness. Tom Crowley
received a slashing tear across his face that sent him
sprawling and moaning in the mud. His cousin, the
horse-blocker, retreating hastily from another lightning
sweep, stumbled over him and fell beneath the nailed
boots of the second Crowley, which trampled upon his
stomach for several moments before he could extricate
himself and roll in breathless agony to the roadside.
Larry Heneghan uttered a vicious oath and then,
abruptly, the four men were alone in the road again, and
the dogs in a howling flurry and scurry had re-crossed
the stone wall and disappeared over the hummock from
behind which they had come.

"Christ Almighty!" panted the horse-blocker. "What
was it at all at all?"

" 'Twasn't a man anyway," said Dermod Crowley, "did yeh see its face, Larry?"

But young Heneghan had vanished. The horse-blocker aided Dermod Crowley to prop his brother—who appeared to be severely injured—against the stone wall and then with a wild yell leaped the wall and raced towards the receding clamour of the chase. For a moment or two Crowley hesitated; his brother was unconscious—perhaps dying. But the instinct to follow that flying thing was too strong. He too jumped the wall and sped hot foot after the horse-blocker.

Towards eight o'clock an excited and partially intoxicated farmer burst into the Constabulary Station at Ballaclare and related a tale so alarming that even the unemotional Head Constable was visibly perturbed. A trap was hastily procured and in this the Head Constable proceeded in person to the spot where Tom Crowley still sat propped against the wall. The injured man was brought in to Ballaclare, where, under the doctor's ministrations, he recovered sufficiently to give a detailed account of the strange affray in which he had received his hurts.

He persisted in stating that his assailant was not a man, but an animal of some sort; an animal like a man, but with a thick hairy coat. Every available man in the barracks was turned out into the night; the Head Constable provided himself with a new pen and several sheets of foolscap, and seating himself with solemnity proceeded to the preparation of a detailed and unimpassioned report.

The doctor returned to his house wearing an expression so grave and so dismayed that his wife, experienced observer of his moods, retired to her little drawing-room with the children, and played and sang to them until their bed-time arrived. When she came downstairs again from the nursery, she learned from the little maid that her husband had been called out again. Instinctively her eyes turned to the spot upon the sideboard where, as usual, she had placed that evening after dinner a small pocket-flask, the customary companion of the doctor upon night cases involving a long drive. The flask was no longer there.

As it was then nearly ten o'clock, and as she was, as I have already stated, a sensible woman, she went almost immediately to bed.

It was some time, however, before she could get to sleep. Every dog in the town, it seemed to her, was barking and howling and growling and snarling that night. It was perfectly ridiculous that so many dogs should be allowed about the place. While she was still wondering for how many of them their owners had purchased licences, she fell at last asleep.

VI

When the doctor, investing himself hurriedly in his driving-coat, had informed the little maid that he was going out again, he had been very careful to leave vague the errand upon which he was bound. And by the time that his willing little brown mare had covered a couple of miles of the Ballincar Road, he had begun to entertain serious doubts as to that errand's wisdom. Somewhere near the spot where Tom Crowley had been found propped against the wall an hour or so before, he drew his trap in to the side of the road, and, lighting a cigarette, took long and anxious counsel with himself.

For many years the share which he had borne in Colonel Harte's dealings with Bernard Mellish had caused him profound regret and uneasiness. The birth of Ulick Harte's son had never been registered and for that omission he must be, and certainly would be, held responsible if the facts of the affair became known. That they had not become known had caused him a surprise that grew, as year followed year, to something like apprehension. Mellish he knew well as an unpopular, surly fellow, cunning enough to keep his mouth shut in his own interest; neither he nor his wife was likely to make any awkward disclosures so long as there was money to be made by remaining silent. But that, some day, some unexpected visitor, some suspicious neighbour, or some momentary carelessness should not make public property the secret of the thing that lurked beneath the Mellish's roof, had always appeared to him a chance so unlikely as to render his own share in that secret at times almost intolerable. Time after time had he resolved to take some step to shake off this incubus that had rested so long and so heavily upon his conscience. He had acted, he told himself, if illegally, still with the best of motives and certainly without gain to himself. After so many years of honoured service in his profession, who would cast in his teeth the mistaken judgment of that long-ago night? A score of times he had thought of at least discussing the matter with old Mr. Hughes. But always his courage had failed him. He had married late in life; he had a wife and children to think of. I offer here no criticism of the doctor's behaviour in this matter. This is simply a statement of his share in his own story.

His intention when he left his snug little surgery that night was to drive out to Mellish's cottage, and to ascertain, if possible, the explanation of the strange attack upon Crowley and his three companions. For from the moment that he had heard Crowley's account of their unknown assailant he had entertained no doubt as to its identity. Somehow or other it had escaped from that shed behind Mellish's cottage in which he knew it passed its dreadful life. For though he had never once in all those seventeen years re-visited the cottage, one of its occupants he had seen and spoken to at frequent intervals. A curiosity which he admitted to me he was unable to control had even led him on many Monday mornings to waylay Mellish on his way to Messrs. Hughes and Lalor's office.

But as he smoked his cigarette the unwisdom of involving himself in any further relations with Mellish at that moment appeared to him plainly. If Mellish's prisoner had, as he believed, escaped from its hiding-place and was now at large, its capture was inevitable. An inquiry would certainly follow; and even if Mellish and his wife did not at once come forward, sooner or later, when silence proved no longer profitable, one or the other of them would divulge the secret which they had kept so closely and so long. Clearly the less he had to do with them the better.

And yet, when his cigarette had burnt itself out, and the little mare, grown restless at the unseemly delay in an unaccustomed place, had been urged once more into her sharp, steady trot, her nose was turned not towards the comfort of her stable, but towards Ballincar and the Doonagh causeway. Something stronger than all prudence and common-sense drew the doctor to Mellish's cottage that night.

As he drove down the hill he heard now at intervals on his left hand, shouting and the barking of dogs, and guessed readily at their explanation. Somewhere out there on the bog was the creature which he had helped to bring into the world, running for its life. Running? How did it run? And then suddenly he recalled that it was blind.

A picture of Ulick Harte's wife as he had known her in all her slim daintiness, with her proud little head and fearless eyes, flashed upon his memory. That blind thing, running God knew how, chivied by dogs—*her* child. It must be stopped. At any cost to himself it must be stopped.

He laid his whip across the mare's quarters with an energy that sent that surprised animal clattering down the last slopes of the hill at a gallop. Mellish first. Mellish knew the bog, knew the thing that was being hunted on it, knew perhaps some way of recalling it when it strayed.

VII

Martin Brett put down his newspaper, and rising from his chair, went for the twentieth time that night to the front door.

"They're huntin' somethin' out there," he said, coming back after some moments and taking his hat from its peg, "there's somethin' up. Come on, Owen, an' we'll go an' see what it is."

The two men procured a stable-lantern, and, despite the tearful protestations of Mrs. Brett, who predicted for herself and her daughter all manner of dire calamities if they were left unprotected, proceeded along the causeway, in the direction of the Ballincar Road, with the intention of striking off across the bog at a point a little short of the Heneghan's dwelling-place. But as they drew near the side-track leading up to Mellish's cottage, they heard the sound and saw the lights of a vehicle approaching them at a rapid pace, along the causeway. The trap, which they had by then recognised as the doctor's—any man in that country could tell the doctor's trap half-a-mile away on the blindest night— drew up beside their lantern and the doctor leant down towards the two faces uplifted to his.

"Anything wrong, Mr. Brett?" he asked, in his usual quiet, cheery tone.

"Well, I dunno rightly, docthor," replied the farmer, unwilling to put into words forebodings that appeared at the sound of that friendly, matter-of-fact voice, suddenly childish. "There's been a lot o' shoutin' an' bawlin' goin' on out there on the bog this two hours back, whatever it is, an' Owen an' me was thinkin' o' goin' to see what it's all about." He paused for a moment. "There's somethin' quare goin' on roun' here anyhow," he added. "Tell the docthor about las' night, Owen, till we see what he thinks of it."

Thus exhorted, the younger Brett, with some diffidence as to his own part in the adventure, related the story of his encounter of the previous night. The doctor listened in silence; whatever his expression may have been, it was hidden from them by the glare of the trap lamp, above which he sat in darkness. But when the elder Brett had supplemented his son's narrative by an account of the screaming which had been heard from Mellish's cottage during the afternoon, the doctor threw aside his driving-rug and got out of the trap.

"Your son had better stay and keep an eye to the

mare," he said quietly. "She's a bit fidgety to-night for some reason or other. You'd better come with me."

Martin Brett took the lantern from his son, and by its light he and the doctor picked their way up the deep-rutted track that brought them, a few minutes later, to the door of Mellish's cabin. The door was open. They passed through the living-room, calling out as they did so, but receiving no reply. A fire still smouldered in the hearth and on the table lay the débris of a meal. Having satisfied themselves that there was no one in either of the two bedrooms, they passed out into the yard behind the house. At the sound of their footsteps a horse whinnied, and a cat, appearing from the darkness with arched back and vertical tail, came to rub itself against Brett's leggings, mewing plaintively. While the farmer bent down to stroke it amicably, the doctor approached the door of a small outhouse which stood ajar, and pushing it wide open, passed into the interior darkness.

"Bring that lantern here, Brett, will you?" he said after a moment.

The farmer obeyed. "God a'mighty!" he said, sniffing, as he thrust his head through the doorway. "Did ever yeh smell such a stench in all yer days?" Then, as the feeble light spread over the floor of the outhouse, he started back with an exclamation of horrified dismay. The doctor seized the lantern and went down on his knees beside the motionless figure that lay face downwards in a litter of filth indescribable.

"Dead," he said briefly. "Dead as a doornail."

Between them they carried Mellish's body into the house and laid it on the table, face upwards. Around its throat ran a tell-tale ring of blue-black bruises. Not until then had they noticed that the clenched right hand of the dead man gripped a cart-whip.

"What's them marks on his neck?" asked Brett in an awed whisper. "It's like as if he's been sthrangled."

But the doctor volunteered no opinion then.

"You say it was a woman's screaming that your wife and daughter heard?" he asked abruptly, and when the farmer nodded corroboration, took up the lantern and went out into the yard again. But it was not until they had grown weary and half-resolved to postpone further quest until the daylight, that they came on Mrs. Mellish, lying on her back in a little patch of cabbages. There was no mark of violence upon her, but she had been dead, the doctor thought, for some six or seven hours when they found her. Heart failure, probably. The mask that stared up at them from amongst the cabbage stalks was, by the flickering light of their lantern, that of Fear itself.

As they stood looking down at it, a cuckoo-clock in Mellish's kitchen struck ten.

VIII

Meanwhile, backwards and forwards across the black expanse of Doonagh Bog there was wild work forward. In broad daylight, even for a man born and bred on it, the bog is difficult and perilous ground to travel over, where one must often journey a hundred yards round to go ten forward, and even then must chance many a jump that asks for a stout heart and judging eye, since there is no take off and a treacherous landing. In the stark darkness of a black winter's night, unless one cares to face the certainty of a plunge in five or six feet of icy water, it becomes one to move with extreme caution indeed. And of this fact Dermod Crowley, hastening unwarily towards the sound of the dogs, assured himself in the most convincing way by falling headlong into a narrow sheer-sided trench. From this pitfall he extricated himself with considerable difficulty and the loss of his hat. Somewhat sobered by his mishap, he resumed his pursuit with cautious feet, moving without any sense of direction save that afforded by the distant lights of two cottages, the nearer of which he concluded rightly to be Martin Heneghan's, the farther Martin Brett's. For half an hour or so, he wandered about aimlessly as his groping footsteps led him, pausing occasionally to listen to the dogs, which had now apparently separated and scattered across the bogs in several small groups. Of Larry Heneghan and the horse-blocker he could divine nothing. He was very wet and cold, and a bad headache had succeeded to the joyous exhilaration of the earlier portion of the evening's proceedings. To attempt to retrace his path across that bewildering maze of waterways without some guiding landmark appeared to him hopeless. He decided to make for the light of Heneghan's cottage, consoled for the greater distance to be covered by the greater certainty of keeping his direction. To look for anything in that place and in that light appeared to him now quite clearly a foolish and futile proceeding.

It so happened, curiously, that a precisely similar decision had formed itself at precisely the same moment in the stalwart breast of Constable Hickey, who just then had realised that for him too, return by the devious ways by which he had reached his present unknown and comfortless position was a thing too improbable to be seriously thought of. He was then about a hundred yards south-west of Crowley. Five minutes later they became aware of each other, and just one minute after that they met. Of the encounter which ensued neither of them ever cared to speak afterwards.

By now the chase had swelled to considerable proportions, and lanterns had begun to flitter backwards and forwards in the direction of the causeway. Between nine and ten o'clock there must have been close on fifty men on the bog, straying about in twos and threes, splashing and stumbling and cursing, seeing none of them, save one, the thing they hunted. When the chase ended, Larry Heneghan and one dog, a gaunt brindled lurcher, were the sole spectators of its ending.

For three and a half hours those two had kept company, taking the same falls, jumping side by side, united by the bond of tireless muscles and untroubled wind. Never once in all that time had more or less than twenty yards separated them from the indistinct shape in front that, for all its shambling gait, covered the ground with a speed exasperating in its steadiness. The dog, doubtless, could have closed, had it chosen. But it preferred to regulate its pace by its human companion, waiting for him, when a stumble or a patch of sticky ground detained him for a moment, and trotting always with its muzzle level with his knees.

The end came quite suddenly. The dog came to an abrupt stop, yelped and ran back a little, and Heneghan felt, at the same moment, his feet and his legs to mid-shin gripped as if in a closing vice. As the truth flashed upon him, he made a mighty effort and, freeing himself from that deadly hold, sprang backwards and sideways, throwing out his arms as his body turned, and so hauled himself by aid of a clump of heather to solid earth again. Rising to his feet and peering into the darkness, he could just discern that in front of him lay a small sheet of water, or rather of watery mud, oval in shape, some fifty yards across at its narrowest part. Close beside him three jagged tree-stumps rose from the edge of the mud. He recognised the spot instantly, and, as he afterwards admitted, was seized with such a fit of shivering and faintness at the thought of the danger from which he had escaped that he was unable to stand steadily and seated himself on the clump of heather beside the now whimpering dog. Once, many years before, in company with some school-fellows, he had watched a cat disappear in the oozing slime of the Sucking Pool. He remembered still that cat's eyes just before the mud covered them.

Some way out in the pool he could just distinguish the vague bulk of the doomed thing that was fighting desperately for its life, splashing frantically and uttering incessantly a strange chattering noise that turned the listener's blood cold. The chattering continued long after the splashing had ceased. Doubtless the creature's fore-arms or fore-legs had been in their turn imprisoned in that dread and merciless embrace. Whether fore-arms or fore-legs young Heneghan's confused impressions did not clearly decide. In the brief furious melée on the Ballincar Road he had caught a glimpse of a face, hideously human, it was true—but human certainly. Yet no human cry or sound came from the thing now, as it struggled. Anger and excitement had died in him, somehow: an odd feeling, half of pity, half of the instinct to save a fellow-creature, brought him to his feet again. But even as he rose the chattering ceased abruptly, and where something darker than the darkness had been there was nothing. He crossed himself and without further ado made off across the bog towards Hartstown Ridge as fast as his nimble legs could carry him.

And so ended the hunting on the Doonagh Bog.

IX

This is the story which the doctor told me on a January day beside the Sucking Pool, as we sat on perhaps the very clump of heather upon which young Heneghan sat the night of the hunting. The last chapter of it is a brief one. Among the passengers on the ill-fated Leinster was a Mrs. Cruikshank, a middle-aged woman, who was last seen in the lifeboat that was still swinging from the davits when the second torpedo struck the vessel's side, just beneath it. Mrs. Cruikshank was the little girl who had clung to her mother's skirts under the elms of Hartstown Avenue on that long ago June afternoon upon which the doctor's story began.

"The Mermaid Hunter" is Casey Prescott's first published short fiction (it appeared in The Yacht magazine, if you're wondering), but the paperback edition of his espionage novel Asset in Black filled prominent portions of airport newsstands last year. I recommend Asset in Black to anybody who appreciates both excellent writing and storytelling so subtle that it takes a moment to absorb the shock of what you've just read.

Which are the same virtues this vignette displays.

THE MERMAID HUNTER

Casey J. Prescott

The waters of Waquoit Bay were silver after sunset, and the man who headed out into them in his Zodiac had to forcefully remind himself that he wasn't on the Tyrrhenian Sea or the Arabian Gulf or the Sea of Japan, that the black strip of light-dotted land in the far distance was only Martha's Vineyard.

To either side, the high walls of the inlet widened, receding, fingers of a hand forced to let him go. Ahead, beyond the black rubber of the Zodiac, was the calm summer surface of the bay, the gray of stainless steel now as the dusk slowly faded.

Darkness came over the man, the boat, and the sea, like some anodizing compound, merging them into a blackness where only shape and depth mattered, while the Zodiac glided over the shallows, between the calm flats and the sand bars, its powerful motor purring like a big cat set free to hunt in the night.

His name was Ellis, and he felt all constriction drop away with the land behind and the light above. The house he'd bought, a couple miles up the inlet where it

173

narrowed, wasn't anything more than a staging area for these night hunts. He'd secured a rope emergency ladder above the ten-foot drop from the edge of his property to the shallows, so he could scramble down to the Zodiac he kept there for nights like this.

Ellis had a bigger boat, a sixty-foot motor-sailor, moored to the west, where the bay was right for it, but he didn't want the big boat tonight.

Tonight was the night; he could feel it. Everything was right: the rare calm summer sea, the five-knot wind, the excitement in his gut. He wasn't going to screw up the hunt, the chase, by forgetting some crucial detail.

He'd failed enough times that he knew what not to do: don't make a hell of a racket, don't disturb the surface any more than necessary; don't use Loran, or scuba gear (he'd never determined whether it was the bubbles, or the rubber); don't even wear a watch with a luminous face.

Mermaids wouldn't come near a guy in a wet suit, a guy with tanks, a guy wearing a watch that glowed in the dark. Ellis knew it. He'd proved it to himself on a dozen stalking expeditions launched on every sea he'd traveled in twenty years of foreign service.

But he'd never seen a mermaid again, not since the first time, while he'd still been a SEAL stationed in the Gulf of Sidra. He'd gone to see some friends who knew where the river-Arabs used to dive for pearls in the Arabian Gulf, and they'd tried it.

Diving with only a weighted rope and a lungful of air, he'd opened his eyes when the rock brought him to the bottom, and there she was. Flowing hair like golden wrack, eyes of abalone, and all woman in mother-of-pearl.

To the hips, that is. From the hips on down, she was pure dolphin, but he hadn't noticed that until he'd reached out a hand. She'd jackknifed, then fled with a flip of tail he still felt in his dreams . . .

God, he'd loved the sea before that, but not so intimately. He'd grown up in a beach house where the winter wind slapped the spume against his bedroom window so hard at night that he was sure, at age eight, some sea demon was coming to get him. So he'd made a deal with the sea gods. If they wouldn't take him, he'd do them proud.

He'd labored for his gods in every contested venue known to the U.S. Navy, and then as Foreign Service officer in the Gulf States. But since he'd seen the mermaid, he'd wanted nothing else. He'd dived off every oil platform in the Arabian Sea, learned to say "mermaid" in Russian, in Farsi and generic Arabic.

He'd blown time and money mounting expeditions, covering his reasons with likely lies; he'd hooked up with the Woods Hole Oceanographic people once he'd reached retirement age, and made lots of mistakes as he learned.

Ellis was methodical, a good seaman, a good intelligence collector. The mermaid was like any other target: you collected and collated data. Mermaids didn't like high tech, he'd realized after a near miss off Sardinia on leave one August, when he'd been sure he'd seen a flash of mother-of-pearl breast off Costa Smeralda, come in empty-handed and drunk, and encountered a "psychic" that night at a glitzy party.

The psychic frowned at him, shook her head, and said through wrinkled lips, "What are you looking for, my American friend, must be found without artifice. As you found her the first time."

He'd shaken it off then with a polite but skeptical comment. Later he'd realized that he'd never asked the psychic about the mermaid, never mentioned any "she." Still later, he went over his notes and decided he'd been going at this all wrong, with more and more sophisticated equipment.

What he was looking for was a creature from the very heart of the sea, perhaps from the sea gods of his youth. You don't find something like that with parallel circuits and side-scanning sonar.

When he'd seen her that one time, all he'd had on was a pair of bathing trunks, not even flippers. And the boat above, where the rope disappeared out of the water, was ancient and quiet, a thing of sail and oar.

He'd gone at it all wrong. No wonder the mermaid was avoiding him. He didn't know why he'd chosen this spot, except that there were numerous mermaid sightings in New England legend, or why he thought he could find the same mermaid here as he'd seen half a world away. It made sense when you subjected it to gut analysis. As for Beysian analysis and other tools of his one-time trade—in those terms, diving alone at night in New England waters without so much as a face mask didn't make any sense at all.

Ellis had lived a long and strenuous life in which the thing that made most sense for him was the sea. It focussed him, calmed him, shrank his onshore problems to defeatable size. Did so, because he'd learned, in a life of manipulation, negotiation, and winning by intimidation, that none of it meant anything more than he was able to believe that it meant.

On the ocean he could believe in anything, even himself. The sea rolled up on the beaches, scoured new channels on its floor and silted up old ones, and never needed to find a meaning, a justification, beyond its process. That existential liberty buoyed him—no matter what man did, the sea was going to be there, doing what it did, for reasons of its own, throughout humankind's forever.

The ocean washed way all his sins by shrinking them to inconsequence, whenever he was sane enough to let it.

And it had shown him the mermaid. Which was more than most men had ever seen.

He reached back, bare feet slipping on the steel plate of the Zodiac's deck, and cut his motor. Halfway from nowhere to nowhere, he let the Zodiac drift away from the sound and churning of its own passage.

In a little while, he'd drop anchor. Use the anchor itself as his diving weight. Touch his feet to the silky bottom. Open his eyes and wait as long as he could.

Maybe this time she'd come. He'd tried to save the

oceans, after he'd quit trying to save specific parts of them, which was after he'd quit trying to save a life here or there, a piece of policy here or there, a bit of American prestige abroad that had sufficient priority for him to be called in as trouble-shooter. He managed, every time, to save only himself.

Maybe an individual could make a difference, change history or nudge fate, in the short term. That, after all, was what Ellis's life had been about. But you realized, after you toted up your successes and failures and quantified the sum, balancing it against what a man learns of history, and politics, and the nature of other men, that history is much like the sea.

Man at his best or at his worst isn't strong enough to change history over the long term, except the history of man himself. History, Ellis was sure now, was just destiny in deep cover. Like the ocean itself, it merely tolerated man's attempts to alter, harness, adulterate, or even destroy it.

And then it surged in like a changing tide, wiping away the sandcastles left on the beach, returning everything in its path to a pristine state as if nothing had ever happened.

"Snaps back," Ellis said out loud to himself, nodding. That was what history did, no matter how hard you tried to shape a better future. The real nature of the future was all around him, stretching out, black and silver, infinitely varied and yet, ultimately, infinitely homogeneous.

Life was the sea and when he was in touch with it, Ellis felt nothing less than harmony. You couldn't be frustrated by the size of a particular wave or its refusal to acknowledge you and get the hell out of your way.

You could only be frustrated with your own selfish, amnesiac failure to find the mermaid.

And yet, tonight he wasn't even that—not impatient, not regretful over past failures, not even cold although the wind was blowing up.

Tonight he knew he was going to find her. He'd

Giant insect stories have been a staple of science fiction for long enough that when "The Beetle Experiment" appeared in Amazing in 1929, the editor (T. O'Conor Sloane) gave it an extremely defensive blurb. Sloane insisted that this story was very different from the usual insect story, and that it was well worth the time it would take even a busy man to read.

He was right on both counts; and his statements still remain true.

THE BEETLE EXPERIMENT

Russell Hays

Few people ever visit the Filmore Museum. It is a musty, gloomy place, occupying the whole second floor of old Marvin Hall; the building itself was long since condemned. Fewer still notice the one really startling object in the whole collection. It is a beetle placed all alone in a small glass case to the right of the entrance. A gigantic beetle, nearly four inches long, and with pale yellow markings on its metallic grey wing sheaths.

Even then it presents no mystery. Tropical insects often reach such proportions. But, if one be entomologically inclined, he marvels when he reads the label beneath it, for *Cicindela Clymene* is a local, night-preying species of tiger beetle, barely half an inch in length.

Nor does the matter end here.

Often of evenings when a drowsy lulling quiet has settled on the campus, an elderly, stooped little man dressed severely in dark blue serge, lets himself into the museum with a pass-key. Glancing furtively about the shadowy room of mammals, he stops before the

181

beetle, with something akin to horror on his thin, shrunken face. For as long as fifteen minutes at a time he will stand there, running his bony fingers agitatedly through his snowy white hair.

"Oh, you devil you! You heartless, bloody devil!" he whispers. The pupils of his mild grey eyes become pinpointed with a look of intense regret, and there settles on his wrinkled face an expression of unbearable anguish.

Should any late visitor chance to enter the museum at such a time, the little man will start guiltily, clutch at his fleshless throat, and flee precipitately from the building.

Inquiry among the students discloses the fact that he is old Asa Stephens, professor of entomology. Admittedly, he is a little queer. And it is something of a shock to discover that he is still in his early forties. This premature aging is attributed to a nervous breakdown some half dozen years ago. At that time, Asa had achieved considerable national prominence in his chosen field, through his work in determining the functions of insect ganglia or nerve centers.

The strain of the long, irregular hours spent in this research is supposed to have proven too much for him. So far, no one has ever thought to connect the sudden bleaching of his hair with the vampire murders, which so terrorized the little college town at that time.

Some four years before his breakdown, Asa had devised a microscope especially adapted for studying living insects. It was under this instrument that he performed the operations by which he definitely worked out two accessory systems to the ganglionic chain. Following his now famous successes at ganglionic research, he endeavored to locate the ductless glands, corresponding to the thyroid and pituitary in human beings, which controlled the growth and development of insects in the larva stage. Eventually he located them. One, he found to be at the base of the brain, the other was a cream-colored protuberance on the side of the third ganglia.

To prove the functions of these glands, he weakened or destroyed them, thereby stunting the grub and the resultant moth or beetle. While experimenting along these lines, he discovered quite by accident that a weak alkaline solution, notably of a potassium compound, had an irritating effect upon the glands, causing them to grow abnormally.

"Now if that's the case," mused Asa, his grey eyes narrowing contemplatively, "what's going to happen to the grub? Will it grow abnormally, too?"

Happening to have a number of tiger beetle larvæ in his laboratory at the time, Asa immediately commenced testing his new theory. All but three of these grubs failed to survive his treatments. These three, as Asa continued to stimulate their endocrine glands by repeated hypodermic injections of alkaline solution, soon grew far beyond the normal size of *Cicindela Clymene* larvæ. They continued to grow! Asa was elated. He visioned the growth of a giant beetle that would set the whole scientific world to gasping.

However, there was still considerable doubt in his mind as to whether the grubs would pupate normally, carrying out that wonderful alchemy of nature whereby ugly, slow moving grubs and caterpillars build for themselves papery cells and wind cocoons from which they emerge as fully developed beetles and butterflies.

At this time, all three grubs had reached a length of approximately five inches. Asa ceased his injections on two of them and waited impatiently to see what would happen. For a week they went on eating voraciously. Then one day they drew down into their holes in the sandbox by the laboratory window, and commenced to pupate. How long it would take them, Asa had no idea. In the meantime, he continued injecting the remaining grub.

By the time it had grown to be a foot long it was a huge, malformed slug that hung in the neck of its burrow with only its ugly, dirt-colored head showing. Feeding it had become quite a problem. Asa had to spend more and more time each morning with his net, capturing an increasing number of insects to satisfy the grub's insatiable appetite. Obviously, he could not go on feeding it this way indefinitely. One evening, by way of experiment, he brought home several mice from the zoology department.

"Either you change your diet, or your growing days are over," he informed the malignant eyes that glared from either side of the oblong, earthy plate set like a trapdoor in the level surface of the sandbox. It seemed to him that a look of cunning understanding came in the baneful eyes.

Taking a mouse from its cage, Asa dropped it in the box. As though warned instinctively, the mouse ran frantically around the sides of the pen, keeping well away from the dark plate near the center. The grub eyed it hungrily, fixedly. Asa made as if to grab at it. The mouse dodged back, racing across the middle of the box. The trapdoor suddenly opened. Asa caught a glimpse of fearful, gleaming shear-like teeth, shooting up from a pale brownish maw. The mouse gave a terri-fied squeak. Then the hideous trap had snapped shut, and the grub's beady eyes glowed triumphantly, as it dragged its struggling victim down into its den.

"You bloody devil, you!" cried Asa. And because he was really a very meek and timid sort of a person, he felt a cold shiver run down his spine.

As the weeks passed and the grub's appetite contin-ued to grow in direct proportion to its size, Asa grad-ually shifted its diet to bits of raw beef. To avoid inquisitiveness on the part of the local butchers, he bought the meat at different shops. And finally, when the grub had reached a length of nearly three feet, he took to driving over to Parker City, where he would buy a quarter of a beef at a time, giving out that he had charge of a road-camp commissary.

Housing the larva also presented a problem. As it grew, it enlarged its den accordingly, throwing sand carelessly out across the laboratory floor. It had nearly emptied the larger box which Asa had provided for it.

Besides, it gave off a strong, sweaty odor now, which made the laboratory nearly uninhabitable.

"I can't keep you in here?" Asa pondered.

Still he could hardly put it out in the yard. Despite the isolation of the cottage he had rented at the outskirts of the village, occasional passers-by would be coming over to see what he was doing. Asa had no intention of getting a flock of rabid newspaper men and fellow scientists on his trail until his experiments were successfully completed. Consequently, he solved the matter by placing the grub in the earth floor of a small woodshed, just off the rear porch.

Nor was the injection of the alkaline solution any longer an easy task. The only way Asa could get the larva out of its den was to dig it out. Constantly, he had to be on the lookout for its ugly head. Once it curled and side-swiped viciously at his arm, its toothed jaws cutting the flesh nearly to the bone.

"Yes, you would! Been trying to do that for a long time now!" Asa cried, as he clutched his bleeding arm. "You treacherous devil!"

Thereafter, he dug down beside it and placed a sort of harness about its wrinkly, hairy body. The grub's skin had become thick and tough. Asa handled it roughly, using a hypodermic with an unusually large needle to keep it from being broken by any sudden squirming. Eventually, the grub grew to be almost six feet long, the frightful trapdoor head a foot and a half across. Its rapacious appetite was astounding. In fact, feeding its very greedy maw was becoming somewhat of a strain on Asa's slender stipend. He decided to let it go ahead and pupate.

Even after ceasing his injections, however, the grub continued to grow. The better part of a month passed before it finally drew its fat body down out of sight in the depths of its burrow, sealing the mouth of the hole behind it.

Standing breathlessly in the shed, Asa could hear it turning and turning, some six feet beneath the floor, as it spun and wound its cocoon-like pupal cell. For nearly two weeks the unceasing labor continued. Then, when it had finally stopped, Asa dug down to the pupa. From the portion of it which he uncovered, it appeared to be a giant, bean shaped cell about three feet through of some brittle material the color and consistency of hard rubber. No sound came from inside of it. Only when he tapped sharply on the wall of the cell were there sluggish movements. The pupa was alive all right!

For a while Asa debated taking it up and burying it in a sand pit in his laboratory. Yet on second thought, he decided it might be best to leave the cell as it was, as nature had intended it to stay during this changing stage.

Now that the larva had gone into its pupal cell, there was nothing he could do but wait until it should emerge a beautiful glistening creature, such as man had never seen before. The two smaller grubs had already issued from their cells as adult tiger beetles a few weeks previously. They were marvelously handsome little creatures, fully four inches long. Their grey bodies were sharply marked with smooth edged blotches of palest yellow. They ran swiftly about the glass cage Asa had provided for them, on incredibly long and graceful legs. When startled, they would fly about with darting quickness, looking at first glance like huge queerly shaped humming birds.

It is one of these, the first to die, which is still to be seen in its case at the Filmore Museum.

While he waited for the giant grub to pupate, however, Asa was not idle in his researches. He wrote a voluminous report of the whole experiment to be presented before the National Entomological Association when the giant tiger beetle should have completed its metamorphosis, indubitable proof of the correctness of his theories.

Asa did considerable dreaming in those days. Long hours of evenings he would sit beside the great buried cell, feeling the faint pulsations of life inside it, while he visioned a gaping world, astounded by the marvel that would some day be paraded before its awed gaze. He had other dreams, half formulated plans of breeding a giant race of ants that would be trained to do man's manual labor. It was an inspiring thought!

He made countless experiments.

The months slid swiftly by. Almost a year had passed since the grub had spun its pupal cell. Asa had no way of knowing when it would come out as an adult, since his experience with the smaller larvæ had shown him that the period of pupation was lengthened abnormally by the increased growth. Yet as spring came around again, he had a growing conviction that the pupa had nearly completed its change.

Lying on the woodshed floor, he could hear slight scraping sounds, impatient movements as though the beetle were tiring of its cramped cell. Could it be getting ready to emerge? For the first time, Asa thought seriously of just how he would handle it when it did come out. He looked about the woodshed. It was a staunch building. Yes, it would hold the beetle for the time being. He would muzzle its fearful jaws, and perhaps clip one of its wings. No trick to do that. There would be plenty of people willing to help him. Too many, most likely!

"No use worrying about that yet," he told himself. For all he knew the giant beetle might never emerge. Life was full of such disappointments.

In that respect, however, he need have had no worry. The monster emerged all right! But not in the placid manner Asa had expected. And yet he should have anticipated it. He was something of an authority on the habits of *Cicindela Clymene*. Consequently, there was really no excuse on his part for what happened. But Asa realized this too late.

It was sometime during the morning of May 17th when the monster beetle ate the end out of its pupal cell and climbed up into the woodshed to dry its waxy wings. The day is etched with painful grooves on Asa's memory. Arising late, he had had time only for a glimpse into the woodshed before he hurried off to his classes.

A wondrous spring morning, it was, the very air rich
as rare old wine and the damp earth springy beneath
his feet. Lilacs were in full bloom along the short cut to
the campus; and the sky above was just as clear as
beautiful, unflawed turquoise.

The morning and afternoon passed uneventfully, except for a growing presentiment on Asa's part. Could
anything have happened to the pupa? Could it have
come out? Asa fidgeted restlessly in his chair, repeating
his lectures automatically, without thought. As soon as
the last of them was finished, he grabbed his hat and
went hurrying home. Getting the key from the kitchen,
he headed out to the woodshed; then stopped, gaping
fearfully, before he reached it.

A great ragged hole had been torn in the side of the
shed. The boards were crushed and splintered as though
they had been cut by the dull, jagged blade of a pair of
enormous shears. Asa clutched suddenly at his throat.
No man had ever made a hole like that! He ran toward
it wildly, leaning over the broken board ends to peer
into the shed. The building was empty.

Asa stepped through the hole and stumbled over the
clods that had been thrown carelessly across the floor.
In the center of them was a black hole a yard in diameter, running straight down into the earth. The little
scientist got down on his knees the better to stare down
into the newly opened den.

"It's come out—got away!" he whispered. "But it
can't have gone far. I'll catch it somehow."

A musty, sweetish odor, like that of wet silk, came up
out of the hole. Probably from the newly opened cell,
he decided. He turned to gaze calculatingly at the hole
torn in the side of the shed. Judging from that, the
beetle must be larger than he had thought it would be.
A monster of a creature! Asa ran his fingers nervously
through his thick brown hair. The sooner he caged it,
the better!

His thin brows pulled together in a worried scowl.
There was something of fiendish ruthlessness in the
way huge clods and splintered boards lay scattered

about the shed. "Looks like it'd just tried to tear things up," he muttered dubiously. "Must be strong as a horse! And if it runs and flies as fast as the little ones . . . !"

A horrible fear clutched at Asa's heart. He commenced appreciating, for the first time, the awful strength and speed of the monstrosity he had grown. The thought was appalling. He wet his lips, struck by a sudden more direful thought. Ah, surely not! It wouldn't do that? Yet it had to eat? And here he was standing idle. Asa leaped over the rubbish and went racing back to the house. Here he got a double barrelled shotgun and loaded it with buckshot. Once he got within range of the beetle, he promised himself, he would cripple it by shooting off a wing. If that didn't stop it, he'd blow a leg off.

As an afterthought, he looped a coil of rope over his arm. It might come in handy for muzzling those jaws.

So armed, Asa stepped out into the yard again. Being completely familiar with the habits of *Cicindela Clymene*, he was under no uncertainty as to where to look for the escaped monster. These tiger beetles, he knew, hunted chiefly at night, hiding out during the day beneath sticks and rubbish. Consequently, the beetle, huge as it was, would probably be hiding somewhere in a thicket. Perhaps along the brush-like banks of Willow Creek; a curve of which pushed over into Asa's back yard.

Since there were few such uncultivated spots in the vicinity of Filmore, it was at least a likely place to look. Of course, if he didn't find it soon, he supposed he would have to get some of his students to help him. There were several that would be willing. And the beetle couldn't get away for long, not if everyone were on the lookout for it. He might even offer a reward? Yes, that would probably be the simplest way to handle the matter.

As the afternoon passed and he found no trace of the beetle, Asa became more and more convinced that this latter plan was the only logical one to follow. Returning to the cottage, he got into his car and drove over to the Filmore post office. At the writing desk, he printed a notice on the back of a small poster.

$100.00 REWARD

*Will be paid for the capture of a giant tiger beetle,
escaped from my laboratory. This creature, which
has been grown to a probable body length of between five and six feet, through stimulation of its
endocrine glands, will likely be found hiding in
thick underbrush during the day, issuing forth at
dusk to hunt. Supposed at the present time to be
hiding along Willow Creek.*

ASA STEPHENS, *Professor of Entomology,
Filmore College*

This would set the busybodies to talking, Asa mused
as he signed the notice. Plenty of them, no doubt,
would consider him cracked. The little scientist's thin
lips drew back in an amused smile. Well, once they saw
the beetle, they'd have an opportunity to change their
minds!

There was a group of men talking excitedly by the
door as he came into the office. In his own preoccupation, Asa had taken no notice of them. Glancing at them
now, he smiled again. The bulletin board was to one
side of them. He would go over and stick up his notice.
They would want to know what it was all about. It was
as well to start the ball rolling. He moved over to the
board and was digging out a thumb tack when a hoarse
exclamation caught his ear.

"A madman! That's what done it!" said one of the
men in an awed tone. "Why, old Jim was chopped up
like he'd fell in a separator! The awfulest look on his
face. I never seen nothin' like it!"

Asa paused, a ghastly premonition coming to him.
He thrust the reward notice guiltily behind his back.
Could it be possible? My God, if it were! He stood
there scarcely breathing.

"The Callahan girl was the same way!" another exclaimed. "Why her eyes were almost popping out of her
head. And she was white as a ghost!"

"White, you say? So was Jim. Like as though the

blood had all run out of his body—hangin's too good for a fiend like that!"

Nausea gripped at Asa's vitals. A fiend, was it? A fiend that sucked the blood from the mutilated bodies of its victims! That would account for the blanched faces, the terror fixed eyes. It could hardly be coincidence. He moved closer to the group. "Do they know who did it?" he asked timidly.

"Not yet," Mills, the tall, hawk-nosed proprietor of the Filmore Hotel, answered him. "But he can't get away. The constable's got three posses out scourin' the country."

"Where—where did it all happen?"

"Right down below your place, about a mile. Along Willow Creek. What gets me though, is that whoever done it would tackle old Jim right out in the middle of a field. Sneaked up and grabbed him off a plow, it looks like."

"Oh, my God!" gasped Asa. What surer proof could there be than that? *Cicindela Clymene* always stalked their prey in the open! Asa shuddered. The hotel man was looking at him queerly. "And the girl?"

"Caught her as she was crossing Fintel's bridge! Her brother found her when he went out to see why she didn't come home. She as lying there, right in the middle of the road."

"Her clothes all torn off!" put in another man.

Asa swallowed hard and turned away. Could Mills suspect him? He walked over to the waste paper basket and tore the reward notice to small bits. On second thought, he pocketed the pieces. It would never do to have someone piece them together now! He had an impulse to run wildly out of the post office, to flee from this naked tragedy before he was found out. Anywhere, anywhere to get away. He looked into his mail box, and with an effort walked casually out to his car parked at the curb.

Getting in it, he drove back to the cottage. What could he do? And the night was only started. He remembered with horror the insatiable appetites of the

smaller beetles. Ever ravenous, they were! How often
he had seen one of them pounce upon some helpless
ground beetle, cutting through the soft portions of its
armor with those powerful pincher-like teeth, then greedily drinking the blood from the still quivering carcass.
Half a dozen victims would fall before the killer's savage
attack, before its bloodlust was even partially satisfied.

Asa felt deathly sick, sick at heart. He closed his eyes
tightly to shut out the grim picture that had come to him.

Arriving at the cottage, he went inside and locked
the door. He tried to think sanely, calmly—to reason
with himself. What would he say, for instance, should
one of the posses visit him? If they killed the beetle,
would they not immediately suspect him? Was there
nothing he could do? No way to stop the carnage? To sit
here helpless was maddening! He snatched up the
shotgun and ran distractedly out into the night.

An hour or more he prowled aimlessly along the
brushy borders of Willow Creek. Once, he imagined he
heard the sharp whir of giant wings. He cringed down
against a wild rose bush, holding his cocked gun with
palsied fingers. Another time, he saw a group of approaching lights. Guessed that it was one of the posses.
He turned on his backtrack, heart jumping, and ran
frantically through the brush. Somehow, he got off the
trail and went crashing through a blackberry thicket.

The thorns tore his clothes, biting through at his
flesh. This would never do. He must keep his head! He
stumbled back on the trail and stood there trembling.
He reached up to his throbbing brow. It was wet with
perspiration.

"Oh, my God, my God—what have I done?" he sobbed.

He made his way back to the cottage and tramped
frenziedly back and forth, across his unlighted laboratory. What was the beetle doing now? Had it claimed
more victims? How many? Whom? Had they found out
yet what it was? Did they suspect him? Asa gave a
tremulous groan. He couldn't go on this way! Better to
know the worst than to stay cooped up here with his
thoughts.

Still clutching the shotgun, he got in his car and drove to town again. A milling crowd of townsfolk and students was gathered about the lighted doorway of Samson's Mortuary. Asa parked the car, leaving the engine running, and joined the tense, queerly silent group that stood on the sidewalk. They looked at him suspiciously. Looked at each other suspiciously. Two more people had been struck down by the unknown fiend—a fiend that might even now be searching for other victims. There was no clue to its identity. Yet Asa found no solace in the fact.

He listened woodenly to the story a raspy-voiced man was telling. One of the victims had been a child. Its playmate had told an incoherent tale that might have been lifted wholly from some medieval witch book. The two boys had been walking along a path crossing the corner of a pasture. A great shiny bird with many long stiff legs had come flying toward them. Had dropped down on the boy in the lead. The other had seen it plainly in the evening light, before he had fled in terror.

Despite the incredulity of his listeners, the boy had stuck to his story. It had been a bird. A great, shiny bird! A short distance from the path, searchers had found the torn body of the playmate!

The raspy-voiced man branded the tale as the wild imaginings of a child. There could be no such hellish thing as a monstrous blood-sucking bird. Yet for all his logic, the crowd about the mortuary shifted uneasily. There were whisperings of a vampire. Hadn't the bodies been only lifeless husks? But it was impossible! There was no such thing.

The body of the farmer, the first to be killed, had been brought to the mortuary. Asa pushed his way to the door. A crowd was packed about the body. Asa climbed up on a chair and peered over their heads to where it lay stretched out on a table. The county sheriff and a deputy were there examining it. They seemed to be at a loss to account for the weapon that had been

used. The body was terribly mangled. Asa felt himself
trembling violently.

The fault was his! It was as though he had made those
ghastly wounds with his own hands. It was he who was
the merciless destroyer that terrorized the night!

He got weakly down from the chair. The temptation
to cry out his guilt, to confess himself the murderer,
came to him. He bit his lips. What good would it do?
Better by far if he could somehow end this reign of
death—somehow kill this abnormity that his own bloody
hands had reared. Or let it kill him, too! He fought his
way madly through the mob pressed about the door.
One of his students spoke to him, but he passed on
unhearing.

A murmur passed through the crowd. Word had just
been phoned in that a student had been found mur-
dered near the edge of town. Asa shrank back as though
the beetle's terrible pinchers had closed on his own
sweaty body.

"Another," he whispered in agony. "Five now! Mother
of God, when will it end?"

Asa walked drunkenly down the street to his car. His
thoughts were an unintelligible jumble. A nightmare!
To think that he should be the unintentional cause of
this catastrophe! He, who felt a pang of remorse even at
the killing of a mouse in his experiments.

He discovered, as he went into his house, that he
was still carrying the shotgun. Must have carried it into
the mortuary with him. What difference? He held it in
his hands and stared at it blankly, unseeingly. The
shadows of the room seemed alive with accusing phantoms. Phantoms that waved grotesquely mocking arms.
He would have sworn that faint screams came to his
tortured ears from out of the night. He slumped down
in a chair to rock tirelessly back and forth. He couldn't
endure this—sitting here all alone. He would go mad.

Asa got resolutely to his feet.

Still in his shirt sleeves, he flung himself out the
door. Dark clouds had blown in from the west, blotting
out the dim radiance of the moon. The air was warm

and sultry, smelt of rain. Asa clutched his gun tightly as
he moved furtively down a cow-path that followed the
grassy, meandering bank of Willow Creek.

Fire-flies played through the air, mystic golden dots
that flashed for a moment like falling meteors. Asa
stared agitatedly into the inky shadows. A mantle of
black, thick air seemed pressed down against the earth.
A line of lightning zig-zagged across the tumultuous
crest of a cloud. A peal of thunder crashed deafeningly.
Presently, it commenced to rain, a slashing driving
downpour that beat against the earth in wind lashed
waves.

Asa stalked through it unminding. Up and down the
tangled banks of Willow Creek, he wandered. The hours
flew magically by. After a while the rain stopped, yet
he continued to beat his way through the water drenched
brush. Dawn broke in the east, pink as a Cherokee rose.
Asa stopped to look up at the sky, breathing heavily.
His mind was chaotic. Years seemed to have passed
since the bright, sunny morning the day before, when
he had hurried eagerly to his classes. All life, all vitality
had drained from his weary body.

"It's no use, no use," he whispered.

As well go home now. He would clean up, then go
into town and tell the sheriff everything. They would
probably think him crazy. No, not after what had happened! He took a path back to the cottage, tottering
along like an old, old man, his thin shoulders slumped
in abysmal despair.

The path was muddy, his clothes torn and bedrag-
gled. He moved slowly across his yard to the open door
of the house. In front of it, he turned to stand gazing
soberly at the newly risen sun, as it shot its golden rays
down through the pure white blossoms of a plum thicket
at the edge of the yard. A metallic grey gleam beyond
the blossoms caught his eye. He held his breath as he
stared at it.

"Can it be?" he gasped. He bent sideways to see the
better.

Outlined behind the blooms was a grey shield marked with smooth edged blotches of palest yellow. Asa cocked both barrels of the shotgun, half crouched. He brought the gun up to his shoulder. As though it had read his intention, the monster moved out of its cover.

Fast as light it moved. Stood there just outside the thicket, eyeing the little scientist malignantly from great, protruding, pale greenish eyes. In even that moment, Asa could not but feel the awful beauty of the creature. It stood on slender, shining legs, seeming tensed, ready to spring. Looking up at it, Asa could see the vivid bronze coloring of its plated stomach, a full seven feet above the ground. A giant, cruel beak, that opened horizontally, was thrust out from between the eyes, jagged, horny shears nearly a foot long, shining like amber in the morning light, and stained red from the blood of its victims.

Of the gleaming metallic grey sheaths that covered the wings, Asa had only a glimpse. Then the beetle was racing toward him, so swiftly that it seemed to fly rather than run.

The scientist shrank back in horror. A mad, babbling cry was wrenched from his bloodless lips. It all seemed an impossible nightmare. He aimed his gun blindly at the flashing body. He felt the stock kick back against his shoulder as it spit out its leaden death. He pulled the trigger of the other barrel. Even as it went off, he was flung sprawling to the ground. Unconsciously, he closed his eyes, waiting for the monster's gory mandibles to close on his wretched body.

A mighty threshing was going on beside him. A great hooked claw caught him across the chest, tearing through his coat as though it were paper. He opened his eyes. The giant beetle was darting, racing wildly about the yard. It crashed against the side of the woodshed. Asa stared at it uncomprehendingly. Then he saw that the gelatinous eyes had been torn open by the buckshot.

Asa gave a shrill, triumphant cry. Strength flowed back into his trembling body. He grabbed up the shotgun with suddenly steady fingers; put in another cartridge as he got to his feet.

The beetle was standing still now, as though trying to reason out what fate had overtaken it. Its blinded front was turned upon the little scientist. Its long whip-like antennae waved in lashing circles, picking up the scent of its man victor. Suddenly, it came floundering toward him, purposefully, jaws spreading wide in a demoniac lust for vengeance. A gleaming, blood-mad colossus! Asa sprang sideways to avoid its lunging rush. Its dripping head banged against the side of the house. Asa stepped in close to the wide spread legs and emptied both barrels into the soft tissue back of its head.

The monster leaped high into the air, spasmodically— flew for nearly a hundred feet, giant wings roaring. Then it crashed to the ground—made an effort to get to its feet, and collapsed, a shining dead heap.

Asa gazed at it dully. The shotgun dropped from his nerveless fingers. Dead, yes, it was dead. But the damage was already done! Five innocent people had paid with their blood for his mistake. He could never right that. His thin face worked tortuously. What good to tell the truth now? He had done all he could. Presently, when he had got his breath, he dragged the heavy carcass into the woodshed. Shoving it down into its pupal pit, he shoveled the hole full of dirt again.

Then he went calmly, resolutely into the house. Taking the huge report he had compiled on his experiment, he thrust it into the stove and touched a match to it.

He heated some water and washed his hands. As he looked into the mirror above the wash bowl, he saw that the hair above his temple had turned a lifeless white.

Henry Kuttner was one of the most prolific SF writers of his day; one of the most technically proficient; and one of those most willing to attempt stylistic innovations. For most writers, "Home is the Hunter" would have been an extraordinary achievement because of the amount of background the author manages to pack into a short, utterly headlong story.

For Kuttner, it was a typically excellent job.

HOME IS THE HUNTER

Henry Kuttner

There's nobody I can talk to except myself. I stand here at the head of the great waterfall of marble steps dropping into the reception hall below, and all my wives in all their jewels are waiting, for this is a Hunter's Triumph—my Triumph, Honest Roger Bellamy, Hunter. The light glitters on the glass cases down there with the hundreds of dried heads that I have taken in fair combat, and I'm one of the most powerful men in New York. The heads make me powerful.

But there's nobody I can talk to. Except myself? Inside me, listening, is there another Honest Roger Bellamy? I don't know. Maybe he's the only real part of me. I go along the best I can, and it doesn't do any good. Maybe the Bellamy inside of me doesn't like what I do. But I have to do it. I can't stop. I was born a Head-Hunter. It's a great heritage to be born to. Who doesn't envy me? Who wouldn't change with me, if they could?

But it doesn't do any good at all.

I'm no good.

Listen to me, Bellamy, listen to me, if you're there at
all, deep inside my head. You've got to listen—you've
got to understand. You there inside the skull. You can
turn up in a glass case in some other Head-Hunter's
reception hall any day now, any day, with the crowds of
populi outside pressing against the view-windows and
the guests coming in to see and envy and all the wives
standing by in satin and jewels.

Maybe you don't understand, Bellamy. You should
feel fine now. It must be that you don't know this real
world I have to go on living in. A hundred years ago, or
a thousand, it might have been different. But this is the
Twenty-first Century. It's today, it's now, and there's
no turning back.

I don't think you understand.

You see, there isn't any choice. Either you end up in
another Head-Hunter's glass case, along with your whole
collection, while your wives and children are turned
out to be populi, or else you die naturally (suicide is
one way) and your eldest son inherits your collection,
and you become immortal, in a plastic monument. You
stand forever in transparent plastic on a pedestal along
the edge of Central Park, like Renway and old Falconer
and Brennan and all the others. Everyone remembers
and admires and envies you.

Will you keep on thinking then, Bellamy, inside the
plastic? Will I?

Falconer was a great Hunter. He never slowed down,
and he lived to be fifty-two. For a Head-Hunter, that is
a great old age. There are stories that he killed himself.
I don't know. The wonder is that he kept his head on
his shoulders for fifty-two years. The competition is
growing harder, and there are more and more younger
men these days.

Listen to me, Bellamy, the Bellamy within. Have
you ever really understood? Do you still think this is
the wonderful young time, the boyhood time when life
is easy? Were you ever with me in the long, merciless
years while my body and mind learned to be a Head-

Hunter? I'm still young and strong. My training has never stopped. But the early years were the hardest.

Before then, there was the wonderful time. It lasted for six years only, six years of happiness and warmth and love with my mother in the harem, and the foster mothers and the other children. My father was very kind then. But when I was six, it stopped. They shouldn't have taught us love at all, if it had to end so soon. Is it that you remember, Bellamy within? If it is, it can never come back. You know that. Surely you know it.

The roots of the training were obedience and discipline. My father was not kind any more. I did not see my mother often, and when I did she was changed, too. Still, there was praise. There were the parades when the populi cheered me and my father. He and the trainers praised me, too, when I showed I had special skill in the duel, or in marksmanship or judo-stalking.

It was forbidden, but my brothers and I sometimes tried to kill each other. The trainers watched us carefully. I was not the heir, then. But I became the heir when my elder brother's neck was broken in a judo-fall. It seemed an accident, but of course it wasn't, and then I had to be more careful than ever. I had to become very skillful.

All that time, all that painful time, learning to kill. It was natural. They kept telling us how natural it was. We had to learn. And there could be only one heir. . . .

We lived under a cloud of fear, even then. If my father's head had been taken, we would all have been turned out of the mansion. Oh, we wouldn't have gone hungry or unsheltered. Not in this age of science. But not to be a Head-Hunter! Not to become immortal, in a plastic monument standing by Central Park!

Sometimes I dream that I am one of the populi. It seems strange, but in the dream I am hungry. And that is impossible. The great power plants supply all the world needs. Machines synthesize food and build houses and give us all the necessities of life. I could never be one of the populi, but if I were I would go into a restaurant and take whatever food I wished out of the little glass-fronted cubbyholes. I would eat well—far better than I eat now. And yet, in my dream, I am hungry.

Perhaps the food I eat does not satisfy you, Bellamy within me. It does not satisfy me, but it is not meant to. It is nutritious. Its taste is unpleasant, but all the necessary proteins and minerals and vitamins are in it to keep my brain and body at their highest pitch. And it should not be pleasant. It is not pleasure that leads a man to immortality in plastic. Pleasure is a weakening and an evil thing.

Bellamy within—do you hate me?

My life has not been easy. It isn't easy now. The stubborn flesh fights against the immortal future, urging a man to be weak. But if you are weak, how long can you hope to keep your head on your shoulders?

The populi sleep with their wives. I have never even kissed any of mine. (Is it you who have sent me dreams?) My children?—yes, they are mine; artificial insemination is the answer. I sleep on a hard bed. Sometimes I wear a hair shirt. I drink only water. My food is tasteless. With my trainers I exercise every day, until I am very tired. The life is hard—but in the end we shall stand forever in a plastic monument, you and I, while the world envies and admires. I shall die a Head-Hunter, and I shall be immortal.

The proof is in the glass cases down there in my reception hall. The heads, the heads—look, Bellamy, so many heads. Stratton, my first. I killed him in Central Park with a machete. This is the scar on my temple that he gave me that night. I learned to be defter. I had to.

Each time I went into Central Park, fear and hate helped me. Sometimes it is dreadful in the Park. We go there only at night, and sometimes we stalk for many nights before we take a head. The Park is forbidden, you know, to all but Head-Hunters. It is our hunting ground.

I have been shrewd and cunning and skillful. I have shown great courage. I have stopped my fears and nursed my hate, there in the Park's shadows, listening, waiting, stalking, never knowing when I might feel sharp steel burning through my throat. There are no rules in the Park. Guns or clubs or knives—once I was caught in a mantrap, all steel and cables and sharp teeth. But I had moved in time, and fast enough, so I kept my right hand free and shot Miller between the eyes when he came to take me. There is Miller's head down there. You would never know a bullet had gone through his forehead. The thanatologists are clever. But usually we try not to spoil the heads.

What is it that troubles you so, Bellamy within? I am one of the greatest Hunters in New York. But a man must be cunning. He must lay traps and snares a long way in advance, and not only in Central Park. He must keep his spies active and his lines of contact taut in every mansion in the city. He must know who is powerful and who is not worth taking. What good would it do to win against a Hunter with only a dozen heads in his hall?

I have hundreds. Until yesterday, I stood ahead of every man in my age group. Until yesterday I was the envy of all I knew, the idol of the populi, the acknowledged master of half New York. Half New York! Do you know how much that meant to me? That my rivals loathed me and acknowledged me their better? You do know, Bellamy. It was the breath of life that True Jonathan Hull and Good Ben Griswold ground their teeth when they thought of me, and that Black Bill Lindman and Whistler Cowles counted their trophies and then called me on the TV phone and begged me with tears of hate and fury in their eyes to meet them in the Park and give them the chance they craved.

I laughed at them. I laughed Black Bill Lindman into a beserker rage and then half-envied him, because I have not been berserker myself for a long while now. I like that wild unloosening of all my awarenesses but one—the killing instinct, blind and without reason. I could forget even you then, Bellamy within.

But that was yesterday.

And yesterday night, Good Ben Griswold took a head. Do you remember how we felt when we learned of it, you and I? First I wanted to die, Bellamy. Then I hated Ben as I have never hated anyone before, and I have known much hate. I would not believe he had done it. I would not believe *which* head he took.

I said it was a mistake, that he took a head from the populi. But I knew I lied. No one takes a common head. They have no value. Then I said to myself, it can't be the head of True Jonathan Hull. It can't be. It must not be. For Hull was powerful. His hall held almost as many heads as mine. If Griswold were to have them all he would be far more powerful than I. The thought was a thing I could not endure.

I put on my status cap, with as many bells on it as the heads I have taken, and I went out to see. It was true, Bellamy.

The mansion of Jonathan Hull was being emptied. The mob was surging in and out. Hull's wives and children were leaving in little, quiet groups. The wives did not seem unhappy, but the boys did. (Girls are sent to the populi at birth; they are worthless.) I watched the boys for a while. They were all wretched and angry. One was nearly sixteen, a big, agile lad who must have nearly finished his training. Someday I might meet him in the Park.

The other boys were all too young. Now that their training had been interrupted, they would never dare enter the Park. That, of course, is why none of the populi ever become Hunters. It takes long years of arduous training to turn a child from a rabbit to a tiger. In Central Park only the tigers survive.

I looked through True Jonathan's view-windows. I saw that the glass cases in his reception hall were empty. So it was not a nightmare or a lie. Griswold did have them, I told myself, them and True Jonathan's head besides. I went into a doorway and clenched my fists and beat my head against the brownstone and groaned with self-contempt.

I was no good at all. I hated myself, and I hated Griswold too. Presently it was only that second hate that remained. So I knew what I had to do. Today, I thought, he stands where I stood yesterday. Desperate men will be talking to him, begging him, challenging him, trying every means they know to get him into the Park tonight.

But I am crafty. I make my plans far ahead. I have networks that stretch into the mansions of every Hunter in the city, crossing their own webs.

One of my wives, Nelda, was the key here. Long ago I realized that she was beginning to dislike me. I never knew why. I fostered that dislike until it became hate. I saw to it that Griswold would learn the story. It is by stratagems like this that I became as powerful as I was then—and will be again, will surely be again.

I put a special glove on my hand (you could not tell it was a glove) and I went to my TV phone and called Good Ben Griswold. He came grinning to the screen.

"I challenge you, Ben," I said. "Tonight at nine, in the Park, by the carousel site."

He laughed at me. He was a tall, heavily muscled man with a thick neck. I looked at his neck.

"I was waiting to hear from you, Roger," he said.

"Tonight at nine," I repeated.

He laughed again. "Oh no, Roger," he said. "Why should I risk my head?"

"You're a coward."

"Certainly I'm a coward," he said, still grinning, "when there's nothing to gain and everything to lose. Was I a coward last night, when I took Hull's head? I've had my eye on him a long time, Roger. I'll admit I was afraid you'd get him first. Why didn't you, anyway?"

"It's your head I'm after, Ben."

"Not tonight," he said. "Not for quite a while. I'm not going back to the Park for a long time. I'll be too busy. You're out of the running now, Roger, anyhow. How many heads have you?"

He knew, God damn him, how far in advance of me he was—now. I let the hate show in my face.

"The Park at nine tonight," I said. "The carousel site. Or else I'll know you're afraid."

"Eat your heart out, Roger," he mocked me. "To-night I lead a parade. Watch me. Or don't—but you'll be thinking about me. You can't help that."

"You swine, you rotten cowardly swine."

He laughed; he derided me, he goaded me, as I had done so many times to others. I did not have to pretend anger. I wanted to reach into the screen and sink my fingers in his throat. The furious rage was good to feel. It was very good. I let it build until it seemed high enough. I let him laugh and enjoy it.

Then at last I did what I had been planning. At the right moment, when it looked convincing, I let myself lose all control and I smashed my fist into the TV screen. It shattered. Griswold's face flew apart; I liked that.

The connection was broken, of course. But I knew he would check quickly back. I slipped the protective glove from my right hand and called a servant I knew I could trust. (He is a criminal; I protect him. If I die he will die and he knows it.) He bandaged my unharmed right hand and I told him what to say to the other servants. I knew the word would reach Nelda quickly, in the harem, and I knew that Griswold would hear within an hour.

I fed my anger. All day in the gymnasium I practiced with my trainers, machete and pistol in my left hand only. I made it seem that I was approaching the berserker stage, the killing madness that overcomes us when we feel we have failed too greatly.

That kind of failure can have one of two results only. Suicide is the other. You risk nothing then, and you know your body will stand by the Park in its plastic monument. But sometimes the hate turns outward and there is no fear left. Then the Hunter is berserker, and while this makes him very dangerous, he is also good quarry then—he forgets his cunning.

It was dangerous to me, too, for that kind of forgetfulness is very tempting. The next best thing to oblivion itself.

Well, I had set the lure for Griswold. But it would take more than a lure to bring him out when he thought he had nothing to gain by such a risk. So I set rumors loose. They were very plausible rumors. I let it be whispered that Black Bill Lindman and Whistler Cowles,

as desperate as I at Griswold's triumph over us all, had
challenged each other to a meeting in the Park that
night. Only one could come out alive, but that one
would be master of New York so far as our age group
counted power. (There was, of course, old Murdoch with
his fabulous collection accumulated over a lifetime. It was
only among ourselves that the rivalry ran so high.)

With that rumor abroad, I thought Griswold would
act. There is no way to check such news. A man seldom
announces openly that he is going into the Park. It
could even be the truth, for all I knew. And for all
Griswold knew, his supremacy was in deadly peril before he had even enjoyed his Triumph. There would be
danger, of course, if he went out to defend his victory.
Lindman and Cowles are both good Hunters. But Griswold, if he did not suspect my trap, had a chance at one
sure victory—myself, Honest Roger Bellamy, waiting in
berserker fury at a known rendezvous and with a right
hand useless for fighting. Did it seem too obvious? Ah,
but you don't know Griswold.

When it was dark I put on my hunting clothes. They
are bulletproof, black, close-fitting but very easy with
every motion. I blacked my face and hands. I took gun,
knife and machete with me, the metal treated so that it
will not catch or reflect the light. I like a machete
especially. I have strong arms. I was careful not to use
my bandaged hand at all, even when I thought no one
watched me. And I remembered that I must seem on
the verge of berserker rage, because I knew Griswold's
spies would be reporting every motion.

I went toward Central Park, the entrance nearest the
carousel site. That far Griswold's men could track me.
But no farther.

At the gate I lingered for a moment—do you remember this, Bellamy within me? Do you remember the
plastic monuments we passed on the edge of the Park?
Falconer and Brennan and the others, forever immortal, standing proud and godlike in the clear, eternal
blocks. All passion spent, all fighting done, their glory
assured forever. Did you envy them too, Bellamy?

I remember how old Falconer's eyes seemed to look through me contemptuously. The number of heads he had taken is engraved on the base of his monument, and he was a very great man. Wait, I thought. I'll stand in plastic too. I'll take more heads than even you, Falconer, and the day that I do it will be the day I can lay this burden down. . . .

Just inside the gate, in the deep shadows, I slipped the bandage from my right hand. I drew my black knife and close against the wall I began to work my way rapidly toward the little gate which is nearest Griswold's mansion. I had, of course, no intention of going anywhere near the carousel site. Griswold would be in a hurry to get to me and out again and he might not stop to think. Griswold was not a thinker. I gambled on his taking the closest route.

I waited, feeling very solitary and liking the solitude. It was hard to stay angry. The trees whispered in the darkness. The moon was rising from the Atlantic beyond Long Island. I thought of it shining on the Sound and on the city. It would rise like this long after I was dead. It would glitter on the plastic of my monument and bathe my face with cold light long after you and I, Bellamy, are at peace, our long war with each other ended.

Then I heard Griswold coming. I tried to empty my mind of everything except killing. It was for this that my body and mind had been trained so painfully ever since I was six years old. I breathed deeply a few times. As always, the deep, shrinking fear tried to rise in me. Fear, and something more. Something within me—is it you, Bellamy?—that says I do not really want to kill.

Then Griswold came into sight, and the familiar, hungry hatred made everything all right again.

I do not remember very much about the fight. It all seemed to happen within a single timeless interval, though I suppose it went on for quite a long while. He was suspicious, even as he entered the gate. I thought I had made no sound, but his ears were very sharp and he moved in time to avoid my first shot that should have finished the thing then and there.

It was not a stalk this time. It was a hard, fast, skillful fight. We both wore bulletproof clothing, but we were both wounded before we got close enough to try for each other's heads with steel. He favored a saber and it was longer than my machete. Still, it was an even battle. We had to fight fast, because the noise might draw other Hunters, if there were any in the Park tonight.

But in the end, I killed him.

I took his head. The moon was not yet clear of the high buildings on the other side of the Park and the night was young. I looked up at the calm, proud faces of the immortals along the edge of the Park as I came out with Griswold's head.

I summoned a car. Within minutes I was back in my mansion with my trophy. Before I would let the surgeons treat me I saw that the head was taken to the laboratory for a quick treatment, a very quick preparation. And I sent out orders for a midnight Triumph.

While I lay on the table and the surgeons washed and dressed my wounds, the news was flashing through the city already. My servants were in Griswold's mansion, transferring his collections to my reception hall, setting up extra cases that would hold all my trophies, all True Jonathan Hull's and all of Griswold's too. I would be the most powerful man in New York, under such masters as old Murdoch and one or two more. All my age group and the one above it would be wild with envy and hate. I thought of Lindman and Cowles and laughed with triumph.

I thought it was triumph—then.

I stand now at the head of the staircase, looking down at the lights and the brilliance, the row upon row of trophies, my wives in all their jewels. Servants are moving to the great bronze doors to swing them ponderously open. What will be revealed? The throng of guests, the great Hunters coming to give homage to a greater Hunter? Or—suppose no one has come to my Triumph after all?

The bronze doors are beginning to open. But there'll

be no one outside. I can't be sure yet, but I know it, I'm certain of it. The fear that never leaves a Hunter, except in his last and greatest Triumph, is with me now. Suppose, while I stalked Griswold tonight, some other Hunter has lain in wait for bigger game? Suppose someone has taken old Murdoch's head? Suppose someone else is having a Triumph in New York tonight, a greater Triumph than mine?

The fear is choking me. I've failed. Some other Hunter has beaten me. I'm no good. . . .

No. *No!* Listen. Listen to them shouting my name! Look, look at them pouring in through the opened doors, all the great Hunters and their jewel-flashing women, thronging in to fill the bright hall beneath me. I feared too soon. I was the only Hunter in the Park tonight, after all. So I have won, and this is my Triumph. There they stand among the glittering glass cases, their faces turned up to me, admiring, envious. There's Lindman. There's Cowles. I can read their expressions very, very easily. They can't wait to get me alone tonight and challenge me to a duel in the Park.

They all raise their arms toward me in salute. They shout my name.

Bellamy within—listen! This is our Triumph. It shall never be taken away from us.

I beckon to a servant. He hands me the filled glass that is ready. Now I look down at the Hunters of New York—I look down from the height of my Triumph—and I raise my glass to them.

I drink.

Hunters—you cannot rob me now.

I shall stand proud in plastic, godlike in the eternal block that holds me, all passion spent, all fighting done, my glory assured forever.

The poison works quickly.

This is triumph.

Research is fun for me. At least it's fun when I'm interested in the subject. I don't have warm feelings about the hours I've spent in the Deed Room, checking land titles.

"Calibration Run" required a lot of research, because when I plotted the story, I knew very little about the Pleistocene mammals of Africa. (The fauna was quite different from that of North America at the time, a fact that was so obvious that it escaped a reviewer who took me to task for saying some sabertooths had tails, when North American species didn't.) As I said, the hours I spent learning about hyraxes and giant giraffes were pure pleasure.

What I knew, before I started the story, about the beginnings of mankind was also cursory: newspaper reports of new finds and out-of-date smatterings. I gained new knowledge which shaped "Calibration Run"; and which made the story very disturbing to write.

But moral decisions can be expected to be disturbing.

CALIBRATION RUN

David Drake

The sabertooth sprang from cover just as Vickers bent to pick up the partridge he had shot. Holgar Nilsen had been dynamiting rock samples a hundred yards away. He shouted as he leveled his Mauser. The blond Nilsen would have had an easy shot—except that Vickers' own body blocked the Mauser's line of fire.

The thud of the cat's paws crossing to leap again warned Vickers an instant in advance of Nilsen's cry. The sandy-haired guide was holding his shotgun at the balance, not ready to fire—and not that bird-shot would have affected the 500-pound killer.

The cat swung down its lower jaw, locking out of the way everything extraneous to stabbing with its six-inch upper canines, as it made its third and final leap. Its bared palate was white as bone.

Vickers flung himself backwards, trying desperately to raise the shotgun. The sabertooth's hide was mottled brown on black, its belly cream. As it sprang, its forelegs splayed and the ten black claws shot out of the pads. Every tense muscle of the cat's body quivered in

215

the air. Its weight slammed Vickers' torso against the stony ground while the blast of Nilsen's rifle rumbled about them.

The cat's eyes were a hand's breadth from Vickers' face as they glazed and the life went out of them. A shudder arched the creature's back, rocking the serrated fangs downward. Vickers screamed but the points were not piercing his chest, only compressing it, and the thrust itself was a dying reflex. Blood had been spurting from the cat's throat where the Brenneke bullet had entered. Now the nostrils drooled blood as well and the cat's muscles went limp.

Holgar Nilsen ran to the linked bodies, cursing in Norwegian. Vickers could not breathe. The carcase sagged over him like a bag of rice, pinning him so tightly that he could not move his index finger enough to put the shotgun on safe. The weapon was pressing against his right leg. It would blow his foot off if it fired now. Nilsen tugged at the sabertooth ineffectively, his panic little less than that of his partner trapped under the cat. The big Norwegian was waving his Mauser one-handed while his eyes scanned the brush in quick arcs. "There was another one," he gasped, "the male. But it ran off when I fired."

"Here, let me help," said Linda Weil, dropping the first aid kit to seize one of the sabertooth's fangs. The curved inner edges of the teeth could shear flesh with all the cat's brutal strength behind them, but they did not approximate real knife blades. In any case, the fangs were the only hand-holds available on the slack carcase. Weil was a short, broad-hipped woman. She twisted, using the thrust of her legs against the passive weight of the sabertooth. The great, brown-and-black body slumped away fluidly. Its haunches still covered Vickers' calves. Nilsen stopped groping blindly and looked down. He gripped a clawed foot and rotated the cat's hindquarters away from his partner.

Vickers was sucking deep breaths. His face and tunic front were covered with blood. He put the shotgun on safe and cocked an arm behind him to help him rise.

"No, no," said the dark-haired woman, touching the guide's shoulder with a restraining hand. "Just wait—"

Vickers lurched upright into a sitting position. "I'm all right," he wheezed. Then, "It was my fault. It was all my fault."

"The buckle," said Nilsen. "Look at your pack buckle." The Norwegian's composure was returning. His left index finger touched one strap of the pack Vickers had been wearing to hold small specimens. The steel buckle was warped like foil against its padding where it had blocked the thrust of the sabertooth's fang. The brushing contact of Nilsen's finger caused pain to stab Vickers.

"Damn," muttered the older guide as Linda Weil helped him off with the empty pack and unbuttoned his tunic. The blood that sprayed Vickers was the cat's, but he knew from the pain that he might well have a cracked rib of his own. The female paleontologist's fingers were cool and expert. She had been chosen as an on-site investigator for the Time Intrusion Project as much for her three years of medical school as for her excellent series of digs in the Sinai with a University of Chicago team.

A square mark larger than the buckle's edges was stamped in white above Vickers' left nipple. "I don't hear anything grating," Weil said. "We'll strap it. Maybe when we get back to Tel Aviv they'll want to drain the hematoma."

"It was waiting for me like I was a goddam antelope," Vickers said. He was a stocky man of thirty-five who usually looked as calm as a fireplug. Now he rubbed the back of his hand over the sockets of his pale eyes, smearing the splotches of tacky blood. "Holgar," he said, "I wasn't ready. I wouldn't have had a snowball's chance in Hell except for you."

"Holgar, we'll want the skull and limbs of this macheirodont when you have a chance," said Linda Weil, pointing toward the sabertooth as she stood. She looked back at Vickers before she continued, "And frankly, I think that if anyone's error can be said to have led to this—problem, near disaster—it was mine. Both of you are used to animals that've had hundreds of thousands of years to learn to fear man. That's not the case here. As you said, Henry, we're just meat on the hoof so far as the bigger carnivores here are concerned. *I'm* the one who should have realized that."

Vickers sighed and stood up carefully. He walked over to the spur-legged partridge, ten feet away where he had dropped it when the cat struck. Raising the heavy bird, he gestured with it to Weil. "It's a francolin like the one we got in the snare two days ago," he said. "I thought I'd roast it for dinner instead of keeping it for a specimen."

The dark-haired paleontologist nodded back. "After I get you bandaged," she agreed. "I think we could all do with a meal and a chance to relax."

Hyenas had already begun to call in the sullen dusk. Time spent in the African bush gave the ugly, rhythmic laughter a homely sound to the pair of guides, but Linda Weil shuddered with distaste.

Holgar Nilsen laughed. He patted the paleontologist on the thigh with a greasy hand. "They are only predators like ourselves," he said. "Perhaps we should invite them to join us for dinner one night, yes? We have so much in common."

Weil switched the francolin drumstick to her left hand and squeezed Nilsen against her thigh with her right. "I don't question their right to exist," the woman said. "It's just that I don't like them." She frowned, scientist again. "We could use a specimen, though. There's a good enough series of hyena fossils known Topside that fresh examples ought to be more datable than most of what we've gathered."

"You know," said Vickers, speaking in a conscious effort to break out of the shell of depression that surrounded him, "I've never quite understood what use the specimens we bring back were going to be. For dating, that is. I mean, taking radiation levels from the igneous rocks should give them the time within a few thousand years. And if I understand the Zeiss—" he gestured with his thumb—"its photographs ought to be down to the minute when they're compared to computer models of star and planet positions."

The 200-mm reflector bolted to the intrusion vehicle was lost in the darkness, as was the normal purr of the motor drive that rotated it by microns along the plane of the ecliptic. As Vickers gestured the mechanism gave one of its rare clicks, signalling the end of an exposure as the telescope reset itself to lock on another portion of sky. The click might have been that of a grenade arming for the level of response it drew from Holgar Nilsen, though the younger guide kept the edges of his anger sheathed in bluff camaraderie. "Come, come," he said, "machines fail. Anyway, the sky could have been overcast for months, for years, for all they knew Topside. And for the rock dating to work, they must compare the samples we bring back with samples from the same rock a million years in the future. How are they to be sure of that, hey? When they only *think* so far we are inserted into the same place, with latitude and longitude changing as the continents move."

Vickers nodded, realizing why his partner reacted so defensively. "Sure," he said, "and the more cross-checks, the better. And I suppose the astronomical data is going to be easier to correlate if they've got a fair notion of where to start."

"Besides," said Linda Weil harshly, "I don't think anyone realized quite how useless anything I came back with would be for the intended purpose. Oh, it'll have use—we've enormously expanded human knowledge of Pliocene life-forms. But as you say, Henry, for dating—"

She paused, looking out over the twilit hills. They had been fortunate in that their intrusion vehicle, an angular block of plates and girders, had been inserted onto high ground. During daylight they had a good view over the brush and acacias, the short grass and the beasts that lived there. Now the shadows of the trees and outcrops had merged with the greater shadow of the horizon, and the landscape was melding into a velvet blur. "The whole problem," Weil said toward the darkness, "is that we've got an embarrassment of riches. Before—when I was Topside—a femur was as much as you were likely to get to identify an animal, and a complete skull was a treasure. We decided what the prehistoric biomass looked like by reconstructing a few fragments here, a few fragments there. . . ." She chuckled ruefully and looked back at her male companions. "And here we are, in the middle of thousands and thousands of animals, somewhere in the past I've been studying for years . . . and I'm nowhere near being able to accurately place the time we've been inserted, the way I've been hired to do—because I can't swear that a single species is one that we 'know' from fossils. I feel as if I've spent my working life throwing darts at a map and convincing myself that I've travelled to the places the darts hit."

"Well, you've travelled here, for certain," said the blond man, "and *I* at least am glad of it." He raised his hand to Weil's shoulder and tried to guide the woman closer to him for a kiss.

"Holgar . . . ," the woman objected in a low voice, leaning free of the big hand's pressure.

"I'll get a couple hyenas tomorrow," Vickers said morosely. The fire he stared at glinted from his face where grease from the bird smeared him. "Unless I screw up again, at least. Christ, Holgar, maybe I'd have been better off if you were a second slower with your shot. Hunting's about the one thing I'd decided I could handle. If I'm no good for that either, then I may as well be a cat's dinner." Unwatched, the shorter guide's hands turned and turned again the section of francolin ribs from which he had gnawed only half the flesh.

Nilsen looked disconcerted. He lowered his hand from the paleontologist's back and resumed attacking his meal. Absently, Vickers wished that one of the three of them had had the skill to make gravy to go with the mashed potatoes, freeze-dried and reconstituted.

"Ah, Henry," said Linda Weil, "I think that's just shock talking. You aren't incompetent because of one mistake—it's the mistakes that make us human. The planning for this, this expedition, was mostly yours; and everything's gone very well. Except that all I can really say about the time we're at is that we're a great deal farther back than the round million years they intended to send us."

"You see, Henry," Nilsen said, "what you need is a wife." The Norwegian gestured with the fork he had just cleared of its load of canned peas. "You have no calm center to your life. Wherever I go, I know that my Mary is there in Pretoria, my children are growing— Oskar, Olaf, and little Kristin . . . do you see? That is what you need."

Vickers looked at the bigger man. Nilsen had jarred him out of his depression as Linda Weil had been unable to do with her encouragement. The paleontologist's complexion was dark, but it was no trick of the firelight that led Vickers to see a blush on her face. She looked down at her hands. "Maybe I've been looking in the wrong places," Vickers said dryly. "Your wife is British, if I remember?"

Nilsen nodded vigorously as he chewed another mouthful of peas.

"Both of mine were Americans," the older guide said. "Maybe that's where I went wrong." He turned his face toward the night. His profile was as sharp and thin as a half-worn knife. "The sporting goods store I tried to manage was in Duluth," he continued, "and the ranch was in Rhodesia. But I could hunt, that I could do. Well." He looked at Weil again. In a normal voice he added, "Well, I still can. I'll get you a hyena in the morning."

"Actually," said Weil, visibly glad of the change of subject, "what concerns me more is that something's raiding our box traps. Several of those to the west had the lids sprung when I checked them this morning. The rest were empty. Probably *was* a hyena; I don't think a mongoose would be strong enough. But apart from being interested in whatever's doing it, I'd like to have the damage stopped."

"We could lay a sensor from the intrusion alarm

under one of the traps," Holgar said. His enthusiasm rang a little false. It was a reaction to the embarrassment he finally had realized that his earlier comment had caused. "Sleep close with the shotgun."

"I've got a three-bead night sight on the Garand," Vickers said, the problem reflecting his mind away from the depression that had been smothering him. "I can sandbag the gun and the spotlight a hundred yards away. That ought to be far enough we won't disturb whatever it is." He frowned and turned to Linda Weil. "Thing is, I can't make sure of something at night unless I give it a head shot or use soft-points that'll blow the body apart if it's small. What's your preference?"

The paleontologist waved the question away. "Save the skull if you can," she said. "But—we've just seen how dangerous the predators here—now, that is—can be. Are you going to disconnect the warning system around us?"

"Just move one pick-up," Nilsen said with a laugh. His left fingertips caressed Weil's cheek playfully . "Otherwise you might get a closer and sooner view of a hyena than you expected, no? And what a waste that would be."

Vickers noticed that his hands were still trembling. Just as well the administrators Topside hadn't permitted any liquor among the supplies, he thought. Though usually it wouldn't have mattered to him one way or the other. "It's all right," he said aloud. "I probably won't be sleeping much tonight anyway. Holgar, let's rig something now while there's still enough daylight to work with."

They were forced to finish moving and resetting the nearest of the traps by lamplight after all. When the door mechanism was cocked and the trigger baited with nuts and fruit, Vickers made his own preparations. His rifle was an M1 Garand, modified by a Marine armorer to accept twenty-round BAR magazines. He rested it on a sand-filled pair of his own trousers, its sights aligned on a point just above the center of the

trap. The variable-aperture spotlight was set for a pen-
cil beam and also aimed at the trap. The light should
freeze the trap-robber long enough for Vickers to put a
soft-nosed .30-'06 bullet through its chest.

Around 2 A.M. the alarm rang. It was a hyrax which
had blundered into the trap in search of the nuts. The
Hyracoidea had been driven to holes and the night by
the more efficient grazing animals who followed their
family's Oligocene peak. The little creature in the trap
wiggled its whiskers against the electric glare. Vickers
switched off the spotlight, hoping the live bait would
bring the robber shortly. But to his own surprise, he
managed to fall asleep; and it was dawn rather than the
intrusion alarm that awakened him the second time.

Vickers' neck was stiff and his feet were cold. A
sheen of dew overlay his nylon parka and the fluorocarbon
finish of his rifle's metal surfaces. The fire was dead.
Hot coffee was the only reason to kindle another fire:
the sun would be comfortably warm in an hour, a
hammer in three. But hot coffee was a good enough
reason, God knew, and a fire would be the second
priority.

The flap of the tent which Linda Weil shared with
Nilsen opened while Vickers was still wiping the Garand
with an oily rag. It was a habit ingrained in the hunter
before steel could be protected by space-age polymers.
Caring for the rifle which kept him alive was still
useful as a ritual even if it were no longer a practical
necessity.

"No luck?" asked Weil as she pulled on her jacket in
the open air.

"Well, there's a hyrax," Vickers replied. "I guess
that's to the good. I was about to put on a pot of—"

The intrusion alarm pinged. The hunter looked by
training at the display panel, even though most of the
sensor locations encircling the camp were in plain sight
in the daytime. The light indicating the trap sensor
was pulsing. When Vickers flicked his eyes downhill
toward the trap, the paleontologist's breath had already
drawn in.

The guide rolled silently into a prone position, laying his rifle back across the makeshift sandbag. He looked over but not through the Garand's sights, and his index finger was not on the trigger. Weil was too unfamiliar with guns to appreciate the niceties which differentiate preparations from imminent slaughter. She snatched at Vickers' shoulder and hissed, "Don't shoot!"

The guide half-turned and touched Weil's lips with the fingertips of his left hand. "Are they chimps?" he mouthed, exaggerated lip movements making up for the near soundlessness of his question. "They don't look quite right."

"They're not chimps," Weil replied as quietly. "My God, they're not."

The tent passed Holgar Nilsen with a muted rustle and no other sign. When the intrusion alarm rang, the Norwegian had wasted no time on dressing. Neither of the others looked around. They had set the trap where neither trees nor out-cropping rocks interfered with the vantage, and where most of the mesh box itself was clear of the grass. The blade tips brushed the calves of the three beasts around the trap now. They were hairy enough for chimpanzees, and they were only slightly taller than chimps standing on their hind legs; but these creatures stood as a matter of course, and they walked erect instead of knuckling about on their long forearms like apes.

Vickers uncapped his binoculars and focused them. The slight breeze was from the trap toward the humans up the slope. The beasts did not seem to be aware they were being watched. Their attention was directed toward the trap and its contents.

The hyrax was squealing in high-pitched terror now. The top of the trap was hinged and pegged closed so that it could be baited and emptied without reaching through the heavily-sprung end-gate. The traps that had been raided the day before had simply been torn apart. This one—

The tallest of the—hominids, it didn't mean human, the word was already in all their minds—the tallest of the hominids was a trifle under five feet in height. His scalp was marked by a streak of blond, almost white, fur that set him apart from his solidly dark companions. He was fumbling at the latch. Without speaking, Vickers handed the binoculars to Linda Weil.

"My God," she whispered. "He's learned to open it."

The hyrax leaped as the lid swung up, but the hominid on that side was too quick. A hand caught the little beast in mid-air and snatched it upward. The hominid's teeth were long and startlingly white against the black lips. They snapped on the hyrax's neck, ending the squeals with a click.

The other black-furred hominid growled audibly and tried to grab the hyrax. The white-flashed leader in the middle struck him with an open hand. As the follower sprang back yelping, the leader turned on the one holding the hyrax. Instead of trying to seize the prey directly as the lesser hominid had done, the leader spread his arms wide and burst into angry chattering. His chest was fully expanded and he gained several inches of height by rising onto the balls of his feet.

The smaller hominid's face was toward the watchers. They saw his teeth bare as he snarled back, but the defiance was momentary and itself accompanied by a cringing away from the leader. He dropped the hyrax as if he had forgotten it, turning sideways as he did so. As if there were something in the empty air, the follower began to snap and chitter while the leader picked up the hyrax. The mime continued until the white-flashed hominid gave a satisfied grunt and began stalking off northward, away from the human camp. The other hominids followed, a few yards to either side of the leader and perhaps a pace behind. The posture of all three was slightly stooped, but they walked without any suggestion of bow-leggedness and their forelimbs did not touch the ground. The leader held the hyrax by its neck. Not even the binoculars could detail the position of the hominid's thumb to the paleontologist.

"That's amazing," said Holgar Nilsen. He had dressed

while watching the scene around the trap. Now he was lacing his boots. "They didn't simply devour it."

"Not so surprising," Linda Weil said, the binoculars still at her eyes. "After all, there were more traps in the direction they came from. They're probably full." She lowered the glasses. "We've got to follow them."

"Look at the way they quarrelled over the coney," Nilsen protested. "They're hungry. And it's not natural for hungry animals not to eat a fresh kill."

Vickers eyed the sun and shrugged off his parka. If they were going to be moving, he could get along without the insulation for the present so as not to have to carry the warm bulk later in the day. "All right," he said, "they seem to be foraging as they go. It shouldn't be too hard to keep up, even without a vehicle."

"They should have sent a Land Rover with us," complained the Norwegian guide as he stood, slinging his Mauser. "We are bound to make some changes in the environment, are we not? So how can they worry that a Land Rover would be more of a risk to the, to Topside?"

"Well, we'll manage for now," Vickers said, stuffing a water bottle and several packets of dehydrated rations into his knapsack. Despite the bandage, it felt as though his chest were being ripped apart when he raised his arm to don the pack. He kept his face still, but beads of sweat glittered suddenly at the edge of his sandy hair. "I think it's as well that we all go together," Vickers added after a moment to catch his breath. "There's nothing here that animals can hurt and we can't replace; and I'm not sure what we may be getting into."

The three hominids were out of sight beyond one of the hills before their pursuers left camp. Both men carried their rifles. The paleontologist had refused the autoloading shotgun, saying that she didn't know how to use it so it would only be in her way. Weil and the younger guide began pressing ahead at a near run through the rust and green grass. Vickers was more nervously aware than the others of the indigenous predators lurking in these wilds. Aloud he said, "Don't be impatient. They're not moving fast, and if we blunder

into them over a rise, we'll spook them sure." Nilsen
nodded. Linda Weil grimaced, but she too moderated
her pace when the guides hung back.

At the looted trap, the paleontologist herself paused.
Vickers glanced around for a sign, but the ground was
too firm to show anything that could be called a foot-
print. Dark smudges on the otherwise dew-glittering
grass led off in the direction the hominids had taken,
but that track would stand less than an hour of the sun's
growing weight.

Weil turned from the trap. "What's this?" she demanded, pointing. "Did you bring this here when you
set the trap?"

Nilsen frowned. "It's just a piece of branch," he said.

"Holgar, there's no tree within fifty yards," said Vickers
quietly. To the paleontologist he added, "It was pretty
dark when we set up the trap. I probably wouldn't have
noticed it anyway. But I didn't see any of the—others—
carrying it either. For now it's just three feet of acacia
branch, broken at both ends."

Weil nodded curtly. She uncapped her neck-slung
camera and took several exposures of the trap and the
branch lying beside it. She did not touch either object.
"Let's go," she said and began striding along the dim
trail again at almost the pace she had set at the start.

When they crested the next rise, even Vickers felt a
momentary concern that they might have lost their
quarry. Then he caught the flash of sun on blond fur a
quarter mile away and pointed. They watched through
their binoculars as two, then all three hominids moved
about the trunk of a large tree.

"They're trying to dig something out of a hole at the
root of the tree," Vickers said, "and I'll swear they're
using a stick to do it." Then he added, "Of course, a
chimpanzee might do the same thing. . . ."

"Linda," said Holgar Nilsen, "what are these creatures?" He rubbed his forehead with the back of the
hand holding his binoculars. His right thumb tensioned
the sling of his rifle.

Linda Weil at first gave no sign that she had heard

the question. The blond guide's eyes remained fixed on her. At last she lowered her glasses and said, "I suppose that depends on when we are. If we're as far back as preliminary indications suggest we are, those are ramapithecines. Primates ancestral to a number of other primate lines, including our own." She would not meet Nilsen's stare.

"They're men, aren't they?" the younger guide demanded.

" 'Men' isn't a technical term!" snapped the paleontologist, raising her chin. "If you mean, 'They belong to the genus Homo, I'd have to say no, I don't believe they do. Not yet. But we don't have any data." She spun to glare at Vickers. "Do you see?" she went on. "What a, what a laughingstock I'll be if I go back from my first time intrusion and say, 'Well, I've found the earliest men for you, here's a smudgy picture from a mile away'? They drove Dubois into *seclusion* for finding Java Man without an engraved pedigree!"

Vickers shrugged. "Well," he said, "it isn't anything that we need to jump the gun about."

Licking their fingers—the leader still carried the hyrax—the hominids wandered away from the trees again. Weil snapped several photographs, but her camera had only a lens selected for close-ups of animals too large to carry back whole.

The landscape itself was beyond any camera, and the profusion of life awakening with the dawn was incredible. Vickers had been raised on stories of the great days of African hunting, but not even Africa before the advent of nitro powders and jacketed bullets could equal the animate mass that now covered what some day would be Israel. Standing belly-deep in the grass they cropped were several species of hipparion, three-toed horses whose heads looked big for their stocky bodies. The smallest of them bore black and white stripes horizontally on their haunches. When the stripes caught sunlight at the correct angle, the beasts stood out as candid blazes. The horses were clumped in bodies of twenty to forty, each body separated from the others by a few hundred yards. These agglomerations could not be called herds in the normal sense, for they mixed hipparions of distinctly different sizes and coloration.

Indeed, antelopes of many varieties were blended promiscuously among the hipparions as well. Vickers had vaguely expected to see bovids with multiple, fanciful horns during the intrusion. Linda Weil had disabused him with a snort. She followed the snort with a brief disquisition on the Eurasian Cenozoic and the ways it could be expected to differ from the North American habitat which the popularizers were fonder of describing.

Oryx had proven to be the most common genus of antelope in the immediate area, though the region was better-watered than those Topside which the curved-horned antelopes frequented. There were other unexpected antelopes also. On the first day of the intrusion Nilsen had shot a tragelaphine which seemed to Vickers to differ from the rare inyala of Mozambique only in its habits: the lyre-horned buck had stared at the rifle in bland indifference instead of flashing away as if stung.

The hominids were moving on; the human trio followed. Weil was leading as before but Holgar Nilsen had begun to hang back. Vickers glanced at the younger man but did not speak. In the near distance, a buffalo bellowed. The guides had scouted the reed-choked bottom a mile away, beyond another range of undulations, but they had not actively hunted it yet. Earlier, the dark-haired paleontologist had commented that a sampling of bovine skulls and horn-cores might be helpful in calibrating their intrusion. Vickers nodded toward the sound. "On our way back," he suggested, "if it's late enough that the buffs have come back out of the reeds after their siesta, we might try to nail you some specimens."

"For God's sake, let's not worry about that now!" snapped Weil. She stumbled on a lump of exposed quartz which her eyes, focused on the meandering hominids, had missed. Vickers had guided tourist hunters for too many years to think that he had to respond.

The clumps of grazing animals seemed to drift aside as the hominids straggled past, but the relative movement was no more evidently hostile than that of pedestrians on a crowded street. Still, when one of the hominids passed within a few yards of a group resting under a tree, up started a 400-pound antelope of a genus with which Vickers was not familiar. After a hundred yards the antelope turned and lowered its short, thick-based horns before finally subsiding beneath another tree. A jackal might have aroused the same reaction.

The hominids had skewed their course twice and were now headed distinctly southward, though they still gave no evidence of purpose. "Reached the end of their range and going back," Holgar Nilsen said. He spoke in a tone of professional appraisal, normal under the circumstances, and not the edged breathiness with which he had earlier questioned the paleontologist. "Do we still follow them?"

Linda Weil nodded, subdued herself by embarrassment over her outbursts at the two guides. "Yes, but I want to see what they were doing at the base of this tree first," she said, nodding toward the acacia ten yards away. She unlimbered her camera in anticipation.

Vickers stopped her by touching her elbow. "I think we can guess," he said quietly, "and I think we'd better guess from here. Those bees look pretty peeved."

"Ah," Weil agreed. The dots flashing metallically as they circled in and out of the shade crystallized in her mind into a score or more of yellow-bodied insects. Fresh dirt of a pale reddish tinge had been turned between a pair of surface roots. The stick that had done the digging was still in the hole. Up and down it crawled more of the angry bees. "Surely they aren't immune to bee-stings, are they?" the woman asked.

Vickers shrugged, wincing at the pressure in his chest. "I'm not immune to thorn scratches," he said. "But if I'm after an animal in heavy brush, that's part of the cost of doing business."

The hominids were almost out of sight again. "We'd

best keep going," said the paleontologist, acting as she spoke.

While they walked uphill again, Vickers swigged water and handed his bottle around. The water was already hot from the sun on his dun knapsack, and the halogens with which it had been cleared gave it an unpleasant tang. Neither of Vickers' companions bothered to comment on the fact.

"This is where we got the horses two days ago," Nilsen said, gesturing toward the low ridge they were approaching.

Vickers thought back. "Right," he said. "We got here due west from the bottom of the trapline. We've just closed the circuit in the other direction, is all."

They heard the growling even before they crested the rise. Nilsen unslung his Mauser. Vickers touched Linda Weil to halt her. He knelt to charge his Garand, using the slope of the ground to deflect the sound of the bolt slapping the breech as it chambered the first round of twenty. The paleontologist's face was as tense as those of the guides. "All right," Vickers whispered, "but we'll keep low."

In a swale a quarter mile from their present vantage point, Vickers had dropped a male hipparion. It was large for its genus; a good 400 pounds had remained to the carcase after the hunters had removed the head and two legs for identification. Hyenas are carnivores no less active than the cats with which they share their ranges, but virtually no carnivore will refuse what carrion comes its way. A pack of hyenas had found the dead horse. They were still there, wrangling over scraps of flesh and the uncracked bones, as the hominids approached the kill. The snarls that the intrusion team heard were the warning with which the hyenas greeted the newcomers.

"We've got to help them," said Nilsen.

Vickers glanced at the junior guide out of the corner of his eye. He was shocked to see that Nilsen was watching over his electronic sight instead of through his binoculars. "Hey, put that down!" Vickers said. "Christ, shooting now'd screw up everything."

"They'll be killed!" the Norwegian retorted, as if that were an answer.

"They know what they're doing a whole lot better than we do," Vickers said, and at least on that the men could agree.

There were six of the shaggy carnivores. Two of them paced between the remains of the hipparion and the hominids who gingerly approached it. "I'd have thought they'd be denned up at this time of day," Vickers muttered. "When you don't know the animal, its habits don't surprise you. . . . But those'd pass for spotted hyenas Topside without a word. Damned big ones, too. They ought to act like the hyenas we know."

At the distance and through the foreshortening of the binoculars, it was impossible to tell for certain how near the hominids had come to the kill. The foremost of the brindled hyenas was surely no more than twenty feet from the hominid leader. The carnivore turned face-on and growled, showing teeth that splintered bones and a neck swollen with muscles like a lion's. Holgar Nilsen gasped. His hand sought again the pistol grip of his slung rifle.

The white-flashed hominid jabbered shrilly. He squatted down. The hyrax was still clutched in his left hand, but with his right he began to sling handfuls of dirt and pebbles at the hyena. To either side, the other hominids were also chattering and leaping stiff-legged. One hominid held a rock in each hand and was clashing them together at the top of each jump.

The pelted hyena only snarled back. Its nearest companion retreated a few paces to the scattered carcass, its brushy tail lifted as if to make up for the weakness of the sloping hindquarters. The other four members of the pack were lying on their bellies in a loose arc behind the hipparion. One of them got to its feet nervously.

The empty-handed hominid suddenly darted toward the carcass. He almost touched the ribs, streaked white and dark red with the flesh still articulating them. The nearest hyena leaped up snapping. Its jaws thumped the air as if a book had been slammed. The hominid jumped sideways with a shriek to avoid the teeth, then cut to the other side as the foremost hyena rushed him from behind. Sprinting, the hominid retreated to his starting position with the snarling hyena behind him.

The hominid doubled in back of his leader, still squealing. The carnivore skidded to a halt. The white-flashed leader had dropped the hyrax at last. He hunched with his head thrown forward and his arms spread like a Sumo wrestler's. Each hand was bunched around a heavy stone, held in a power grip between the palm and the four fingers. Unnoticed by the watching humans, the leader had prepared for this moment. The angle hid the hominid's bared teeth from the watchers, but his hissing snarl carried back to them on the breeze.

Only the one hyena had followed through on its rush; now it faced the three hominids alone. Snarling again to show teeth as large as the first joint of a man's thumb, the carnivore backed away. The white-furred hominid hurled a rock that thumped the hyena in the ribs. The beast snapped and snarled, but it would neither attack nor leave its position between the carcase and the hominids. Its powerful shoulders remained turned toward its opponents while its hind legs sidled back and forth nervously, displaying first one spotted flank and then the other to the watching humans. Making as much noise as a flock of starlings, the hominids also retreated. At a safe distance from the hipparion carcase and its protectors, they turned and resumed their leisurely meander southward. The hominid with the pair of stones continued to strike them together occasionally, though without the earlier savage insistence. Chips spalled from the dense quartz glinted like sparks in the air.

Holgar Nilsen let out his breath slowly. Linda Weil lowered her binoculars and said, "Holgar, what's gotten into you? I *know* why *I'm* so tense."

The Norwegian scowled. Vickers glanced at him and then raised his glasses again. He did not know how personal the conversation was about to become. "I—" said the blond man. Then, "Hyenas are terrible killers. I've seen what they can do to children and even to a grown man who'd broken his leg in the bush."

"Well, we're here as observers, aren't we?" said the paleontologist. "I don't understand." Nilsen turned away from her gaze and did not reply. The woman shrugged. "We need to be moving on," she said. Her face, like that of the younger guide, was troubled.

The hyenas had disappeared back into shallow burrows they had dug around the site of the kill. The humans skirted them at a distance, knowing that another outburst might call the hominids back from the rise over which they had disappeared. "Sort of a shame not to bag one now when we know where they are," Vickers said regretfully as he glanced toward the hipparion. The ribs stood up like a beacon. "I'd expected to be stuck with a night shot . . . and nobody's as good in the dark, I don't care what his equipment is." Neither of the others made any response.

No unusual noise gave warning as the intrusion team neared the next crest, but Holgar Nilsen halted them with a raised hand anyway. "They turned their direction to go where they knew carrion was, the horse carcass," he said. The senior guide nodded, pleased to hear his partner use his flawless sense of direction. "But if they are making a large circle, so to speak, and they have been looting our traps west of the camp, then we must be close to where they started."

Nilsen's logic was good; all three made the obvious response. Both men tautened their rifle and binocular straps and got down on their hands and knees. Since the grass was thick and over a foot high, there was no need to go into a true low crawl with their weapons laid across crooked elbows. The paleontologist looked dubious, but she followed suit. Her camera finally had to be tucked into the waist band of her trousers. The ground, prickly with grass spikes and flakes of stone, slowed their progress more than did concern over security.

The hominid camp was in a clump of acacias less than 200 yards down the next slope.

"Oh, the lord have mercy," whispered Nilsen in Norwegian as his eyes adjusted to the pool of shade on which he focused his binoculars. It was hard to tell how many of the hominids were present; anything from a dozen to twenty was possible. Clumps of grass, shadows, and the emerald globes of young acacias interfered with visibility. The three hominids which the intrusion team had been following were standing. The white-flashed leader himself was the center of a clamoring mass of females and infants. Vickers noted that although many hands were stretched out toward the leader and the prey he carried, neither was actually touched by the suppliants.

Much of the confusion died down after a few minutes. The smaller hominids made way or were elbowed aside by additional males. Their external genitalia were obvious, though the flat dugs of the females were hidden by their fur. Most of the males were empty-handed, but one of them was dragging forward what could only be the femur of a sivatherium. The bone was too massive even for the molars of the great hyenas; in time it would have been gnawed away by rodents, but nothing of a size to matter would have disputed its possession with the hominids. Vickers frowned, trying to imagine what the latter with the relatively small jaws expected to do with a bone which was beyond the range of hyenas and the big cats.

But the troop's first order of business was the hyrax. It provided a demonstration that the jaws and limbs of the hominids were by no means despicable themselves. The leader gripped the little animal with his teeth and systematically plucked it apart with his hands. One of the males reached in for a piece. The leader cuffed him away and dropped the hyrax long enough to jabber a stream of obvious abuse at the usurper. With something approaching ceremony, the leader then handed the fleshy hind legs to two males. Despite the confusion, Vickers was sure that at least one of them had been a companion of the leader during the morning's circuit.

Dignity satisfied, the white-flashed hominid continued parcelling out the hyrax. The leader's motions were precise; each twist or slash of nails that still resembled claws stripped away another fragment. As each hominid received a portion, he or she—a foreleg had gone early to a dun-furred nursing mother—stepped back out of the ruck. There was some squabbling as members of the troop bolted their allotments, but Vickers did not notice anyone's share actually hijacked.

"Nineteen with him," Linda Weil counted aloud as the leader stood alone in the widened circle of his juniors. Every member of the troop—Vickers found he had an uneasy tendency to think 'tribe'—every member of the troop had been given a portion of the hyrax. The leader held only the head and a bloody tendril of hide still clinging to it. With a croak of triumph the leader bent and picked up the lump of quartz he had carried since the encounter with the hyenas. He rotated the hyrax head awkwardly with his thumb, then brought his two hands together with a resounding *smack*. Dropping the stone again, the leader began to slurp the brains greedily.

"God damn it, you know they're men," Holgar Nilsen whispered hoarsely.

"It's nothing more than sea otters do," the paleontologist replied, but she kept the glasses to her eyes and would not face her lover.

Vickers looked from the one to the other, Weil tense, Nilsen angry. "I don't think otters share out meat like that," Vickers said. "I don't think I've ever seen animals share out meat that well. Maybe wolves do." He paused before adding, "That doesn't mean they're not animals."

The hyrax was a memory, though a memory that had provided each hominid with a good four ounces of flesh in addition to whatever protein individuals might have scavenged for themselves during the morning. Now the

females were bringing out the results of their own
gathering: roots and probably locust pods, though it was
hard to be sure through the binoculars. Females appeared to be approaching males one on one, though the
distinguishing marks of most hominids were too subtle
for immediate certainty. The dun-colored mother and
an adolescent female whose pelt was a similar shade
stood to either side of the leader, cooing and attempting to groom his fur as they offered tubers of some
kind.

But the males had not completed their own program
as yet. The leader barked something which must have
been more in the line of permission than a command.
Two of the males responded almost before the syllable
was complete, squatting down and chopping furiously
with rocks gripped in either fist.

"I can't see them!" Linda Weil said.

Vickers looked at her. Grass blurred all but the heads
and flailing arms of the squatting hominids. The *crack!*
of stone on bone denser than teak ricocheted up to the
watchers. "Ah, they're breaking up the giraffe thigh
with rocks," the guide said.

"I know that!" snapped the paleontologist. "Of course
they are! And I can't see it!"

Long flakes of bone were spitting upward, catching
stray darts of sunlight that made them momentary jewels. The remaining hominids surrounded the activity in
a chattering circle, the nuts and tubers forgotten. Occasionally one of the onlookers might snatch at a splinter
of bone which would quickly be cast aside again after a
perfunctory mumbling.

Linda Weil stood up, holding her camera.

The motion drew the eyes of one hominid. His chirp
focused every head in the troop. It was the minuscule
whirr of the camera that set off the explosion, however.
The hominids fanned forward like a rifle platoon, the
half-dozen adult males serried out in front while the
young and females filled the interstices a pace or two
behind. Even at a distance, their racket was considerable. Each throat was snarling out a single, repetitive

syllable as loudly as the lungs beneath could drive it. Some of the females threw handfuls of dirt. It pelted the backs of the males, only the wind-blown dust carrying any considerable distance toward the humans.

The males were not throwing anything. For a further icy instant, Vickers studied their hands through the binoculars. Then he dropped the glasses onto their strap and unslung his Garand. One or both fists of each male hominid bulged with a block of stone. The whole troop was beginning to advance.

"Holgar," Vickers said without taking his eyes off the hominids, "you and Miss Weil strike for camp right now. I'm going to follow just as quick as it's safe. *Right now!*"

Both Nilsen and the paleontologist turned to speak, so it was the senior guide alone who saw the rush of the sabertooth from the instant it burst from cover. Dirt flew as the cat's paws hit, its legs doubling under as its spine flexed to fire it along on another leap. In motion, the sabertooth's mottled body looked so large that it was incredible that it could have sheltered behind the small acacia from which it had sprung. Even more amazing was the fact that it had reached the acacia, for the grass to a considerable distance in every direction seemed sparse and featureless.

Despite their noise and apparent concentration, the hominids saw the sabertooth almost as quickly as Vickers did. They had reacted to the humans as if to a territorial challenge; the response evoked by the big cat was one of blind panic. The orchestrated threats dissolved into patternless shrieking. The individual hominids, even the leader, blasted away like shot from a cylinder bore.

The sabertooth was only a leap from its victim, the dun mother. Nothing the troop could have done at that point would have made the least difference.

Nilsen's Mauser was fitted with an electronic-bead sight, awesomely fast for a shooter trained in its use. The rifle was up and on and as suddenly wrestled away as Linda Weil lunged at it. "No!" the paleontologist shouted. "No! *Don't—*"

The dun hominid knew she had been chosen. She plucked off the infant which clung to her with all the strength of its tiny arms. The nearest member of the troop was the adolescent female, possibly an older daughter. To her, poised between love and terror ten feet away, the mother hurled her infant. Then, at the last possible moment, the mother cut against the grain of the charge with an agility that could scarcely have been bettered.

It was not enough. The macheirodont twisted. It was unable to flesh its teeth as it intended, but its splayed forepaws commanded a swath six feet broad. The right paw smacked the hominid in the middle of the chest. Four of the five claws hooked solidly and spun the light hominid into the path along which the killer's momentum carried it. The jaws crunched closed. One of the long canines stabbed through a shoulder blade to bulge the dimple at the base of the victim's throat.

The surviving hominids had regrouped and were scampering away westward like wind-scud. Vickers retrieved his binoculars. The adolescent had already passed her burden onto an adult female without an infant of her own. The males were bringing up the rear of the troop, but the looks they cast over their shoulders as they retreated were more anxious than threatening. The leader still carried the block of quartz he had found near the hyenas. All the rest had dropped their weapons in the panic. The leader continued to call out, his voice a harsh lash driving the troop. Behind them, the sabertooth had begun to feast noisily.

"If you'd shot," Linda Weil was shouting, "it'd be the last time they'd let us get within a mile of them! They're *smart*, I tell you. Smart enough to connect a noise we make with things falling dead!"

The big Norwegian had wrenched away his rifle too late to shoot to any purpose. He stood with the Mauser waist high, half shielded by his body as if he expected the paleontologist to snatch at the weapon again. "It's all right for *you* to frighten them!" the guide shouted back. "When I want to save their lives, what then? You scream, you prevent me! Look at that—" he waved toward the blood-splashed grass beneath the acacias, the muzzle of his rifle quivering as he released the fore-end to gesture. "That could be the end of our race down there!"

After a quick glance at his companions, Vickers had resumed giving his attention to the scene focused in his glasses. Neither of the humans appeared to be immediately dangerous, and the big cat certainly was. It was ripping its prey apart by mouthfuls, pulling against stiff forelegs which pinned the small carcase to the ground. The hominid's bones affected the killer no more than a sardine's bones affect a hungry human. The cat was obviously aware of the humans watching it, but for the moment it had food and did not feel threatened.

"We aren't here to save animals," Weil said, pitching her voice normally in contrast to the shouts she had exchanged with Nilsen a few moments before. "We're here to observe them. Those, ah, primates reacted to me as they would to another troop of primates—display, threats—warnings, that's all. They'll continue to let me come close enough to observe. But if you'd shot, from then on they'd have reacted to us the way they did to the macheirodont—and I damned well doubt any of us can stalk the way that cat did!"

Holgar Nilsen's face was red beneath his hat brim. He turned and spat, knocking dust from the heads of brazen oat-grass. "Observe?" he said. "Meddle! You're going to meddle us all out of existence!"

"It's already been a pretty long day, as early as we started," Vickers suggested with what was for him unusual diplomacy. "I think we've seen about all we're going to see today . . . and if we're going to discuss it, I'd rather it was after a meal and coffee. A lot of coffee."

Vickers led his sullen companions back past the looted trapline. He was not sure whether either of the others noticed that three of the traps were still set, even though the tops of all of them had been unlatched. Since the bait was still there, it meant that the hominids had opened the traps purely for fun.

*   *   *

"All right," said Holgar Nilsen, "I'll tell you just what's bothering me." The blond man's concern had not affected his appetite. He gestured with the remnants of his hipparion chop, an experiment which the others were willing to call a failure. "You play games with me with words, but these *are* men we've found. What I am saying is, what if these are the only ones? What if we do something that gets them all killed? Like we did this morning, drawing their attention to something that shouldn't be in this, in this time at all so that they don't see the tiger waiting to kill them!"

Weil raised her hands in frustration. "I couldn't guess within a million years what time we've been inserted into, Holgar," she said. "You know that. The chances of us being landed on exactly the right time and place to find the absolutely earliest individuals who could be called human—that's absurd! Now, I'm not saying the troop we've observed isn't typical of the earliest, well . . . men."

Vickers swallowed the bite of coarse, musky hipparion flesh he had been chewing for some time. "That's fine, what you say about likelihood," he said quietly. "But I suppose there had to be a first some time. It's an open secret, in the Project at least, that the reason some of the brass Topside are so excited about time intrusion is the chance that it *will* turn out to be possible to change the past."

"You're both still looking for the missing link!" the paleontologist said with more acid than she had intended to show. "There isn't any such thing, isn't, wasn't, whatever. There were at least three primate stocks we know about that could have and would have become homo sapiens in time. One of them did—and both the others, australopithecus and homo habilis so called, were thought to have been direct ancestors during your lifetime and mine. They could have been, they were that close; and if it weren't for competition from our own stock, one or the other of them would certainly

have evolved into a higher hominid that you couldn't
tell from your next-door neighbor."

The younger guide's face was still as a death mask.
"That's all very well," he said, "but would they *be* my
next-door neighbor? Would they *be* my wife, my children? Will there be my farm in the Transvaal as I left it
if we upset the, the past that all that grows from? This
cosmic viewpoint is very scientific, no doubt, but *I* at
least am human!"

Linda Weil swallowed with difficulty though her mouth
held nothing but saliva. "I—" she said. Then, "Holgar,
don't let's talk about this now. I can see you're upset
and I, I'm upset also. This is . . . this is a very big
opportunity for me. I shiver when I think how big an
opportunity it is."

Nilsen looked at her silently, then tossed the rib
bone toward the coals. Ash spurted and the rib spun off
into the grass beyond. "I'm going to shoot a hyena," the
guide said, wiping grease from his hands on the grass.
He gripped his Mauser and stood. They had been eating as they always did, beneath a nylon fly. Sunlight
now bisected the tall man diagonally. "Or perhaps you
want as many as possible carnivores left alive, now, to
kill men?"

Weil's forehead scrunched up, but she would not
call to the Norwegian as he walked away. Vickers said,
"Look, Holgar, hang on a moment and I'll—"

Nilsen's head spun around. "No thank you!" he
said. "I will take no risks—we are both aware of how
dangerous the land is now, are we not? But I will do
this thing alone, thank you."

Vickers shrugged. Technically the younger man was
his subordinate, but they were several million years
from any further chain of command. Vickers' own bad
experience the day before did not make Nilsen's pro-
posal unreasonable. Only the situation was unreasonable, and that wasn't something Vickers could help the
Norwegian with. "All right," he said, "but call in every
half hour on the radio."

The blond man nodded but did not turn around again as he stalked off.

Linda Weil cursed in a dull voice. She looked at the forkful of meat she was holding and put it down again. "Vickers," she said, then paused to clear her throat. "Ah, Henry, I'll need a specimen of these primates before we go back."

The guide met her eyes while continuing to chew. "Tell you the truth," he said, "I don't know that I'm ready to shoot anything quite that, ah, anthropoid, without a good reason. What do you need a specimen for?"

"Oh, of course killing one was out of the question," the paleontologist said. Vickers continued to look at her, blinking but not speaking. Touching her tongue to her lips, Weil went on, "The specimens would be for the same purpose as the others that we've gathered, dating. . . . We're probably dealing with an advanced ramapithecus. I think that's the safest assumption. But a careful examination of dentition and cranial capacity, plus the knee and pelvic joints in particular, could . . . well, it's—possible—that the primates we've observed could really belong in the genus homo after all. If we knew that, we'd know as much about when we are as those macheirodont specimens, for instance, can tell us. Among other things."

Vickers' face softened in a tired grin. "So in terms of the task I've been sent to aid you in," he said, "you're justified in ordering me to help gather primate specimens. You can burn me with the administration Topside if I start—having qualms the way Holgar seems to be."

The woman scowled and looked away. "I'm not threatening you," she said. "You're not the sort who needs to be threatened to get him to do his job—are you? I'm just pointing out that it *is* your job, that yes, I *am* the one who has final say over what specimens are to be collected. That's why they sent a paleontologist."

"All right," said Vickers, "but if you had a notion of retrieving that sabertooth's kill, you can forget it." He stood up and walked to the edge of the fly, where he could observe the tiny dots that were vultures a thousand feet above the plain.

"Umm?"

"Our friend treated it just like a cat with a field mouse," the guide explained. "Ate the whole head while I watched it. Its mate would likely have done the same thing with me—if it hadn't been for Holgar." He paused. "You might find the knee joints. I wouldn't count on anything much higher up."

"Oh," the paleontologist said, her careful eyes on the guide's back. "Well, to tell the truth, that wasn't really what I had in mind anyway." After a moment, Vickers turned around. Weil continued, "There's nothing we need to know that can't be learned as well or better from X-rays of a living specimen. Without hurting it a bit. All we have to do is carry one back Topside."

"Jesus," said the guide in disbelief. "Jesus Christ." He spread his hands, then closed them and looked away from the dark-haired woman. "Did it ever occur to you," he said, speaking toward the heat-shimmer above the fire, "that Holgar could be right? That we mess up this, this *present*, and when we get back Topside there's nothing there?" He jerked his head back to look at Weil. "Or that what is there is as different from us as baboons are from chimps? Does that bother you?"

"It doesn't bother me," Linda Weil said calmly, "because it's absurd. I'm bothered by the realistic problems of completing my task. That's all."

Vickers smiled again. "That's really all?" he asked, letting his eyes brush Nilsen's empty camp stool.

The woman blushed, a dark rush of blood to a face already as tan as Vickers'. "That's neither here nor there!" she said. "Now, how can we capture a specimen?"

"Oh, there's ways," the guide said. He put his hands in his hip pockets and turned away once more. For a moment he whistled snatches of "Blue Water Line" through his teeth. "Yeah, there's ways," he continued, "although it'll be a lot easier if we can get Holgar to cooperate."

"He'll cooperate," Linda Weil said grimly. "I'm going back with my specimen. His choice is whether it comes aboard in a cage or gets packed in sealant like the rest."

"I got two," Nilsen said, thumbing toward the bloody tangle on the collapsible sled he was drawing. "A male and a female, I wanted. But when I dressed them out, both were pregnant, so I just left the other with the offal."

Vickers glanced at what was left of the hyena. For specimen purposes and the need to pack it in alone on the titanium sled, Nilsen had used a heavy-bladed knife to strip the beast to head, spine, and limbs. The ribs, hide, and the whole abdominal cavity had been abandoned at the kill site as useless; and for that matter, this was about the first use Vickers had heard of for any part of a dead hyena. "Just about impossible to sex a hyena, even after you open them up," he agreed. "I know people to this day who'll swear they're hermaphroditic, that if you shut two males in a cage for a week, one'll change so they can screw." Vickers' eyes, but not the Norwegian's, flickered toward the intrusion vehicle where Linda Weil occupied herself with a microfiche catalog of the Pliocene specimens known Topside.

"Well," said Nilsen. He dropped the tow line and walked toward the frame-supported drum which stored their water. It was pumped through plastic line from the stream a thousand feet east of them. The spigot could be adjusted to dribble sun-heated water in an adequate shower. The younger guide leaned his rifle against the trestle set there for the purpose, out of the splash but in easy reach if occasion demanded it. Vickers nodded in approval. The Mauser chambered powerful 9.3 by 64 mm cartridges. Needlessly big for hyena, perhaps . . . but both the hunters were of the school that used what worked for them; and if their tastes were radically different, then they were alike in their scorn for purists who could not hunt without a battery of a dozen guns.

"Ah, Holgar," the senior guide said, knowing that he had to be the one to broach the subject but increasingly uncomfortable with his role, "I think we have to talk about this hominid business."

"I don't want to talk about it," Nilsen said, unzipping his filthy trousers and hanging them on the trestle.

"Well, I don't know that I do either," said Vickers, "but I guess that isn't an option." He picked up the sprayer he had filled when Nilsen approached the camp. It was Vickers' task to seal the specimen since his partner had done the even messier job of dressing it out. More important, the work gave Vickers something to do with his hands. The stripped carcase was already black with flies, but the sealant would suffocate those it did not drive away. Vickers began to pump. Raising his voice to compensate for distance and the spatter of water, he continued, "While you were getting the hyena, we rigged a net trap down by our water supply. There's a grove of locust trees there, and when we knew what to look for we found plenty of sign that the, the hominids were gathering pods. Maybe the troop we saw, maybe another one. It's hard to guess what their ranges are."

"We ought to leave them strictly alone," the younger man said distinctly. "We ought to get out of here at once, go back on the intrusion vehicle before we do irreparable harm. If we haven't already done irreparable harm." He twisted off the spigot and stepped barefoot away from the muddy patch under the tank.

Vickers set down the sprayer but did not immediately turn the specimen over to cover the other side. "Yeah," he said. "Well. Look, Holgar, we're not going to hurt anything, we're going to capture one ape to study." The sandy-haired man did not at the moment mention Weil's intention of carrying the specimen back Topside. "You know goddam well yourself from baboons that we could take a lot more than that on a one-shot basis and you wouldn't be able to tell the difference in five years' time."

Nilsen was toweling himself off without speaking.

Vickers noticed that Linda Weil, a hundred feet away, was no longer even pretending not to be watching the men from the platform. Sucking on his lips in frustration, Vickers went on, "I cut a section off the end of the drive net we used for small animals. We've got it sprung between a pair of trees; and it's command-released so there's no chance of it being tripped by a pig or going off when the, the hominid we want's in a position to maybe get hurt. But that means that one of us has to be watching it in the morning when the foragers are out."

The younger guide left his bloody, sweat-stained clothes hanging and padded back toward the tent and his foot locker. "Holgar," Vickers said, trying to control the tremor in his voice. His skin prickled on the inside with the dry anger he had not felt since his second wife left him. "I'm talking to you. Don't walk away like that."

The Norwegian turned at the tent flap, rolled up during the day. "You haven't said a thing that touches me, you know," he said. "Not a damned thing."

"The *hell* it doesn't touch you!" the older man shouted back. "Somebody's got to watch the trap, and somebody's got to squire Linda around tomorrow. She wants to poke through their old camp and see if she can locate the new one. . . . And that's her *business*! Now, you can do whichever you want, but if you think you're going to pretend you're nowhere around—look, buddy, I wouldn't have to be a lot madder than I am before I'll put a soft-nose through the chest of one of the god-damned animals and get a specimen that way. We've got jobs to do, and sulking like a little kid who didn't get the bike he wanted for Christmas doesn't cut it!"

The bigger man slung his towel to the ground between them as if it were a gage of battle. "That slut up there," he shouted, "she has everything to gain from meddling, does she not? And you—I know you, I've watched you—you have nothing to lose, that's your trouble. But what about me and all the people like me? When we get back Topside, will it be all right for us if everything is the same—except the people all have purple skins and tails?"

"Holgar, you've heard the options," Vickers said in a voice as hard as a gunlock.

"All right, I'll mind the trap!" Nilsen stormed. "You didn't really think I'd go off with her, did you?" Still nude, the Norwegian snatched up his sleeping bag in one hand and his foot locker in the other, dragging them out of the tent. "And may God have mercy on your souls!"

"Yeah," said Vickers tiredly. "We all need a little mercy." He walked away from the half-prepared hyena, scanning the horizon. He wished he saw something there that he had an excuse to kill.

"Will the macheirodus still be at the camp site?" Linda Weil whispered in the near darkness.

"Possibly," Vickers said, more concerned with his footing than he was with the question. Early morning had seemed a likely time to observe hominids revisiting their former camp, so the guide and paleontologist had set out as soon as there was enough light to shoot by. "Frankly, I'm a lot more worried that it may be somewhere between here and there."

"Oh," Weil said. Then, "Oh—*that's* what you meant when you said we couldn't leave before you could see to shoot."

The guide looked over his shoulder. "Good lord, yes," he said in amazement. "You didn't think I was planning to shoot one of *them*, did you?"

There was more sky-light now than there had been only minutes before. The paleontologist stepped around Vickers and a thorny shrub without pausing. "I don't interfere with the hunting decisions you and Holgar make, you know," she said. "The animals I've worked with all my life are bones that can't hurt you unless you drop them on your foot. Or you let them lead you to an assumption that makes your colleagues say you're a fool—that can hurt too."

"I'd better lead," said Vickers after a glance behind
that assured him that the sun was still below the horizon.

There were several minutes marked by the whispering of grass against leather and the occasional clack of
stones slipping under a boot sole. At last the guide said,
"That hominid can't have gone more than eighty pounds
on the hoof, so to speak. Dressed out, maybe half that
. . . and that's counting a lot that that sabertooth eats
and you and I wouldn't. Now, I've seen lions gorge
forty pounds in a sitting, and they were a lot smaller
than our friend. Still, it's a good five days before a
lion that full even thinks of moving on. . . . All things
considered, and assuming that the sabertooth kept eating the way it started yesterday while we watched it,
I'd expect to find the fellow snoozing under the trees
where it made the kill."

"Oh," said the paleontologist. "Ah, do you think—I'd
still rather call them primates—do you think they'll
come back even if the macheirodont is gone?"

Vickers laughed. "And do I think there's life on Saturn?
Look, how would I know?" By using common sense,
the right half of his brain told him. It was always easier
to plead ignorance, though. . . . "All right," the guide
said slowly, "there was nothing permanent about that
camp. The troop probably roams the area pretty widely.
And they dropped everything when they took off, but
everything wasn't—anything, really. We saw some of
them carrying rocks, but they were as like as not to
drop them. And the roots and such they'd gathered,
that wasn't anything they were storing, just a day's
supply and as easy to replace as recover. So no, I don't
think they'll come back."

Vickers missed Weil's muttered response, but it might
have been a curse. "You mean," she said more distinctly, "that the chances are we won't be able to get
near the camp site because the cat's still there; and even
if the cat's gone, there won't be any real chance of
seeing living hominids there again."

"Well, don't worry about the sabertooth," Vickers
said, smiling at the term "hominid" which the other had

let slip. "I— " his expression sobered. "Look," he went on, "I blew it bad the other day and let that cat almost get me. That doesn't mean I can't nail one if it's sleeping in a place you want to look over."

Weil nodded, though the guide in front of her could not see the gesture. "How is your chest?" she asked.

Vickers shrugged. "It hurts," he said. "That's good. It reminds me how stupid I can be."

They were in sight of their goal now, though the paleontologist did not yet recognize the clump of acacias from this angle. The anvil tops of the trees, forty feet in the air, were already a saturated green in the first light of the sun. Vickers touched Weil's shoulder and knelt down. The dark-haired woman crouched and studied the scene. At last she recognized the swell of the hill to the right from which they had watched the camp and the kill the day before. "All right," she whispered to the guide. "What do we do now?"

"We wait," said Vickers, uncapping his binoculars, "until I've got a clean shot at that sabertooth or I'm awfully damn sure it's nowhere around." With the lenses just above the thorny shrub between him and the acacias, Vickers studied the blurring gray-on-gray beneath the trees.

Vickers could feel movements all around them. A trio of squabbling finches fluttered into the bush inches away from his face, then scurried back again without having taken any obvious interest in the humans. The grass moved, sometimes in sympathy with a puff of wind, often without. The landscape was becoming perceptibly brighter, its colors returning as pastel hints of the richness they would have in an hour.

Over a ridge a half mile south of the humans ambled a family of sivatheres. As they walked, the beasts browsed high among the thorny acacias. The sivatheres were somewhat shorter than the largest of the true giraffes with which Vickers was familiar, but that difference was purely a matter of neck length. The sivatheres were higher at the shoulder and were greatly more massive in build than giraffes Topside. Males and females alike were crowned with a cluster of four skin-covered horns, blunt as chairlegs. "You know," whispered the guide as he stared at the graceful, fearless creatures, "I ought to be able to get one of those for you if this doesn't pan out. . . ." The stocky man had done his share of trophy hunting in the past, and the old excitement was back in a rush as he watched the huge animals move.

"Quite unnecessary," retorted Linda Weil. "I've compared their ossicones to those of known species, and there's no correlation. These are a new species; and that's no help at all in the question of dating."

Vickers lowered his binoculars. He was conscious of the mechanism that had caused him to suggest the sivatheres as a target. Despite that embarrassment, however, he said, "But it's the pattern of the teeth, not the horns, that's really diagnostic, isn't it? What you mean is, you're more interested in the hominids than you are in doing your job." The woman looked away, then met his eyes silently. "Look," the guide continued, "I tore a strip off Holgar because he wasn't doing his job. But if you're going to pull the same crap yourself in your own way—well, we may as well go back Topside right now."

The guide had not raised his voice, but the iron in it jolted the woman as effectively as a shout could have. She touched Vickers' wrist in a pleading, not a sexual, fashion. "Henry, this may not be exactly what they sent us here to find," she said, "but I'm certain in my own mind that, that even the people in the engineering section will be able to see how desperately important it is. A chance through time intrusion to actually *see* which theories of human nature are true, whether our ancestors were as violent as Chakma baboons or as friendly as Capuchin monkeys. This might be a chance to understand for the first time the roots of the political situation that makes the—men in Tel Aviv so anxious to refine time intrusion into a, well, a weapon."

Vickers shook his head. He felt more frustration than disagreement, however. "The men and women in Tel Aviv," he corrected. "Well, understanding the roots of their problem is fine, but I suspect that they'd trade it for a way to get a nuke into Berlin around '32." He sighed. "But this isn't getting our job done, is it?" Vickers turned his binoculars onto the acacia grove again.

For a moment, Vickers was in doubt about the dark shape at the base of one of the trees. It could have been a root gnarling blackly about a boulder bared by ages of wind and rain. Then the shape rolled over and there could be no doubt at all that the sabertooth had slept where it killed. Vickers let the binoculars hang gently on their strap and lifted his Garand.

Weil's breath sucked in. It was that, rather than her fingers clamping on his biceps, that caused Vickers to slack the finger pressure that would an instant later have sent a 150-grain bullet cracking down range. The guide's seated body held the rigid angle of which the rifle was a part, but his eyes slanted left to where the woman was pointing. "I'll be damned," Vickers mouthed. He lowered the butt of his weapon.

The sabertooth lay 200 yards in front of them, a clout shot at a stationary target. But a hominid was quartering toward the acacias from the left, already as close to the trees as he was to the watching humans. The hominid was sauntering with neither haste nor concern, a procedure which seemed both insane and wildly improbable for any creature his size when alone in this habitat. Vickers had the glasses up again. From the hominid's build, from the way his arms hung as he walked . . . from the whorled grain of his fur that counterfeited two shades in a pelt of uniform gray . . . the guide was sure that this hominid was the one that had made the unsuccessful snatch at the carcase in the midst of the hyenas. That hominid had been present when the sabertooth struck—and therefore he could not conceivably be walking toward those murderous jaws in perfect nonchalance.

Weil's camera was whirring. Vickers suspected that she would learn more through her binoculars than through the view finder, but there are people to whom no event is real unless it is frozen. No doubt many of them worked with bones. The hominid was only fifty yards from the sprawling cat. He stopped, scratched his armpit, and began calling out in a sharp voice. He was facing the end-most tree in the grove as if someone were hiding in its branches. Nothing larger than a squirrel could have been concealed among the thorns and sparse foliage.

The sabertooth's wakefulness was indicated not by its movements but by the sudden cessation of all the tiny changes of position a sleeping animal makes. The great head froze; the eyes were apparently closed but might have been watching the hominid through slitted lids. The cat could not have been truly hungry after the meal of the previous day, but neither had the dun female provided so much meat that another kill was inconceivable. The cat grew as still and tense as the mainspring of a cocked revolver.

Vickers made a decision. He started to raise the rifle again. Linda Weil shook her head violently. "No!" she whispered. "It—it's their world. But if none of the other primates are in sight, ah, afterward, kill the macheirodont before it has time to damage the specimen."

The guide turned his head back toward the grove with a set expression. He held the Garand an inch short of firing position despite his anger. But they were just animals. . . .

The cat charged.

Considered dispassionately, the initial leap was a thing of beauty. The torso which had seemed to be as solid as a boulder was suddenly a blur of fluid motion. Vickers could now understand how he had been so thoroughly surprised by this killer's mate; but the recollection chilled him anew.

The hominid himself was not in the least surprised. That was evident from the way he sprinted away from the cat at almost the instant that the carnivore first moved. There was no way that the hominid could match the sabertooth's acceleration, however. When the fore-paws touched the ground the first time they had cov-

ered half the distance separating killer from prey, and
when the paws touched the second time—

It was as if the sabertooth had stepped into a mine
field, and the mines were alive. Vickers had counted six
adult males in the hominid troop. The cat's leap after
the first had carried it into the midst of the other five.
Sparse as the grass and brush had seemed, it had served
to cloak the ambush not only from the humans but also
from the sabertooth. Murderously intent on its running
prey, the cat's upper canines were bared and its claws
were unsheathed to sweep its victim in. A pair of hominids leaped from either side like the jaws of a trap
closing. If their own fangs were poor weapons in comparison to those of the 600-pound carnivore, then the
blocks of stone they carried in their fists were impres-
sive weapons by any standard. They smashed like sledge
hammers, driven by the strength of the long arms.

Whatever might have come of the tumbling kaleido-
scope, it should have involved the death of the hominid
acting as bait. The cat's paws were spread, certain to
catch and rend even if reflex did not also flesh the long
fangs an instant later. The bait, the Judas goat, made
one last jump that would not have carried him free had
not the white-flashed leader risen behind the sabertooth
and seized the cat's rigid tail.

The hominid's mass could no more have stopped the
flying cat directly than it could have stopped a moving
car; but 120 pounds applied to a steering wheel can
assuredly affect a car's direction. The cat's hindquarters
swung outward with the impact. Mindless as a servo-
mechanism, the same instinct that would have spun
the cat upright in a fall reacted to counter the torque.
The claws twisted away from their target. The sabertooth
landed on the ground harmlessly, and the thud of its
weight was overlaid by the sharper sound of stones
mauling its ribs and skull.

The cat had charged silently. Now it screeched on a
rising note and slashed to either side. Hominids sprang
away. This was not the blind panic of the previous
day. Rather, they were retracting themselves as a rifle's

bolt retracts to chamber another round. The leader still gripped the base of the cat's tail, snarling with a fury the more chilling for the fact it was not mindless. When the sabertooth tried to flex double to reach its slender tormentor, the hominid that had acted as bait smashed a rock against the base of the cat's skull.

The sabertooth would have run then, but its left hip joint was only shards of bone. Escape was no longer an option. The cat tried to leap and failed in a flurry of limbs. Hominids piled onto the flailing body. One of the attackers was flung high in the air, slashes on its chest filling with blood even as the creature spun. That was probably the last conscious action the carnivore took. All that Vickers could see for the next several minutes was a montage of stone-tipped arms rising and falling with a mechanical certainty. They made a sound on impact like that of mattocks digging a grave in frozen soil.

"God," whispered the hunter.

Vickers had seen baboons kill a leopard, and he knew of well-enough attested instances of dholes, the red hunting dogs of India, killing tigers that had tried to drive them off their prey. The calculated precision of what he had just watched impressed Vickers in a way that the use of stones as weapons had not, however.

"Oh, I've died and gone to heaven," breathed the paleontologist. "This is incredible. It's just incredible."

Vickers shivered. He peered through his binoculars but kept a firm grip on the rifle with his right hand. He was checking, not wholly consciously, to make sure he could account for all six males of the troop. He had sometimes felt a similar discomfort in baboon country, though never so intense. "I don't think," he said carefully, "that we'd better track, ah, these further today. They're apt to act, ah, unpredictably. Used to be I thought if worst came to worst and they rushed us, one shot'd stop them. Right now, I don't know that would be a good idea."

Weil looked at the guide's thin profile, measuring his

mind with her eyes. "All right," she said at last, "we'll go back for now instead of seeing where they—" she nodded—"head. We'll see what Holgar has found. But it all depends on Holgar."

"I hope to God you're right," muttered Vickers as he began the task of backing away without arousing the hominids' attention. They were hooting cheerfully around the macheirodus, surely dead by now. The furry arms still rose and fell.

The closest human-sized cover was 200 yards from the locust trees but that was close enough. Nilsen had to admit that his senior had done a masterful job of arranging the trap. The section of netting lay flat. Each pair of corner ropes was slanted across the net to a bent branch on the other side. When the trigger peg was pulled out to release the branches, the net would be snatched upward and rolled shut simultaneously—while still under enough unreleased tension to prevent anything within from escaping unaided. The release line itself led to a patch of brush on a rocky outcrop. It would become unbearably hot by ten in the morning, but by then the hominids should have visited the grove if they were coming at all.

Nilsen desperately hoped that the troop had completely evacuated the region in the aftermath of the sabertooth's attack.

The Norwegian morosely fingered the handle of doweling around which Vickers had clamped the release line. Anyone else would have used nylon cord for the line; Vickers had disconnected the braided steel cable from the winch to use instead. The nylon could easily have taken the strain, but it would have stretched considerably over the distance when Nilsen pulled on it. That could be enough warning to send the hominids scurrying away before the trap released. The steel would require only a single sharp jerk with enough muscle in it to overcome the line's dead weight.

Nilsen studied the watercourse through his binoculars, for want of anything better to do at the moment. A half-squadron of hipparions dashed up to the bank, paused, and dashed away again without actually touching the water. The nervous horses were ignored by the score or so of antelopes already drinking. From their size and markings they appeared to be impalas; but if so, the species was different enough from those Topside for the females as well as the males to bear horns. There was no sign of hominids.

The younger guide had considered failing to spring the trap or deliberately botching the operation—perhaps managing to frighten them away permanently without capturing one. But even though this was Holgar Nilsen's first expedition with Vickers as his partner, he knew already what result such sabotage would bring. If Vickers found the trap had been released at the wrong time, or that it had not been released when there was sign in the grove that hominids had been present . . . well, the senior guide was accurate out to 500 meters with his Garand. There was not the slightest chance that he would not shoot a hominid if he thought Nilsen had tried to call his bluff.

The half-light had become true dawn. Even the gray of the bush pig's hide was a color rather than a shade. The sow watched as her piglets drank and stamped at the edge of the water, light glinting on the spikes of her tusks.

Something was moving in the grove.

Even before he shifted his glasses, Nilsen knew that the hominids had arrived as he had feared they would. There were three of them, all females. Two were fully adult, each carrying a nursing infant. The third was shorter and slighter, the adolescent who had received the infant from the tiger's victim. Now she was holding a large leaf or a swatch of hide. Fascinated, Nilsen forgot for a moment why he was stationed there, forgot also his fear and anger at the situation.

The adult hominids were gathering locust pods from the ground. When each had a handful, she dropped it onto the makeshift platter which the adolescent carried.

Nilsen swore under his breath. An incipient basket

was a more frightening concept to him than was an
incipient axe. They were men, they were ancestors of
him and of all the billions of other humans living Topside, who *had* been living Topside before the intrusion
team started meddling. . . .

One of the adults moved off to the left, hunched over
and momentarily hidden by bushes. The other adult
chittered happily. Ignoring the thorns, she began to
climb the trunk of one of the trees that armed the trap.

The trap. The adolescent was holding her bundle in
one hand and with the other hand was plucking curiously at the nylon meshes on which she stood. Nilsen
touched the release handle. He did not pull it. Then he
had a vision of the hominid as she would look through
the sights of Henry Vickers' rifle, the front blade bisect-
ing her chest and the whole head and torso framed by
the ring of the rear aperture. Nilsen jerked the line.

The whittled peg flipped from its socket and the two
anchor lines slashed against the sky. Their twang and
the victim's shriek of alarm were simultaneous as the
net looped crosswise in the air. It hung between the
branches, humming like a fly ambushed and held by a
jumping spider.

The two adult hominids and their infant burdens
disappeared screaming like children near a lightning
strike. The Norwegian hunter could not be sure that
the one who had been climbing had not been flung
from her perch and killed when the trap sprang. There
was no time to worry about that now. Snatching up his
Mauser and the sled, Nilsen began running through the
grass toward the grove. Antelope exploded from the
water. Hipparions joined the rout with less grace but a
certain heavy-footed majesty.

Nilsen pounded into the grove, panting as much from
nerves as from the 200 yards he had run. The net was
pulled tight enough to bulge the meshes around the
captive, though not so tight that it choked off the hominid's helpless bleats. Locust pods spilled from a horse-
hide apron were scattered on the ground beneath the
trap.

"Sweet Jesus," the guide muttered. "Oh, my children, my Mary."

Vickers had planned a safe method of completing the capture single-handedly as well. It proved as effective in practice as the trap itself had. The hominid hung six feet in the air, only eye height for the Norwegian. He flung a second square of netting over the taut roll. Then, through the edges hanging low enough to avoid the captive's teeth and claws, he wove a cord back and forth in a loose running seam. When Nilsen had reached the hominid's feet, he pulled the cord and tightened the outer net over the inner one like cross-wrapped sheets. As soon as he tied off the lace, the guide had a bundle which the captive within could not escape even after the tension of the branches was released. Holding the head end of the bundle with his left hand, Nilsen cut the anchor cords one at a time, dampening the backlash and ultimately supporting the hominid's weight with his own unaided strength. She mewed and twisted within the layers of net, baring her teeth but unable to sink them into the Norwegian's arm.

Nilsen found it easier to think of the creature as a beast now than it had been when he watched her moving freely at a distance. She was small, and small without the softness of a human child of the same size. Her jaw was prominent, her forehead receding, and her nose little more than the bare nostrils of a chimpanzee. Most of all, the covering of coarse brown fur robbed the captive of her humanity.

And the fur was as specious an indicator as the rest of them, which the guide knew full well. The hominid had no more hair than Nilsen did himself. Only the fact that the body hairs of later-evolved hominids were short and transparent by comparison to those of the captive permitted Nilsen to pretend the captive was inhuman. That did not matter. The fact that Nilsen *could* pretend to be dealing with a beast and not an ancestor was the only thing that allowed him to do what circumstances forced him to do.

The big man set his captive down gently. With prac-

ticed speed he extended the titanium frame of the sled
and locked its members into place. He picked up the
hominid again, lifting her off the ground one-handed
instead of dragging her as a smaller and weaker man
would have had to do. The sled had integral tie-downs
with which he fastened his burden securely despite her
squirming. It would be to no one's benefit for her to
break halfway loose and injure herself. The best Nilsen
could hope for now was that Weil would examine the
hominid briefly and release her. Unharmed, the creature could go on about whatever business she would
have accomplished had the time intrusion not occurred.

The guide settled his slung rifle and began trudging
toward camp at a pace that would not upset the sled on
the irregular ground. As a matter of course, he glanced
around frequently to be sure that he was not being
stalked by a predator. He paid no particular attention to
the brush surrounding the locust grove, however.

Nilsen would have had to look very carefully indeed
to see the glint of bright eyes hidden there. The eyes
followed him and the captive hominid step by step
toward his camp.

"I'll put a kettle of water on and do the dishes,"
Henry Vickers said. "No need for you two to worry
about it."

The firelight brought out attractive bronze highlights
in Linda Weil's dark hair. It softened the lines of her
face as well. "Oh, I don't think that will be necessary,"
she said with a comfortable smile. "We can carry them
Topside dirty and let somebody there worry about them."

Both men turned and stared silently at the beaming
paleontologist. The hominid whimpered outside the circle of firelight. She was in a cage, the largest one
available but still meant for considerably smaller specimens. Weil ignored the sound. She turned to Holgar
Nilsen who stared glumly at his hands. "Holgar," she
said, "you did a great job today. I know how much you
hated doing it, but you did it splendidly, professionally,

anyway. Because of that, we're able to return Topside first thing tomorrow and not—not interfere with the creatures living here any further."

Nilsen looked up slowly. His face was as doubtful as that of a political prisoner who has just been informed that the revolution has made him president. "Do you mean," he asked carefully, "that you're already done examining, ah, it?" A quirk of his head indicated the cage at which Nilsen had refused to look ever since he had transferred his captive to it.

The paleontologist gave a brief head-shake, a tightening around her eyes showing that she was aware of what was about to happen. "No," she said, "we'll carry the specimen back with us Topside. The sort of testing necessary will take years."

"No," said the Norwegian flatly. Then he cried, "God in heaven, *no!* Are you mad? Henry—" turning to the senior guide who would not look at him, stretching out both hands to Vickers as if he were the last hope of a drowning man—"you cannot permit her to do this, will you?"

"Look, one cull from a troop," muttered Vickers to his hands. "Not even breeding age. . . ."

Nilsen's eyes were red with rage and the firelight. "I—" he began, but the alarm pinged and cut off even his fury.

Both men focused on the panel, their hands snatching up their rifles. Linda Weil was trying to place the source of the sound. The indicator for Sensor Five, northeast of the camp, was pulsing. From the dial, the intruder was of small to medium size: an impala, say—or a hyena.

The guides exchanged glances. The Norwegian shifted his rifle to a one-hand hold, its butt socketed on his hip. He picked up the spotlight. Vickers leveled the Garand, leaning into it with all the slack in the trigger taken up. He nodded. Nilsen flicked on the light and slashed its narrow beam across the arc the sensor reported. Nearby bushes flashed white as the spot touched them; further out, only shadows pivoted about the beam. According

to the sensor, the intruder was still there, 150 meters
out in the night. It did not raise its eyes to give a pair of
red aiming points when the light touched them.

"Turn it out," Vickers whispered across the breech
of his rifle.

After-effects of the fierce white beam shrank the firelit
circle to a glow that scarcely cast the men's shadows
toward the bush. The sensor needle quivered as the
intruder moved. Vickers fired into the night.

The crack of the .30-'06 made Weil scream in surprise. The muzzle flash was a red ball, momentary but
as intense as a bath in acid. Chips of jacket metal spun
burning into the night like tiny signal rockets. The
sensor jolted, then slipped back to rest position as the
intruder bounded back into darkness.

"What was it?" Linda Weil demanded. Her palms
were clamped to her ears as if to squeeze the ringing
from the drums.

"I don't care so long as it's gone," Vickers said, slowly
lowering the Garand. "I've seen a man after a hyena
dragged him out of his tent by the face."

"The world might be better off if we *were* killed
here," said Holgar Nilsen bitterly.

Vickers looked at the younger man. He did not speak.
Nilsen spat on the fire. "I am very tired now," he said.
"I will sleep." He nodded toward the intrusion vehicle,
its supporting beams sunk to knee height in the ground.
The metal glowed with a soft sheen of oil where rust
had not already crept. "There. I wish you both comfort."

The blond man's footsteps could be heard on the
steel even after his form had blurred into the night. "I
shouldn't care, should I?" said the woman, speaking
toward the fire but loudly enough for Vickers to hear
her.

Vickers walked to the water tank and began filling
the eight-liter cauldron. The stream rang from the gal-
vanized metal until the water buffered itself. "I don't
know," the guide said. "If somebody thinks he's ac-
complishing anything by sleeping on steel planking, I

guess that's his business." He set the pot directly on the coals, twisting it a little to form a safe seat.

"After all, I was only recreation anyway, wasn't I?" the dark-haired woman resumed. "What was a twenty-seven-year-old man going to want with a woman five years older when he got back to a place with some choice? Even if he didn't already have a family!"

"Look, that's out of my field," said the guide. He had already switched magazines in the Garand. Now he checked his pockets to see if they held a loose round to replace the one he had just fired into the night.

"Well, he can *have* his damned security!" Weil said. "*I've* got success that he couldn't comprehend if he had to. Do you realize—" her index finger prodded the air toward Vickers—"just how big this is? By bringing back this specimen, I've just become the most important researcher into human prehistory in this century!"

The guide's expression did not change. Linda Weil pulled back with a slight start. "Well, we all have in a way," she amended in a more guarded voice. "I mean, I couldn't have done this here without you and, and Holgar, of course. But the . . . well, it's my *field*, of course."

Vickers laid the Garand carefully across the stool on which he had been sitting. He tested the dishwater with the tip of a thumb. "You know," he said, "I've got some problems about carrying her—" he gestured toward the dull whimpering—"back with us, too. Look, you've got your camera, and they aren't expecting us back Topside for three more days anyhow. Why don't we stay here, you do your tests and whatever, and then—" Vickers spread his hand with a flare toward the hills, completing the thought.

The look that flashed across the paleontologist's face was as wild as the laughter bubbling from the throat of a hyena. Weil had control of herself again as quickly. "Do you really want to keep her three days in a cage she can't stand up in, Henry?" the woman asked. "And you *know* that we couldn't accomplish anything here, even with a reasonable length of time—which that isn't.

Quite aside from the fact that they'd all suspect I'd made the story up myself. A few photos for evidence!"

"Holgar and I are here as witnesses," Vickers said. He lifted the cauldron's wire handle with a stick.

"Marvelous! And where did you do *your* post-graduate work?" Weil snapped. She softened at once, continuing, "Henry, I know my colleagues. They'll doubt, and they *ought* to doubt. It's better than another Piltdown Man. Oh, there'll be another expedition, and it may possibly be as incredibly fortunate as we've been—but then it'll be their names on the finds, not mine. And it's not fair!"

Water sloshed as Vickers shifted the pot. A gush of steam and flying ashes licked his boots. "I don't think she's human," he said quietly, "but if she is, I don't think we've got any business holding her. Not here, not Topside. You know they'd never be able to find this, this slot in time close enough to put her back in it once she leaves."

"Henry, for God's sake," the dark-haired woman pleaded, "we're not talking about some kind of torture. Good grief, what do you think her life span's going to be if we leave her? Five years? Three? Before she winds up in a sabertooth's belly!"

Vickers gave the woman an odd look. "I think both the sabertooths in this range," he said, "have eaten their last hominid."

"All right, a hyena then!" the paleontologist said. "Or until she goes into anaphylactic shock from a bee sting. The point is not just that when we go Topside, everything here will be dead for five million years. The point is that the specimen will live a much longer life in comfort that she'll appreciate just as much as you do. And she'll advance our knowledge of ourselves and our beginnings more than Darwin did."

"Yeah," said the guide. He slid the trio of aluminum plates into the water. "I like modern comforts so much that I spend all the time I can in the bush." He stirred the dishes morosely with the tableware before he dropped that in as well. "Okay, I've been wrong before. God knows, I've generally been wrong."

Five distant hyenas broke out in giggling triumph. No doubt they had just killed, Vickers thought. He spat in the direction of the sounds.

Holgar Nilsen swore in Norwegian. He had been doing a last-minute check of his ammunition as they all stood on the sun-struck platform of the intrusion vehicle. As rudimentary as their camp had been, it had taken four hours of solid work to strike it and restack the gear and specimens on the steel. "We can't go yet," Nilsen said. "I can't find one of my cartridge cases—we can't leave it out there."

Vickers had already unlocked the vehicle's control panel. Now he took his hand from the big knife switch, but his voice was sour as he said, "Look, Holgar, have you forgotten to count the one up the spout?"

"No, no, it's not that," the big man insisted. "Of course I don't have a shell in the chamber for returning to Tel Aviv." Nilsen held a twenty-round ammunition box in his left hand. Twelve spaces were filled with empty brass; four still held live rounds, their cases bright where they showed above the styrofoam liner. Only three of the remaining four spaces could be accounted for by the rounds in the Mauser's magazine. "Leaving the brass here—what will it do to the future?"

"Oh, for Chrissake," Vickers said. "Look, we're leaving the lead of every shot we've fired here, aren't we? And this isn't the first team that's been sent back, either."

Linda Weil stood beside the wire-mesh cage. The hominid hunched within, scratching at the dusty floor, did not look up. She had not eaten anything since her capture, despite offers of locust pods and what must have been to her an incredible quantity of antelope haunch. The paleontologist looked up from her specimen and said, "Yes, and after all, we've been evacuating wastes, breathing, sweating ourselves. I think it's wise at this point to clean up as much as we can, but I don't think we need be concerned over details."

"When I want your opinion, slut, I'll ask for it!" Nilsen shouted.

Earlier that morning the younger guide had ignored Weil's occasional, always conciliatory, comments. Now his face was red and the tendons stood out in his neck. The woman's face distorted as if she had been struck.

"Damn it all anyway," said Vickers. "We're about five minutes away from never having to see each other again if we don't want to. Let's drop it, shall we?"

The other guide took a deep breath and nodded. Vickers reached for the control switch again. Actually, he wouldn't have minded going on further intrusions with Nilsen if the big man could get over his fear of possible future consequences. Nilsen was hard-working, a crack shot . . . and besides, he had already saved Vickers' life once.

"Oh, hell," Vickers said. He dropped his hand from the switch. "We forgot to pick up those goddam rock samples in the confusion. Hell. I'll get them."

Nilsen held out a hand to stop the senior guide. "No, let me," he said. Giving Vickers a sardonic smile, he inserted another fat cartridge into the chamber of his rifle. He had to hold down the top round in the magazine so that the bolt would not pick it up and try to ram it into the already-loaded chamber. "After all," he continued as the action snicked closed, "it was I who forgot them. And besides, I don't care to stay with the— remaining personnel."

"Do you think I care?" Linda Weil shrieked. The blond man ignored her, his boots clanking down the two steps to the gritty soil. Far to the west a storm was flashing over a rocky table, but here around the intrusion vehicle not a breath stirred. The grass was scarred by signs of human use: the blackened fire-pit and the circle cleared around it; the trampled mud, now cracking, beneath the shower frame; the notches in the ground left by the sled's sharp runners. A hundred yards away was the outcrop shattered by Nilsen's dynamite a moment before his shot saved Vickers' life. Like the other damage they had done to the land, this too was transitory. It only speeded up the process that frost and rain would have accomplished anyway over the next five million years.

Nothing in the landscape moved except Holgar Nilsen, striding purposefully toward the broken rock.

"Something isn't right," Vickers muttered. His eyes narrowed but they saw nothing to justify what he felt. Reflexively, he charged his Garand. The bolt rang like an alarm as it stripped a round into the chamber.

"What's the matter?" Linda Weil demanded.

"Stay here," Vickers said. "*Holgar!*"

The Norwegian turned and waved. He had almost reached the outcrop. He continued walking.

Vickers swung over the stairs, his left hand locking him to the rail while his right controlled the weapon. "Holgar!" he shouted again. "Stop! There's something—"

When the younger guide paused a second time, the hominids sprang from ambush.

Vickers set his feet and dropped the fore-end of the Garand into his waiting left palm. Nilsen's eyes widened, but the leveled rifle was a warning more certain than a shout. He was already swinging the Mauser to his shoulder as he spun to face his attackers. The six male hominids were strung in a line abreast, ready to cut him off whichever way he dodged. Their hands held stones. In the center of the rushing line, the blond-flashed leader was only twenty feet from Holgar.

The big Norwegian dropped his rifle and turned. "Don't shoot them!" he screamed to Vickers. "You'll wipe—"

Nilsen crumpled, limp all over. The hominid standing over him raised his stone for another blow, white fur and white quartz and bright blood spattering both. Vickers fired three times, so swiftly that the last shot was still echoing before the brass of the first had spun into the bronze-red grass. He aimed for their heads because there was no time for anything but certainty and nothing but a head shot is instantly certain. Fresh brains are not gray but pinkish-white, and the air was pink as the three nearest hominids collapsed over the body of Holgar Nilsen.

The survivors were dashing away with the gracefulness of deer, their torsos hunched slightly forward. Vickers pounded like a fencepost running. He carried the Garand across his chest with its safety still off. After a long moment watching, Linda Weil picked up the medical kit and clambered down the steps to follow the men.

At the tangle of bodies, Vickers slung aside one hominid still arching reflexively in death. Beneath him the leader was as rigid as the block of quartz still locked in his right hand. Neither the entrance nor the exit wound of the bullet had damaged the white fur. Vickers rolled that carcase away as well.

Holgar Nilsen was still breathing.

The crown and brim of Nilsen's hat had been cut by the force of the blow, and the back of the Norwegian's head was a sticky mass of blood and short blond hair. But the skull beneath seemed whole when Vickers probed it, and the injured man's breathing was strong if irregular.

"Why did you kill them if you cared so much?" Linda Weil demanded as she knelt panting in the bloody grass. "He told you not to shoot, didn't he? *He* didn't want it."

The guide shifted to give Weil more room. He did not speak as she soaked a compress from her canteen and held it to the gash. His index finger crooked up to put his rifle on safe, but his eyes had resumed their search of nearby cover.

The dark-haired woman stripped a length of tape from the dispenser and laid it across both scalp and compress. "Do you want to know why?" she said. "You killed them because you hoped he was right. You hoped that you wouldn't be a failure when we got back to the future because there wouldn't *be* a human future any more. With all your talk, you still tried to wipe man off the planet when you got an excuse." Her fingers expertly crossed the initial length of tape with two more.

"Take his feet," Vickers said. "The quicker we get him Topside, the quicker he gets to a hospital."

"I'm sure he wouldn't want to be touched any more," said the paleontologist as she stood. Not by a slut like me." She closed the medical kit. "Besides," she added, professionally rotating the head of the hominid leader to look at it, "I have my own duties. I'm going to carry this one back."

Vickers looked at the woman without anger, without apparent emotion of any sort. Holgar Nilsen outweighed him by fifty pounds; but when Vickers straightened with his partner locked in a packstrap carry, the motion was smooth and perfectly controlled. The stocky man reached down with his free hand and gripped the sling of Nilsen's Mauser. He began walking the hundred yards back to the intrusion vehicle. His steps were short but regular, and his eyes kept searching the bush for danger.

There was no couch but the steel floor of the intrusion vehicle on which Nilsen had slept the past two nights. Vickers laid his partner down as gently as he could, using a sleeping bag as a pillow beneath the side-turned head. Only then did the guide let himself relax, dragging great shuddering gasps of air into his lungs. His Garand leaned against him, held by the upper sling swivel. He wondered whether his arms were strong enough even to level the weapon if danger should threaten.

Linda Weil had given up her attempt to carry the dead specimen. She was now dragging it by the arms, her back to the intrusion vehicle. Vickers started to go back to help her; then he looked down at Nilsen. He eased back on his heels.

The hominid had begun sobbing.

Enough of the fatigue poisons had cleared from Vickers' muscles that he was willing to move again. He knelt beside the specimen. Her long, furry hands covered her eyes and muzzle. A tear dripped through the interstices between her fingers and splashed on the floor. Vickers' eyes followed the drop to the starburst it made in the dust. He was still heavy with fatigue. The tear had fallen beside one of the patterns the hominid had scratched in the dust with her fingertip. The guide stared dully at the marks. The abstract design suddenly shifted into a pair of stick figures. Once his mind had assimilated the pattern as a mother and child, Vickers could not believe that he had not seen it before.

"Jesus," the guide prayed.

Long fingers could reach the latch of the cage through the mesh, so Nilsen had wired it shut in lieu of a padlock. Vickers leaned his rifle against a stack of labeled cartons and began to untwist the wire with both hands.

"Vickers!" cried the paleontologist. "What are you doing?"

The latch clicked open. Vickers dropped the door of the cage.

"Omigod!" the paleontologist shrieked, letting her burden fall so that she could run the last twenty yards to the vehicle.

The hominid looked from the opening to Vickers through the mesh. Her eyes were brown and shining with more than tears. She leaped instead of crawling through the opening and hit the platform running. She broke stride when she straightened—the cage had been only a meter high—but her leap from the intrusion vehicle landed her ten feet out in the grass. Linda Weil made a despairing clutch at the little creature, but the hominid was yards away before the paleontologist's arms closed. The adolescent ran in the direction the adults had taken after the ambush, and she ran with the same loping grace.

Linda Weil stumbled forward until she caught herself on the edge of the intrusion vehicle. The sounds she was making were not words, nor were they obviously human. Vickers stepped down and touched her shoulder. "You've still got your specimens," he said quietly. "I'll help you load them."

The woman raised her head, dripping tears and mucus and despair. "You did that because you hate me, didn't you?" she asked in a choking voice.

Vickers' face was very still. "No," he said, "I did it because I don't hate anybody. Anybody human."

From the bush came the sound of joyful voices. The words themselves were not intelligible to humans born five million years in the future.

Have You Missed?

DRAKE, DAVID
At Any Price
Hammer's Slammers are back—and Baen Books has them!
Now the 23rd-century armored division faces its deadliest
enemies ever: aliens who *teleport* into combat.

55978-8 $3.50

DRAKE, DAVID
Hammer's Slammers
A special *expanded* edition of the book that began the
legend of Colonel Alois Hammer. Now the toughest, mean-
est mercs who ever killed for a dollar or wrecked a world
for pay have come home—to Baen Books—and they've
brought a secret weapon: "The Tank Lords," a brand-new
short novel, included in this special Baen edition of *Hammer's Slammers*.

65632-5 $3.50

DRAKE, DAVID
Lacey and His Friends
In Jed Lacey's time the United States computers scan
every citizen, every hour of the day. When crime is detected, it's Lacey's turn. There are a few things worse than
having him come after you, but they're not survivable
either. But things aren't really that bad—not for Lacey and
his friends. By the author of *Hammer's Slammers* and *At
Any Price*.

65593-0 $3.50

**CARD, ORSON SCOTT; DRAKE, DAVID;
& BUJOLD, LOIS MCMASTER**
(edited by Elizabeth Mitchell)
Free Lancers (Alien Stars, Vol. IV)
Three short novels about mercenary soldiers—never be-
fore in print! Card's hero leads a ragtag group of scientific
refugees to sanctuary in Utah; Drake contributes a new
"Hammer's Slammers" story; Bujold tells a new tale of
Miles Vorkosigan, hero of *The Warrior's Apprentice*.

65352-0 $2.95

DRAKE, DAVID
Birds of Prey

The time: 262 A.D. The place: Imperial Rome. There had never been a greater empire, but now it is dying. Everywhere its armies are in retreat, and what had been civilization seethes with riots and bizarre cults. Against the imminent fall of the Long Night stands Aulus Perennius, an Imperial secret agent as tough and ruthless as the age in which he lives. But he stands alone—until a traveller from Earth's far future recruits him for a mission so strange it cannot be disclosed.

55912-5 (trade paper) $7.95
55909-5 (hardcover) $14.95

DRAKE, DAVID
Ranks of Bronze

Disguised alien traders bought captured Roman soldiers on the slave market because they needed troops who could win battles without high-tech weaponry. The leigionaires provided victories, smashing barbarian armies with the swords, javelins, and discipline that had won a world. But the worlds on which they now fought were strange ones, and the spoils of victory did not include freedom. If the legionaires went home, it would be through the use of the beam weapons and force screens of their ruthless alien owners. It's been 2000 years—and now they want to go home.

65568-X $3.50

DRAKE, DAVID, & WAGNER, KARL EDWARD
Killer

Vonones and Lycon capture wild animals to sell for bloodsport in ancient Rome. A vicious animal sold to them by a trader turns out to be more than they bargained for—it is the sole survivor of the crash of an alien spacecraft. Possessed of intelligence nearly human, it has two goals in life: to breed and to kill.

55931-1 $2.95

DAVID DRAKE

"Drake has distinguished himself as the master of the mercenary sf novel."—*Rave Reviews*
